DATE DUE		

A S
YOUNG
A S
WE FEEL

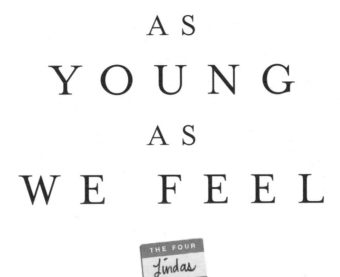

THE FOUR

Lindas

═══ *BOOK ONE* ═══

MELODY CARLSON

David C Cook®

transforming lives together

AS YOUNG AS WE FEEL
Published by David C. Cook
4050 Lee Vance View
Colorado Springs, CO 80918 U.S.A.

David C. Cook Distribution Canada
55 Woodslee Avenue, Paris, Ontario, Canada N3L 3E5

David C. Cook U.K., Kingsway Communications
Eastbourne, East Sussex BN23 6NT, England

David C. Cook and the graphic circle C logo
are registered trademarks of Cook Communications Ministries.

The Web site addresses recommended throughout this book are offered as a
resource to you. These Web sites are not intended in any way to be or imply an
endorsement on the part of David C. Cook, nor do we vouch for their content.

This story is a work of fiction. All characters and events are the product of the author's
imagination. Any resemblance to any person, living or dead, is coincidental.

LCCN 2009943353
ISBN 978-1-4347-6497-3
eISBN 978-1-4347-0187-9

© 2010 Melody Carlson
Published in association with the literary agency of Sara A. Fortenberry.

The Team: Andrea Christian, Erin Healy, Amy Kiechlin,
Sarah Schultz, Jaci Schneider, and Karen Athen
Cover Design: The Designworks Group, Tim Green
Cover Photos: The blonde girl on the right is Getty
Images, Hulton Archive, Rights Managed.
The other three girls are Veer Images, Zefa Photography, Rights Managed.
All other images are from Photo Library, royalty-free.

Printed in the United States of America
First Edition 2010

1 2 3 4 5 6 7 8 9 10

122109

=Chapter 1=

MARLEY PHELPS

Marley had hoped that her former high-school friends might've grown up by their thirty-fifth reunion. Unfortunately she was disappointed. Oh, most of them had matured somewhat, at least externally. She observed more bald heads, wrinkles, and gray hair than she recalled from their last gathering, and she was relieved to see that many had let go of old cliques and social boundaries. But others, like Keith Arnold, were still jerks. That surprised her, since rumor was he'd done time for embezzlement. Marley figured that alone would've knocked the former football jock down a peg or two, but once he'd poured a few Kamikazes into that paunch belly of his, he started acting like he was still the king of Clifden.

"It can't be!" he said loudly as a heavyset woman entered the room. "Are you really Abby Franklin? The cute little cheerleader I used to hoist over my shoulder?"

Abby did appear to have put on some weight since high school, but Marley wondered who hadn't. Still, Abby looked uneasy as she glanced around the crowded lounge as if she wanted to make a fast break. And who could blame her?

"Hey, Abby." Marley moved between Abby and Keith the Jerk. "It's so good to see you again. You're still living in town, right? How's it going?"

"Pretty good." Relief washed over Abby's face.

"Don't mind that big baboon," Marley said quietly. "He's been doing his best to offend everyone."

"I almost didn't come."

"I'm glad you did." Marley nodded over to where Keith was ordering another drink from the bar. "I've observed that Keith has a pattern. He either insults you or ignores you. He hasn't said a word to me. But since you were part of his crowd, he must've felt the need to include you in some good old public humiliation."

"I feel so honored." At the bar Keith and a couple of guys were gathered around a tall, attractive blonde. "Is that Caroline McCann?"

"The life of the party, as usual."

"I swear that woman *never* ages. She doesn't look a day over thirty."

"A lot of us look good from a distance."

"Does she look worse close up?" Abby almost sounded too eager.

Marley laughed. "Not really. Oh, a little older perhaps, but she's still gorgeous."

Abby eyed Marley now. "You're not looking bad yourself. I like your hair."

"Why thank—"

"Abby Franklin!" cried Caroline as she recognized her old friend. "Get yourself over here, girlfriend!"

"Oh dear!" Abby grabbed Marley's arm. "I don't know if I can do this."

"Sure you can," Marley assured her. "Just be yourself and let the good times roll."

Marley felt mildly surprised that she'd actually had a conversation with Abby. They'd been friends once, long ago, back in grade school. But then Abby got popular and turned into a somewhat stuck-up cheerleader, whereas Marley had always considered herself to be more of a free spirit—at least back then. How times and people had changed!

"I don't envy *her*," commented a classmate that Marley barely remembered. The slender woman nodded toward Abby, who was now socializing with the lovely Caroline and obnoxious Keith.

"I'll bet you used to," Marley teased.

She snickered. "Maybe so. It's funny how the tables turn after high school. I just saw Brenda Jones in the bathroom, and let me tell you, that woman won't need to use her AARP card for ID. It's written all over her face. I suppose it's nature's way of leveling the playing field."

"But underneath our older exteriors, we're the same people," Marley pointed out.

"Except that some of our exteriors just look better."

"Right." Marley couldn't recall this woman's name, and the light was too dim to read her name tag, but since she'd made so many catty remarks, Marley mentally named her Cat Woman. Cat Woman continued to make her witty observations, sparing no one. As Marley was trying to think of a graceful way to escape her, another woman joined them. It took Marley a moment to recognize her old friend, but then Joanna hugged her, and they exchanged greetings.

"It's been so long," Joanna said.

"It's hard to believe it's been thirty-five years." Marley shook her head. "Honestly I just don't feel that old."

"I do." Joanna made a weak smile.

"Some of our friends are a lot older than at our last reunion." Cat Woman directed this observation to Joanna. "In fact I think the last five years must've been hard on certain people."

"While others like Caroline McCann"—Joanna sighed in a tired way—"look as good as ever."

"Can you believe we're older than the president of the United States?" Cat Woman took a sip of her margarita.

"We need to quit focusing on age." Marley stood a bit straighter. "Really, what difference does it make? Aren't we as young as we feel?"

"I don't know about you, but I'm feeling about eighty at the moment." Joanna pointed to her feet. "And these shoes are killing me."

"Take them off," suggested Marley.

"If I take them off I might not be able to get them back on again." Joanna frowned. "Ever since I entered menopause, I've had a horrible time with everything from hot flashes to night sweats to water retention."

Marley looked at Joanna's puffy feet and nodded with sympathy.

"Why don't you go sit down?" Cat Woman suggested.

Marley suspected that Cat Woman didn't care to be seen with Joanna. There was no denying that Joanna had changed a lot. Marley found it difficult to believe that this woman with the frowsy gray hair and bad pantsuit had actually been hip at one time. Marley could still remember how the two of them used to hang out in the art department, sometimes sneaking around back to smoke a joint when Mr. Monroe was distracted.

"I think I will sit down and put my feet up."

"And I think I'll get another drink," Cat Woman said.

"And I'd like to mingle a bit," Marley added. Not that she needed anyone's permission. Still, she felt a sliver of guilt for not joining her old friend as Joanna sat on the sidelines of The Cliffs Hotel lounge. But it seemed obvious that Joanna was not enjoying herself, and Marley had come here with the intention of having some fun. In fact she was overdue for some good times.

"Hey, it's Hippie Girl," said Caroline McCann after Marley squeezed in next to her to order a cabernet.

Marley forced a smile. "And it's Cheerleader Girl."

Caroline laughed. "Dang, I forgot my pom-poms again."

Marley realized she was starting to act like Cat Woman now and decided to nip it in the bud. "Caroline McCann," she exclaimed, "I just have to say, you look amazing. You haven't aged a day since our last reunion. What's your secret?"

Naturally Caroline beamed at the compliment. "Why, thank you, Marley. I guess it's just good genes. But I could say the same thing about you."

"You could." Marley chuckled. "If you were a liar."

"No, you really *do* look good. And youthful too. And you've changed your hair." Caroline reached over and touched Marley's spiky brown hair and giggled. "It's so short, it must be easy to care for."

Keith leaned into the conversation. "Watch out, Marley, you might be mistaken for butch." He laughed like he thought that was funny.

Marley just rolled her eyes.

But Caroline punched him in the arm. "And if Marley was butch, what's it to you anyway?"

"Then I'd just have to say you girls make an interesting couple." Keith draped his arm around Caroline's shoulders as he gave Marley the once-over. "But hey, I don't recall you girls being friends in high school."

"In case you haven't noticed, we're not in high school anymore," Marley pointed out.

"I know that. But didn't you used to hang out with that artsy-fartsy crowd?" he said to Marley. "Kind of the dippy-hippie bunch?"

Marley ignored him as she paid the bartender for her wine. Why bother to engage?

"For your information," Caroline told him, "Marley and I have been friends since we were in first grade."

"Well, sort of on-and-off friends," Marley clarified.

"Do you remember the Four Lindas?" Caroline exclaimed suddenly. Marley laughed. "Our secret club."

"Huh?" Keith looked confused now.

"It's a secret," Caroline said in an almost-seductive voice. "If we told you, we'd have to kill you."

"So why don't you kill me on the dance floor, baby doll?" Before Caroline could answer, he pulled her out to where several couples were dancing to oldies from the seventies. Marley watched for a bit, then turned to see Abby Franklin making her way toward her.

"Well, we've all survived Keith," Marley said.

"Unfortunately what he said is true." Abby patted her rounded hips. "I have put on a few pounds since our last reunion. Not that I need Keith to remind me."

"And not that he has room to talk," Marley told her.

"But I had been doing Jenny Craig back then, and I stayed busy with my garden and walking. Now it seems I sit around too much, and I probably enjoy my own cooking a little too much too."

"So you like to cook?" Marley couldn't even remember the last time she'd turned on her oven or enjoyed a home-cooked meal.

"I really do." Abby nodded, then smiled. "I have to tell you, Marley, you're looking good."

Marley nodded toward the dance floor. "Not as good as Caroline McCann. Can you believe her?" Caroline looked as limber as ever as she moved on the dance floor. Her pale blue dress must've had some beads or sequins on it, because it sparkled from the lights bouncing off the disco mirror ball. She really did look like Hollywood.

"No one looks as good as Caroline. And Paul can't take his eyes off of her."

"You're still married to Paul?" Marley remembered how shocked she'd been when Abby and Paul married right after high-school graduation. For some reason she'd always assumed it wouldn't last. Not that she was much of an expert on such things.

"Thirty-five years in June."

"Wow. Congratulations."

Abby just shrugged. "How about you?"

Marley was tempted to lie, but then wondered, *Why bother?* "John and I divorced about four years ago."

"I'm so sorry."

"Don't be." Marley held her head high. "It was for the best."

"Well, it hasn't always been easy for Paul and me either. But we've weathered the storms, and I'm pretty sure we'll be growing old together. At least I hope so."

"Is that him dancing with the class prez out there?" Marley asked.

"Yes, and it's my fault." She laughed. "I told Paul I needed a break, and I grabbed Cathy Gardener to take my place."

"Does Cathy still live in Clifden too?"

"Yes. She's been the city manager for more than ten years now, and she's really quite good at it."

"She always was a great diplomat."

Abby nodded. "Class president, valedictorian, girl most likely to succeed. She's sure lived up to the predictions. How about you, Marley? Do you still do your art?"

"Not like I wish. After the divorce I had to get a nine-to-five job. But at least I work in a gallery. Now instead of making art, I just sell it."

"That sounds like a fun job. Sometimes I think about working outside of my home, but then I consider all that I'd miss: cooking, sewing, gardening. And I just can't bring myself to do it." She frowned slightly as she watched the dance floor. Marley followed her gaze, observing that the current song was a slow one. Abby's husband had switched partners and was now dancing with the lovely Caroline.

"So is Caroline still doing the actress thing?" Marley asked.

Abby turned back to Marley. "She told me she hasn't had any good roles for a while, but she still seems to be happy down there in LA. I can't imagine it myself. I sometimes watch reruns of that reality series, the one with the housewives. And when I see the shows set in Orange County, I cannot believe what a rat race it must be down there. Everyone is so focused on looks and being skinny and rich. I swear I wouldn't last a week."

"So how about Clifden?" ventured Marley. "I assume you still live here?"

"Oh, yes. We finished our new house a couple years ago. It's in North Beach—a new community that Paul developed."

"Ocean view?"

Abby nodded. "And beach access, too. It's quite lovely."

"And you're still happy to be living in Clifden?"

"Honestly there's no place I'd rather be."

"I noticed that town has some new shops."

"Yes. They come and go." Abby nodded at a tall redheaded woman who was just entering the room. "Isn't that Janie Sorenson?"

Marley studied the elegant-looking woman dressed in a light-colored two-piece suit. "I think so. I still can't get over how much she's changed since high school. Can you believe it?"

Abby nodded. "I remember that frizzy red hair and braces, and bad skin. Poor thing. I used to try to be friendly to her, but she was so shy, I could hardly get her to speak."

"Except when it came to speech class and debates," Marley reminded her. "That's when the real Janie came out."

Abby waved to Janie. "Paul told me she's a partner in a big New York law firm. Who would've thought?"

"How we've all changed."

Janie joined them. "Have I missed anything interesting?" she asked in a way that suggested she didn't really care.

"Not really," Abby told her. "Did you fly from New York today?"

Janie nodded with tired eyes. "I left Kennedy at seven this

morning, then got stuck in Denver for nearly three hours. I almost decided to just spend the night in Portland, but then, here I am." She frowned. "Although I'm not sure why exactly. I really wasn't friends with these kids."

"I'm glad you came," Marley told her. "It does everyone good to see how people can change."

Janie brightened slightly. "Yes. I suppose you're right."

"I was sorry to hear about your parents," Abby said gently.

"What happened to your parents?" asked Marley.

"Mom passed away last February, and Dad followed her in July. I'm still working out the details of their estate."

"I'm sorry." Marley put her hand on Janie's arm. "My parents both passed away about five years ago, within two months of each other."

"It's kind of sweet, isn't it?" Abby sighed. "To love someone so much that you don't want to stick around after the other one is gone. I think Paul and I might be like that."

Janie took in a quick breath and seemed on the verge of tears.

"Are you okay?" Marley asked quietly.

"I'm sorry," Abby said. "Was it something I said? I'm always sticking—"

"No, no, it's okay." Janie retrieved a handkerchief from a sleek brown bag that Marley suspected was terribly expensive. "It's just that I lost my husband, too." She dabbed her nose.

"Oh, I'm sorry." Abby put an arm around her.

"How long has it been?" Marley asked with concern.

"He passed on about six months before my parents started going downhill."

"Wow, you've had a hard couple of years," Marley said. "Are you holding up okay?"

"Not at the moment." Janie glanced around uncomfortably. "But it might have to do with being back here. And I'm tired. I think I'll visit the ladies' room to freshen up, if you'll excuse me."

"Poor Janie," Abby said after she was gone. "Seems she's had it rough."

"Did you notice how thin she is?"

Abby nodded. "And those dark shadows beneath her eyes."

"I hope she's not having health problems."

"I shouldn't have said that bit about couples dying together." Abby shook her head. "Sometimes I just don't think before I—"

"Is there a doctor in the house?" someone hollered from the dance floor.

"Call 9-1-1!" yelled someone else. "We need an ambulance!"

Abby and Marley both rushed over to see what was wrong. There on the dance floor was Cathy Gardener, eyes closed and motionless. Paul and a couple of others hunched over her, trying to help.

"Let me in!" demanded the bartender. "Everyone back up and give the lady some room to breathe!" The young man pushed his way to Cathy's side and, like a pro, immediately began to administer CPR.

"Come on," the bartender said between breaths and counts. "Come on!"

"It looks like he knows what he's doing," Abby said quietly.

"Thank God for that," Caroline said.

"Do you think she'll be okay?" Marley stared down at the lifeless woman in the pinstriped dress, noticing that one of her shoes, a sensible navy pump, was missing.

"Let's pray for Cathy," Caroline said.

"Yes," agreed someone else.

Just like that, several of them bowed their heads and actually began to pray out loud, as if it were the most normal thing in the world. Marley stood among them, but praying was not her specialty. So she tried to send positive thoughts and good karma in Cathy's direction. Before long she could hear sirens approaching the hotel, and then the paramedics burst into the lounge and took over.

"Everyone back off," the bartender commanded the crowd. "Give the medics room to work."

By now the house lights were on, the music had stopped, and everyone stood at the sidelines. Quietly they huddled into small groups. Some continued to pray. Others simply watched with helpless expressions, and a few talked in worried whispers.

Janie came over to stand with Marley, Abby, and Caroline. "Did you see what happened?" she asked quietly.

"She just collapsed," Caroline explained. "One moment she was dancing with Keith, and then she just went down."

"Do you think it's her heart?" Janie asked.

"I don't know," Caroline said sadly. "Although she had a pained expression in her face."

"I've never heard of her having any kind of medical problems before," Abby told them. "She's always been such an active, energetic person. I'm sure she'll pull through."

"I wonder if she has family or anyone who should be notified."

Janie glanced around the crowd. "Is she with someone tonight? Her husband perhaps?"

"She's single," Abby explained. "She was married for a few years, but that was a long time ago. And I know she doesn't have kids. From what I've heard, she's always been married to her job."

The paramedics had Cathy connected to machines now. With grim expressions, they lifted her onto the gurney, quickly adjusting the medical equipment and taping various tubes as they secured her for the trip to the hospital. But as they worked, Cathy's face remained pale and her body lifeless. Marley thought the circumstances really did not look hopeful. The entire lounge grew quiet as everyone helplessly watched their former class president being wheeled out.

After she was gone, the Clifden High School Class of 1973 looked at each other with expressions of shock and confusion. For some reason Marley thought everyone suddenly seemed strangely out of place in the starkly lit lounge. It was hard to imagine that just twenty minutes ago, they were laughing and joking. A few people moved to the door, gathering purses and coats as if preparing to leave. Others didn't seem to know what to do, but everyone seemed equally uncomfortable. It was clear: The party was over.

=Chapter 2=

CAROLINE MCCANN

"I'm going to the hospital," Caroline announced. "Cathy shouldn't be alone. Who wants to come?" As she gathered her jacket and purse, she wondered why she was acting so authoritative. Normally she let others call the shots. But at the moment, it seemed that someone needed to take control, and she was worried about Cathy. This was no time for a single person to be alone.

"We'll come too." Abby glanced at her husband. "Right?"

"Sure." Paul reached in his pocket for his keys.

Caroline grabbed Marley's hand. "Do you want to come too?"

"Well, I—"

"I do," Janie said. "Cathy was a good friend to me when I needed one."

"Okay," Caroline commanded, "let's get this show on the road." She led the way down the stairs and through the lobby. When they reached the parking lot, Caroline continued giving directions. "Marley and Janie can ride with me and we'll meet you guys there, okay?" And just like that, they were on their way.

"Do you think Cathy will be okay?" Marley asked from the backseat.

"She sure didn't look too good." Caroline turned down Driftwood Drive. Going forty-five in the twenty-five zone, she sped toward the hospital and hoped no cops were out tonight.

"Seeing Cathy just lying there," Janie said quietly, "looking so helpless and almost childlike ... well, I had this flashback."

"What kind of flashback?" Marley asked.

"It's something I haven't thought about for ages. But it was the beginning of sophomore year, and Cathy and I were in band together and, as usual, one of the guys in the brass section started teasing me."

"Kids can be so brutal," Marley said in a way that sounded bitter. "And some don't even stop once they've grown up."

"Anyway, Cathy stood up and defended me," Janie continued, "and she did such a brilliant job that the teasing stopped—in band anyway. I was always so grateful to her. But I'm not sure I ever told her thanks." Janie made a sniffing sound and Caroline wondered if she was crying.

"Cathy was—I mean *is*—a real leader," Caroline said. "In the truest sense of the word. She was always kind and helpful to everyone."

"I'll bet she never had a single enemy," Marley said.

Caroline pulled into the hospital's front parking area, snagging a spot near the entrance.

"Wow, I didn't know they built a new hospital," Marley said. "Swanky."

"Yes, it's actually pretty nice," Caroline said as she got out of the rental car. "I know because my mom's been here a couple of times."

"Does your mother have health problems?" Janie asked as they hurried in.

Caroline tapped the side of her forehead as the automatic door slid open. "Mostly just mental ones."

"Oh." Janie frowned. "Is it dementia or Alzheimer's?"

"They're not sure yet. But something upstairs has gotten a little whacked-out in the past couple of years." Caroline blinked as they entered the brightly lit lobby.

"So your mom still lives in town?" Marley asked. The group crossed the shiny laminate floors.

"Yep. Same old house." Caroline almost started to explain that the same old house was about to fall down around her mother's ears but stopped herself short. She just wasn't sure how much to disclose to women she barely knew at all, even though she'd technically known them for decades. In fact this whole racing-to-the-hospital scene seemed a bit surreal. And yet Caroline felt like she was still in charge. And so she headed directly to the information desk and, after several minutes of computer search, was finally informed that Cathy was being treated in the ER.

"It's down that way," Caroline told the others.

"This is so weird," Marley said as they quickly moved down the corridor. "Being here with you guys, I mean. Visiting Cathy in the hospital. Unreal."

"I just hope she's okay," Janie said as they entered a waiting area to see that Abby was already there—pacing.

"Man, you guys must've really sped over here," Caroline said.

"Paul took the short cut," Abby explained. "Then he parked by the ER entrance. He's talking to a nurse right now."

"So you don't know anything yet?" asked Janie.

Abby just shook her head.

A few minutes passed before Paul came over to join them. "We might as well sit down," he said. "The nurse said it's going to be a while."

"But is Cathy conscious?" asked Marley.

He shrugged. "They won't give me details. Apparently Cathy's sister lives about an hour south of here, and she's on her way right now. Anyone want coffee or anything?" They put in their orders, and Paul went off to see what he could find.

"This sure isn't how I expected to spend the evening." Janie slipped off her creamy linen jacket, folded it inside out (probably to keep it clean), and laid it across her lap. Caroline glanced at the designer label as she watched Janie smooth a perfectly manicured hand over the satin lining. *Gucci. Well, of course,* Caroline thought. *Janie is a successful attorney. Why wouldn't she wear Gucci?*

Caroline leaned forward ever so slightly, hoping to discretely check out Janie's pretty shoes, but to her dismay she actually gasped. "*Your shoes,* Janie!"

"What?" Janie looked down in alarm.

"Why, they're absolutely gorgeous!"

Now everyone was staring down at the high-heeled, sleek leopard-print pumps. Janie chuckled as she crossed one slim leg over the other, revealing a flash of bright red sole underneath.

"*Christian Louboutin!*" exclaimed Caroline.

Janie looked slightly embarrassed. "I don't normally indulge a shoe fetish, but I splurged for the reunion."

"Those are so hot." Marley nodded approval.

"They must've cost a fortune," Abby said. "But then, you're single and a successful career woman. Why not?"

Caroline studied Abby. For some reason Caroline had always assumed that Abby was quite well off. Paul was an established developer in Clifden, plus his family had always been wealthy. But judging by Abby's appearance, Caroline wasn't so sure. She would've expected that Abby might've fixed herself up a bit more for their reunion. And yet Abby's sandy brown hair was dull and tinged with gray and seemed to be in need of a good cut. Her limp blue-denim sundress looked like it might've come from a discount store, and her brown leather sandals had definitely seen better days. And yet Abby was still pretty. Those big brown eyes and that warm smile sparkled. But why had she let herself go?

Caroline turned her attention to Marley. She actually looked better than ever. Her short haircut seemed to draw attention to her eyes, and she seemed fitter than Caroline recalled. Marley's clothing, a jewel-toned paisley broomstick skirt and black velveteen lace-trimmed tank, looked stylish if slightly bohemian. And her jewelry, while not exactly Caroline's style, looked handmade and kind of cool. Maybe even costly. Caroline wasn't much of an expert when it came to that sort of jewelry. She was more a gold-and-pearls sort of girl. Although she didn't have much of that to show for herself.

Marley slapped her forehead. "Do you guys know what we have here?"

"A bunch of middle-aged women, waiting to see if an old friend is going to be okay," ventured Abby.

"No!" Marley firmly shook her head. "We have the Four Lindas!"

"Oh-mi-gosh!" exclaimed Caroline.

"That's right," Janie said quietly.

"Can you believe it?" Abby smiled. "After all these years, the Four Lindas are reunited."

"I wonder how long it's been since we started our little club," mused Caroline.

"Let's see." Janie appeared to be doing the mental math. "Forty-seven years," she proclaimed.

"Boy, does that make me feel old." Abby sighed.

"Age is just a number, baby," Marley told her.

"So do you guys remember that day in Miss Spangle's class?" Caroline asked. "When she took that first roll call and nearly fell out of her shoes?"

"She thought it was a joke," Janie reminded them.

Now Caroline pointed to Abby. "Roll call, *begin.*"

"Linda Franklin," said Abby with a twinkle in her eye, "here!"

Caroline went next. "Linda McCann. Here."

"Linda Phelps," Marley said with a chuckle, "here!"

"Linda Sorenson," Janie said finally, *"here."*

"The Four Lindas, present and accounted for," said Caroline. "I call this meeting to order." And then they all giggled like they were in first grade again.

"I feel terrible," Abby said as she wiped tears from her eyes. "We're out here laughing and Cathy is in there ... well, who knows?"

They all nodded, quickly sobering up.

"But you have to admit that it's funny," Caroline whispered. "I mean the four of us here together."

"Who would've thought?" Marley just shook her head.

"I'm surprised none of us ever went back to using our first names." Janie spoke quietly. "I know I considered it briefly during law school, but it just didn't feel right. I'd gone by my middle name for so long that I couldn't even imagine being called Linda. Although when I'm working, I go by Jane, not Janie. It sounds more authoritative."

"I've never been that crazy about being called Linda either," admitted Marley. "I actually tried using both my first and middle names together after my divorce for a while. But being Linda Marlene felt odd. And the name Linda just never sounded very artistic to me."

"Thank goodness for middle names." Caroline opened her bag to fish out a lipstick. She wondered if Janie would guess that her purse was a fake D&G, since it was actually a pretty good imitation that had even fooled her shopaholic neighbor.

"Do you know I looked the name up online once?" Janie told them. "Linda was the second most common name for girls born in the fifties."

"Big surprise there." Caroline touched up her lipstick, taking her time to press her lips together.

"What was the first?"

"Mary."

"Mary?" Abby frowned. "Was anyone in our class even named Mary?"

They all shook their heads.

"Maybe it was a regional thing," suggested Janie. "The Lindas were out West and the Marys were back East."

They were still chatting about their common name when Paul

returned with their drinks. "I thought I heard a party going on down this way," he said as he handed out paper cups. "Does that mean Cathy is better?"

Abby frowned. "No. We haven't actually heard anything yet."

He looked curiously at them. "But you all sounded so merry."

"I think we kind of forgot where we were," Caroline admitted.

"And I tend to giggle when I'm nervous," Marley told him.

Then Abby explained to him about the Four Lindas.

"You're kidding me," he said. "You're *all* named Linda?"

"And we used to have a club," Caroline explained.

"But it fell apart by sixth grade," Marley filled in.

"Why?" He sat down next to his wife.

"Oh, we started going our separate ways." Abby shrugged. "Caroline and I both got boy crazy, and we started wearing makeup and heels and stuffing our bras."

"And I wanted to be a hippie," Marley said. "That meant *no* bra."

Paul chuckled.

"And I got braces and zits and turned into a social-phobic wallflower," Janie admitted. "I was quite a pathetic creature."

"But here you all are," Paul said, "back together again. And, if I do say so, you're a fine-looking bunch of ladies." He glanced over to the reception area, where a nurse had just emerged from ER and was talking in hushed tones to the woman managing the desk. "Would you like me to check on Cathy again?" he offered.

"Yes," Abby said eagerly. "Please do."

"I wasn't too fond of Paul in high school," Marley told Abby when he was out of earshot. "But I have to admit he's turned out to be a very nice man."

Abby pointed to herself. "Well, thank you very much. I guess I can take a little of the credit for that."

"No doubt you've had a good influence on him," Marley said wryly.

When Paul returned, his expression was solemn.

"What is it?" demanded Abby.

"They haven't been able to revive her."

"Does that mean she's dead?" asked Caroline.

He nodded sadly. "Medically speaking, she *is* dead. There's no sign of brain activity, and it's only the machines that are keeping her vital signs going."

"Oh no!" Janie's hand flew to her mouth and she began to cry.

"But I've heard of people getting revived," Marley said hopefully, "even after they were proclaimed dead. We can't give up on her yet."

"Let's pray," Caroline suggested. And although prayer was still relatively new to her, she wanted to rely on it more. She knew it made a difference. Maybe it would make a difference now. And so they all bowed their heads, but it seemed that only Caroline was praying. Everyone else remained silent. Just the same, Caroline was determined not to give up on Cathy. She hadn't always been a believer. But some things had happened the past few years—things that made her trust the power of prayer. They were still praying when Cathy's sister arrived, rushing in with her husband trailing behind her. But no one was at the desk to answer their questions.

"What's happening to Cathy?" the sister demanded. "Do you guys know *anything?*"

Paul stood up and gave her the heartbreaking details, and the sister immediately broke down into tears. They all did their best to comfort her, but before long everyone was crying again. And that's when the doctor came out and told them that it was over. "We did all we could, but Cathy had already suffered cardiac arrest. She was dead even before the paramedics arrived."

"Her heart?" The sister looked stunned. "But she seemed perfectly healthy."

"Sometimes that's how it seems."

"She had no history of heart problems that I knew of," she persisted. "And she went to the gym three times a week."

"Unfortunately fitness, while good, doesn't exclude anyone from heart disease." The doctor looked at all of them now. "Did you ladies know that heart disease is the number-one killer of women in your age group?"

"I thought it was cancer," Caroline said quietly.

"No, heart disease more than doubles cancer." He sadly shook his head. "Sorry to sound so grim, but so often it's women who don't take the symptoms seriously. A man suffers chest pains and he usually calls the doctor. A woman has the exact same pains, and yet she chalks it up to stress or indigestion." He turned back to Cathy's sister now. "I'll need you to help fill out some paperwork, please."

With tears in her eyes, Cathy's sister thanked them for coming, then she and her husband followed the doctor behind closed doors.

"This is so sad." Caroline blew her nose on a tissue.

"I wonder if we should cancel the reunion barbecue tomorrow," Abby said to no one in particular.

"Doesn't seem there's much else we can do here," Paul told her. "And it's past midnight." He and Abby said their good-byes.

"I'll drive you girls back to the hotel," Caroline told Marley and Janie. "That's where I'm staying anyway."

"So am I," Janie told her.

"I don't have a room yet, but I think I'll stay there tonight too," Marley said.

"I'm not sure there'll be a room left," Caroline warned her. "They seemed pretty busy when I checked in this afternoon."

As it turned out, Caroline was right. Thanks to the reunion, the hotel was full, but Caroline offered Marley the extra queen bed in her room. And then, because all three of them were still feeling upset and unsettled, they gathered in Caroline's room to talk and didn't end up going to bed until nearly two in the morning.

Even then Caroline had difficulty sleeping. Whether it was the doctor's sobering warning about women and heart disease, or the fact that an old friend had just died, Caroline felt reminded of her own mortality. It wasn't a new feeling, but perhaps one she had managed to suppress over the past couple of years. What troubled her most was the feeling that, despite a promise she'd made to herself several years ago, she hadn't really lived her life to the fullest yet.

She wasn't even thinking about her old Hollywood aspirations this time. Caroline was nobody's fool; she was fully aware that real stardom was not only a long shot, but pretty much an impossibility at this stage of the game. There were times she'd thought differently, times when she'd hoped that one small opportunity would lead to another. But it never quite panned out. Not like she'd dreamed anyway.

Out of habit she still read the trade magazines sometimes. She knew of women her age, big-name stars who were already established, who were unable to get cast in anything worthwhile. The truth was, the only roles she'd ever had were walk-ons and bit parts and the occasional commercial, and that was when she'd been younger. Once she hit her fifties, she found herself fighting a depressing, losing battle. The glamour and glitz of her childhood dream had finally tarnished.

The thing that kept her awake tonight was the fact that her life was one great big, fat disappointment. Despite her general optimism, and even her attempt to play the role of a successful Hollywood personality at the reunion, she knew that she was mostly fooling herself—and then only barely. In the raw darkness of night, with death on her mind, she felt painfully aware of her reality. For one thing, she was still alone. No husband, no boyfriend, no significant other. Nada. Add to that the fact that she was unhappily employed. Sure, she worked in an impressive Beverly Hills restaurant, and tips weren't bad, but she was basically a middle-aged waitress. Really, did life get any more pathetic than that?

What troubled her most—and she couldn't even figure this one out—was that she had never owned a dog. As silly as this dog fixation seemed, it was really getting her down tonight. For as long as Caroline could remember, she had *always* wanted a dog. Specifically a golden retriever. But her parents had never allowed it, and later in life she'd lived in apartments and condos where a large, energetic dog seemed irresponsible.

As Caroline silently cried herself to sleep, she wondered if she would live long enough to have a dog of her own.

=Chapter 3=

ABBY FRANKLIN

Abby woke early on Sunday. She got out of bed feeling refreshed and happy and vibrant. And why shouldn't she be? It was a perfect August morning and the ocean stretching outside of her floor-to-ceiling, west-facing windows looked calm and peaceful and bluer than blue. But as she slipped her feet into her slippers, she remembered Cathy Gardener, and her spirits plunged. *Poor Cathy!*

Abby's step felt tired and heavy as she trudged out to the kitchen to make coffee. As it brewed, she stood and stared out at the seascape, yet hardly saw it at all. Although it made no sense, Abby blamed herself for Cathy's unexpected demise. It was all her fault!

Her therapist had once accused Abby of being a guilt monger, taking credit for all the earth's ailments and blaming herself for anything and everything that could possibly be wrong with the world. Of course, she rarely went to her therapist anymore. But in this situation, she thought her therapist (who probably had been friends with Cathy) might agree that Abby truly was the responsible party. After all, who had grabbed Cathy's hand last night? Who urged Cathy out to the dance floor? Who selfishly wanted a break? Who stood by watching as Cathy dropped dead?

"I smell coffee." Paul came into the kitchen in his T-shirt and boxers.

Abby nodded sadly.

"Are you okay?" he asked.

"As okay as one can be while taking a guilt trip."

"And what are you tripping about this time?" Paul filled his favorite mug with coffee, then turned to look at her.

"Cathy Gardener."

He frowned. "Why?"

"*Why?*" She held up her hands as if this were perfectly obvious. "*I'm* the one who dragged Cathy onto the dance floor. *I'm* the one who made her dance with you and I'm—"

"You *made* her?" Paul sort of laughed, but his eyes were sad. "Apparently you didn't know Cathy Gardener as well as I thought you did. No one ever *made* that woman do anything she didn't want to do, Abby."

"But she dropped dead out there, Paul. If I hadn't pushed her to—"

"Then I should share your guilt," he said. "I'm the one who danced with her, not you. And while we're casting blame here, let's not forget Keith Arnold. He's the one who was dancing with Cathy when she collapsed. Maybe we should call the police and have him—"

"Oh, Paul!" Abby slammed her coffee mug so hard onto the marble countertop that she was surprised it didn't shatter. "Don't be ridiculous."

"I was just playing your little guilt game."

"Thanks a lot." She filled her cup and let out a long sigh.

He leaned over and pecked her on the cheek. "Don't be so hard on yourself all the time. Cathy died because it was her time to go. You had nothing to do with it."

"I suppose." She took a slow sip.

"Now, if I'm going to make that tee time, I better get moving."

"You're still playing golf today?" she demanded. "After what happened last night?"

"I'm the one who made the arrangements for the reunion tournament, Abby. I've got to show up."

"What if no one else does?"

"Then I'll just explain the situation and hope that Shore Links will be understanding and not charge me everyone's green fees."

"And what about the beach barbecue?" she asked him. "Should we cancel it?"

"I don't see why. A lot of these people have been looking forward to it. And last night, well, it was a disappointment to everyone."

"But what if no one shows up?"

"You've already ordered the food," he pointed out. "And you've got help coming, and everything's pretty much ready, right?"

"I've been getting ready for this for weeks." It was true. She'd really thrown herself into planning for this barbecue. Despite Paul's urges that she have the entire thing catered, she had done some of the cooking herself, sticking food away in the big freezer so it would be ready. Nowadays, cooking seemed to be one of the few things she really enjoyed doing.

"Then you might as well proceed, just in case a few people do come."

"I suppose." Abby remembered the Four Lindas. "And maybe Janie, Caroline, and Marley will come."

"Yes, I'm sure they'll be here. And maybe we can do something special, you know, in Cathy's memory," he suggested.

"You mean like throw flowers out onto the ocean?"

He smiled sadly. "She didn't die at sea."

Abby closed her eyes. "I just can't believe she's gone."

He set down his cup and wrapped his arms around her. "I know this is hard, Abby. I'm feeling it too. But Cathy wouldn't have wanted us to drop everything for her sake. Think about it: She was always so organized and such a go-getter. How would she feel if the reunion— a reunion she helped to plan—came to a screeching halt?"

"You're right." Abby nodded firmly. "I know you're right."

But after he left, she felt the guilt rising up in her again. She couldn't stop it any more than the little boy who put his finger in the dam could stop the water from flooding the city. That's how it usually went with her and guilt.

Abby used to think these feelings of guilt were just a normal part of motherhood. With three daughters, she had often worried that she wasn't doing everything quite right. Or not doing enough. Whether it was potty training (too soon or too late?) or whether to make them take ballet or piano (or both?), she had never been quite sure. She second-guessed herself if the girls had sisterly feuds or if they complained about their clothes or fretted over their weight. Whatever the problem, Abby almost always felt certain the cause was her fault.

Then, as her daughters grew older, Abby feared that she'd neglected to give them all they needed when they were younger.

When they had problems in adolescence, Abby questioned herself to figure out what she'd done wrong to make them handle life the way they did. Although her daughters hadn't been terribly messed up, they had experienced their share of troubles. Once they got into their twenties, they seemed to level out. For the most part anyway.

It did bother Abby that her oldest daughter seemed to think more highly of her career than she did of her four-year-old daughter, Lucy. If only they lived closer, Abby would happily take care of Lucy during the workweek. Certainly that would be better than being cared for by strangers. She hated the idea of Lucy spending forty hours a week in day care. And she blamed herself for not living closer to her daughter. But to move a hundred miles? Well, Paul had made it clear that wasn't going to happen.

And then there was her middle daughter. Abby tried not to think of Laurie too much since that usually led not only to guilt, but depression as well. Laurie kept her family at a distance for the past couple of years. No one seemed to know why, although Abby assumed it must be her fault. But whenever she brought her concerns up to Laurie, the conversation ended abruptly. Abby's therapist had said Laurie would probably outgrow this kind of thing in her thirties, but that was still a few years away.

Then, of course, there was the youngest daughter, Nicole. Fortunately Nicole was their happy sunshine girl, and the only thing Abby could complain about was that she missed Nicole terribly. Well, that and the fact that Nicole had dropped out of college last year. That had been more upsetting to Paul than Abby, though. But Nicole had decided to live in France for a while, claiming it would help her to focus on art. Abby had tried to sound supportive, but the truth was she wished that Nicole would come home. Why couldn't she focus on art here?

The ringing of the phone interrupted her guilt trip, but when she answered, it took a moment to realize the caller was Janie. "Oh, hi, Janie, how're you doing?"

"All right, considering I'm sleep deprived. Anyway, Marley and Caroline and I were just heading out to get some breakfast in town, and then we wanted to take a walk on the beach. We wondered if you'd like to join us."

Abby considered this. When was the last time a girlfriend had called out of the blue and invited her to do something like this? She couldn't even remember. "Sure," she said eagerly. "Let me throw something on and I'll be right there."

"Caroline suggested Clifden Coffee Company. She said they serve a light breakfast. Does that sound okay?"

"Sounds perfect."

Abby felt unexpectedly happy as she pulled on her khaki capri pants, a plaid shirt, and her faithful old Dansko sandals. She paused to glance at herself in the full-length mirror and frowned. She felt so frumpy and fat compared to the women she was about to meet. She ran a brush through her faded hair, attempting to fluff it and give it some life, but her efforts seemed useless. She even took time to put on some lipstick, but that only made her look slightly haggard, so she wiped it off. She felt like canceling, except she didn't know Janie's number. If only she could turn back the clock and be young and vivacious and energetic again. How did Janie, Caroline, and Marley manage to look so good in their fifties anyway? It probably helped that those women had lives. Abby wished she had a life—a reason to get into shape, to wear stylish clothes, to wake up with a spring in her step.

"Oh, stop being foolish," she told herself. "Go out and meet your friends." She thought about the word *friends* as she slung the strap of her oversized canvas bag over one shoulder. Were those women really her friends? Oh, sure, they'd created a club as kids, but that had fallen to the wayside. Soon Marley would return to Seattle, Janie to New York, and Caroline to LA. All places that seemed so far away, not to mention more glamorous and exotic than little Clifden.

As Abby drove into town, she had to ask herself who her friends in Clifden were. Sometimes she met Jackie for coffee. But Jackie's bed-and-breakfast kept her pretty busy, and really, they had little in common.

Abby remembered how social she'd been in high school. It seemed she'd had friends by the boatload. But she'd married while everyone else was heading for college, and then the kids came. After that she was consumed with her family, and for a long time she'd believed her daughters were her friends.

Feeling cynical, Abby laughed as she parked in front of the coffee house. Yeah, right, her daughters were her friends. Oh, sure, they loved her. She knew that. But they all had friends of their own. The sixty-thousand-dollar question was, why didn't she?

=Chapter 4=

JANIE SORENSON

Janie really didn't think anyone would be checking in with her in regard to work. Not on a Sunday anyway. But she felt the need to have a short break from Marley and Caroline, and because she'd given up smoking after Phil died, her BlackBerry provided her with the next best excuse to step out onto the Clifden Coffee Company's rear deck, which overlooked the ocean. It wasn't that she didn't like Marley and Caroline. But for some reason she felt some kind of unspoken pressure from them. She couldn't put her finger on it exactly, but it was as if they expected something from her. She wasn't even sure what. They kept treating her like she was so smart and accomplished. The big New York attorney. Like they thought every time she opened her mouth, they would experience … what? Brilliance, perhaps?

The problem was, she just didn't feel terribly smart. Truth be told, she was simply a hard worker. A very hard worker. It was her late husband, Phil, who'd had the brains in the family. Well, perhaps her son would live up to his father's legend in time. Being twenty, he had plenty of time. But when it came to her older child, Janie wasn't so sure. In fact she'd rather not think about her daughter at the moment.

"What a perfect day," said a male voice.

She turned to see a middle-aged man sitting in the far corner of the deck. He was smoking a pipe while leaning back on a chair with his feet propped up on the railing. With his trimmed gray beard and faded denim shirt, he was rather picturesque in a beachy, natural sort of way, kind of like a young version of the stereotypical old fisherman.

"I didn't know anyone else was out here," she said, then wondered why she'd thought he needed to know that. "But, yes, I must agree, it's a lovely day. Some people assume just because it's summer that every day at the beach should be this nice. But I know better."

He tipped his sunglasses back on his head and squinted. "Are you from around here?"

"I used to be." She glanced back down at her BlackBerry, although she knew there was nothing much to look at there. "Now I live in New York."

"Where in New York?"

"Manhattan."

He let out a low whistle. "Big city girl, eh? And let me guess, you're actually working right now?"

"Not exactly. Just checking on things."

"But it's too nice of a day to be working. You should be out playing."

She dropped her BlackBerry back into her bag. "And that's exactly what I plan to do." She turned to see that Abby was just coming into the coffee shop. Waving to her, she said. "My friends and I are having breakfast, then we're heading to the beach."

He followed her gaze then looked surprised. "You're friends with Abby Franklin?"

"Yes, as a matter of fact."

He stood and moved closer, peering curiously at her face, then looking back through the window to where Abby was joining Caroline and Marley. "And Caroline McCann is your friend too?"

She sort of shrugged, then wondered why this guy seemed to know everyone. She also wondered at his eyes. They were ocean blue with deep, fanned-out wrinkles at the edges, as if he laughed a lot.

"Who are you, anyway?" he asked. "Are you here for the Clifden class reunion?"

"Guilty as charged," she admitted.

"But I don't recognize you."

"Are you here for the reunion?" she asked in a formal-sounding tone, the kind she might use in court.

"I'm not sure." He chuckled.

"What does that mean?"

"Well, I did graduate with the class, but I didn't really know many people."

A little light bulb went off in her head. "Are you ..." She stared at him in disbelief. "Are you Victor Zilkowski?"

He smiled and the wrinkles by his eyes deepened. "How did you know?"

"I'm Janie Sorenson."

He reached for the table next to him as if he needed to balance himself. "No way," he said as he gaped at her.

She smiled. "It looks like we've both changed." She glanced over to where all three of her friends were watching her now. They looked very curious. "I'm keeping my friends waiting."

"But you were never friends with those girls."

She held a finger up. "But see? That just shows what you don't know. We were all very good friends in grade school."

He nodded but seemed disappointed. "Well, don't let me keep you."

"Why don't you come in and meet—rather, remeet them?"

He seemed reluctant, but Janie did something that surprised herself. She linked her arm in his and tugged him along. "Come on," she told him. "They don't bite."

He chuckled but came willingly.

"And trust me, they've all become much nicer with age." Soon she was introducing Victor to the others, but only Marley seemed to remember him. And only vaguely.

"Don't feel badly," he told them. "I did my best to stay below the radar." He grinned. "I was a small, geeky kid with the worst inferiority complex imaginable."

"Kind of like me," Janie admitted.

"But look how nicely you both turned out," Caroline said with a bright smile. "Are you coming to the reunion barbecue today, Victor?"

He looked unsure.

"Of course you're coming," Janie assured him.

"Oh yes!" Abby said quickly. "Please, *do* come. It's at my house, and I'm so worried that no one will show."

"Why would no one show?"

"Oh, you probably haven't heard the unfortunate news." Janie glanced at her friends, and Abby explained last night's tragedy.

"No, I hadn't heard." He shook his head sadly. "That's really too bad. Cathy was one of the few people I actually knew from our class. Not from high school so much. But she was so kind and gracious when I moved back to town a few months ago. She helped me work out some permits with the city. Wow. I just can't believe she's dead."

"That's how we all feel," Marley told him.

"It puts a real damper on this reunion," Caroline said.

"I'd like to do something at the barbecue today," Abby said slowly. "Something to remember her by. I'm not even sure what exactly. But I do hope you'll come, Victor."

"Yes," Caroline urged him. "Do it for Cathy."

He nodded. "All right, I will."

Abby was already writing down her address on a napkin. "Here, just in case you don't have your reunion packet. It begins at two."

He tipped his head to them. "Nice seeing you ladies. Hopefully I'll see you again later." Then he left.

"Hasn't he grown up into a great-looking man?" Caroline said as soon as he was out the door. "Although I honestly don't remember him from school."

"I'm sure you probably never noticed him," Janie said as she sat down and picked up a small paper menu. "Did you girls order yet?"

"No, we were waiting for you," Marley said.

"When we're ready, we order at the counter," Abby explained. "So were you and Victor good friends in school, Janie?"

Janie looked up and sort of laughed. "Not exactly. I mean, we spoke occasionally. And he was on the debate team. As I recall, he was very smart."

"What does he do now?" Caroline asked.

"I have no idea," Janie admitted. "We didn't really get that far."

"Hopefully he'll come to the barbecue." Caroline chuckled. "And then we can *grill* him good."

They all laughed as they went up front to place their orders. But as she waited for the others, Janie felt caught off guard by a slight twinge of envy toward Caroline. The emotion seemed ridiculous and unfounded, but it was there all the same. As much as Janie hated to admit it, her jealousy was related to Victor. So silly. As juvenile as grade school. In the two years since Phil had died, Janie had not so much as looked at a guy—not once. She didn't plan to start now.

"And for you?" asked the young man behind the counter.

Janie ordered a skinny latte and whole-wheat bagel, plain, and was about to pay when Abby stepped up. "Is that *all* you're having?" she demanded. "Good grief, Janie, that wouldn't keep a bird alive."

"I'm not that hungry," Janie told her. "Besides I don't usually eat breakfast."

"Don't eat breakfast?" Caroline frowned. "Don't you know that's terrible for your metabolism?"

"Doesn't look like it's hurt anything as far as weight goes," Abby said a bit sheepishly. "But it's just not healthy, Janie. You really need to start your morning with a good breakfast—especially as you get older."

"She's right," Marley agreed. "I always like to start my day with protein."

"I'll make Janie eat some of my eggs," Abby said in a sneaky tone.

Janie laughed as she dropped a dollar in the tip jar. "I feel like I'm having breakfast with my mothers."

"Thanks a lot," Abby told her. "But I'm afraid mothering comes naturally to me. I have three daughters and they never listen to me."

Janie patted Abby on the back. "Thanks, I appreciate that you care." It actually was rather sweet to be mothered, especially since Janie's own mother had never seemed overly concerned about Janie's health one way or another. This had always seemed odd to Janie, considering how her mom had been obsessed with health and medicine in general. Except Mom had always fretted over her own health, not the health of others. From as early as Janie could remember, her mother thought she was dying. She'd had Janie late in life and attributed many of her unusual maladies to that fact. When she claimed to have things like malaria and leprosy, though, Janie and her father started to wonder. They did what they could to convince Mom otherwise, but eventually Janie began to understand that her mother simply suffered from a bad case of hypochondria. Ironically she lived to be eighty-seven.

As the four of them ate breakfast together, they joked and reminisced about grade school. "Remember when Bradley Moore hid a snake in Mrs. Denfeld's desk?" Marley was laughing so hard she could barely speak. "And the poor woman was so frightened she actually wet herself?"

"I feel sorry for her now that I'm in my fifties," Abby admitted. "I can see how something like that could happen."

"Or how about when Mr. Peters suspended the four of us just

because we said we'd rather have recess than school?" Caroline reminded them. "My parents were furious."

"Caroline," said Abby, "do you remember when Allen Reynolds held you down and kissed you?"

Caroline made a face. "And that was *before* we were boy crazy. I was so upset, I washed and washed my mouth, afraid that I'd have boy germs forever." She sighed. "I wonder where Allen is now."

Abby laughed. "Last time I saw him, he was bald and wearing suspenders."

"Suspenders?" Caroline made a face. "Seriously?"

"Oh yeah." Abby nodded. "A lot of the good-old boys in these parts favor suspenders."

"Now that's something you don't see in Manhattan," mused Janie. She leaned back and sipped her coffee, listening as the others recalled funny stories she could barely remember. It felt strangely familiar to be with these three friends from her past, and comforting, too. And yet it was all so unexpected.

After breakfast they headed to the beach. Parking their cars at the jetty, they all got out, took off their shoes, and proceeded to walk along the water's edge. After a while they paired off. Marley and Janie walked in front, with Abby and Caroline following.

"I know you live in Seattle," Janie said to Marley, "but I'm not sure what you do."

"I work in a friend's art gallery."

"Oh, that sounds fun."

"I suppose, but I'd rather be doing my own art full time."

"So you still do art?"

"When I get the chance."

"Why don't you do it full-time?"

Marley laughed. "Because I'd rather be selling someone else's art than living as a starving artist."

"Right. So what does your husband do?"

"My exhusband is a commercial pilot."

"Oh, I didn't know you were divorced."

"It's only been a few years. The last reunion I was still with him."

"Has that been hard?"

"Financially. But in every other way, it's been wonderful. I wish we would've divorced ages ago."

"Really?"

Marley paused to pick up a shell, dropping it into her cardigan pocket. "Absolutely. It was a rotten marriage."

"How so?"

Marley sighed. "Well, for starters, John was one of those pilots who felt that being away from home entitled him to sleep with other women. You know, a woman in every port. Airport, that is."

Janie chuckled. "That must've been hard."

She nodded. "But that wasn't the worst of it. He was also emotionally abusive. I mean, I could never do anything right as far as that man was concerned, whether it was having his uniform looking picture-perfect, or dinner, or my hair. Everything was always wrong. Wrong. Wrong. Wrong." She kicked the sand with her bare toe and swore.

"That couldn't have been fun."

"Nope. The main reason I stuck it out for so long was for our son. I told myself that when Ashton graduated high school, I'd leave John."

"How old is Ashton?"

"Almost thirty." Marley shrugged. "Yeah. I stayed with John a little longer than I'd planned. The truth was, I was scared to go out on my own. I'd never really had a career. My excuse was that I was an artist, except I wasn't doing much art. My marriage sort of sucked the life out of me. It's like I never had the emotional energy to do much of anything."

"But you do now?"

"Isn't life funny? Now I have the right kind of energy and a desire to do art. Unfortunately I don't have the time. I put in about fifty hours a week at the gallery."

"Oh."

"But at least I'm happier." Marley turned to Janie. "How about you? What's your story? I know your husband died a couple of years ago, but that's about all I know. Do you have kids?"

"Yes. Two. A girl and boy. Twenty-two and twenty, respectively."

"Respectively," Marley imitated, then laughed.

"I know. Sometimes I sound just like an attorney." Janie took in a deep breath of fresh sea air. "My son, Matthew, is starting his junior year at Princeton."

"Mmm. Princeton. Impressive."

"It was Phil's alma mater. I went to Stanford. Anyway, Lisa is my oldest and she's had, well, some challenges. We're a little out of touch at the moment."

"Out of touch?"

Janie stopped and faced Marley. "I don't normally tell people this. It's not easy to say. Lisa has a drug problem. She's been in treatment twice, but it just doesn't seem to stick. I haven't spoken to her since June." She felt tears in her eyes and wondered why she'd just confessed this dark secret to a woman she barely knew. Even some of her closest coworkers were unaware of what was going on with Lisa.

To Janie's surprise, Marley hugged her. "I'm so sorry," she said quietly. "That has to be really hard."

Janie nodded as the two of them stepped apart. "It is."

"Well, since you told me your secret, I'll tell mine." Marley grinned uncomfortably. "My son, Ashton, is gay."

"Oh." Janie just nodded and the two of them continued to walk.

"I know, you're probably wondering why that would be a big deal to a free spirit like me. Aren't artists supposed to be loose and liberal about these things? The answer is yes, as long as it's someone else's kids. When it's your own kid, well, that takes some getting used to. Fortunately I'm mostly over it now. But the idea of never having grandchildren gets to me sometimes."

"But he can still have—"

"He doesn't want to."

"Oh. Well." Janie sighed. "I guess we can't live our children's lives, can we?"

"No." Marley shook her head. "I have enough difficulty just living my own."

"I hear you." It was true. Janie's life had been nothing but difficult for nearly five years. First it was Phil's diagnosis of colon cancer. Then the treatments. Then Lisa's drug addiction, which she tried to hide from Phil. Then his death shortly after Matthew graduated high school. And most recently her parents' deaths. Sometimes she wondered how much more she could take—she felt like she was hanging on by a frayed thread. If not for her children, she might've given up already.

==Chapter 5==

MARLEY

"Your home is absolutely beautiful," Marley told Abby as she welcomed the three of them into her new home. Marley took in the spacious and well-appointed room, with its hardwood floors, enormous stone fireplace, massive built-in shelves, and furnishings that looked straight out of *Architectural Digest*. Marley noticed the wall of floor-to-ceiling wood-framed windows that overlooked the ocean. Everything about this place really was stunning. Perfection both outside and in. And the view was killer.

As much as the emotion irked her, Marley felt seriously jealous. And she wondered why some people seemed to have all the luck. Abby had married a great guy and now lived in this fantastic house. In comparison Marley's life seemed like a dismal failure. A big, fat disappointment.

"Your view is gorgeous," Janie was telling Abby.

Marley nodded, determined not to fall victim to these waves of envy. "If I lived here, I'd never get anything done, because I'd be glued to the windows all day long."

"If I lived here, I'd get a dog," Caroline said.

Abby laughed. "Yes, I've considered that. But Paul's not fond of indoor pets, and I can't see keeping a dog outside during the winter. It's too wet and cold here."

It had been Marley's idea that they should come early to help with the barbecue, but it seemed Abby had everything under control. "I wanted to do all of the cooking myself," she told them, "but Paul insisted we get some help. Even so, I went ahead and made a few things. But I'll probably just leave them in the freezer for another day." She waved at the trays of food lining her counters and sighed. "Already this looks like far too much."

"This is a delightful kitchen," Marley told Abby. This room, too, looked like it might've been clipped out of a magazine. It wasn't necessarily Marley's style—if Marley really had a style; she wasn't so sure—but the kitchen's warm colors were lovely just the same. And it was far nicer than Marley's tiny galley kitchen, not that she ever cooked.

"I like that it doesn't have that stark feeling of some of the new homes," Caroline told Abby. "You know, the ones that are all granite and stainless steel."

Abby smiled. "I was going for French country." She pointed to a big ceramic rooster perched in a corner of the travertine countertop. "Paul said if I brought one more chicken in here, he was going to start crowing."

"Well, I think it's charming," Marley told her.

"And it suits you," Janie added. "Sweet and homey."

"Would you like to see the rest of the house?" Abby offered. Soon she was giving them the grand tour. "We wanted it to feel roomy and comfortable but not too big," she said as they paused in the large master suite, which also looked out over the ocean. "It's just a little over twenty-four hundred square feet."

Janie laughed. "That sounds big to me. My apartment is less than a thousand, although that's considered roomy by some New York standards."

"And my condo's less than eight hundred square feet," Caroline said.

"I can beat you all," Marley told them. "My studio apartment is only six hundred eighty square feet."

"Isn't it funny how different our lives are from each other's? And so far apart geographically," mused Abby. "And yet we all started out in the same place."

"With the same name," added Marley, making the others laugh.

"Sometimes I wonder what it would be like to move back to Clifden," Janie mused as they stood in the spacious master bathroom.

"Seriously?" Abby looked surprised.

"Well, I still have my parents' home. I need to decide what to do with it."

"Why not keep it for a vacation getaway?" Marley ran her hand over the slate tile that bordered the edge of the oversized tub. She didn't even have a tub in her apartment.

"I've considered that. The truth is, I'm not sure I can afford to keep it with Matthew at Princeton. Plus I'm still paying medical bills that Phil's insurance didn't cover. Well, it might be more sensible to just sell it."

Abby continued the tour, finally stopping off at the den, where a bartender was manning the bar. "Why don't we get something to drink?" she suggested. "Then we can sit out on the deck and relax until the other guests arrive. That is, if they arrive." She looked at her watch. "I expect they'll be finishing up that golf tournament soon."

They got their drinks and went out to soak up some sun.

"This is so beautiful." Marley leaned back into the padded lounge chair. She felt like Pollyanna with all her praise and positive remarks, but it seemed the only way to squelch the screaming, jealous demon inside of her. "What a glorious day."

"It's what Paul calls a real-estate day," Abby told them. "He says you could sell anything to anyone on a day like this."

"You could sell me," Marley admitted. "In fact I was strolling through town after our beach walk, and I started falling in love with Clifden all over again. I love the smallness and the charm, the friendly shopkeepers. Well, it's a lot different than Seattle."

"And Manhattan," added Janie.

"And LA." Caroline sighed.

"Well, don't let this weather trick you," Abby reminded them. "You've all lived here before, so you know that it can be windy, stormy, foggy. Sometimes all in one day!"

"Yes." Caroline nodded. "Like the old *if you don't like the weather now, just wait.* I never appreciated that until I lived in Southern California for a while."

"Or how about the old joke about the coast wind?" Marley said. "How do you know when the wind stops blowing on the beach?"

"Everyone falls down," Janie finished for her.

"Or what about, 'Oregonians don't tan, they rust,'" Abby said.

"Speaking of tanning ..." Janie lowered her sunglasses and

pointed to Caroline. "You must not be too worried about skin cancer with that tan you've got."

Caroline shrugged. "Hey, once you've survived breast cancer, you figure, what's the big deal?"

The other three got quiet.

"You had breast cancer?" asked Marley.

"It's been more than five years," Caroline said cheerfully.

"Congratulations." Abby lifted her hand to give her a high five.

"Thanks." Caroline put her hands beneath her boobs now, giving them a push to reveal a fair amount of cleavage. "And I did get some enhancements out of the deal. These girls are both the result of implants."

"Nice." Marley nodded. "I could use a pair of those myself."

"Well, even though you're a survivor, you should be careful with the sun." Abby held out a bottle of sunscreen. "Anyone need to lather up?"

"Hey, if I get skin cancer, it'll be from the overexposure I had as a kid," Caroline told them. "Do you guys remember that time we floated out with the tide on our air mattresses?"

"Oh, don't remind me." Janie shook her head. "I was grounded for a month after that."

"It wasn't like we did it intentionally." Marley took a sip of her margarita. "We were just having fun."

"Yeah," agreed Caroline. "And girls just want to have fun."

"But it wasn't much fun getting our backs burnt to a crisp." Abby winced. "My mother almost took me to the hospital, I was in so much pain."

"I remember my mom put towels soaked in milk on my back,"

Marley told them. "It actually helped, although I smelled like a cheese factory for a few days."

They all laughed.

Abby set her lemonade down and turned to look at the other three. "You know, I can't remember when I've had so much fun with girlfriends."

"I was actually feeling a little guilty," Janie told them. "I mean, when I think about Cathy Gardener and how we should be in mourning today."

Caroline slapped her forehead. "Oh, I'd almost completely forgotten."

"I know what you mean," admitted Marley. "Last night seems kind of removed from this beautiful, sunny day. It's hard to feel too sad."

"I suppose I've gotten good at it." Janie leaned over to rub sunscreen onto her shins. "It feels like I've been grieving for years now. I guess it just comes naturally to me."

Marley reached over and patted Janie's bent back. "I know divorce isn't the same as death," Marley said, "but it comes with its own kind of grief."

"There are all kinds of grief," Abby said quietly. "Not all related to death."

"You know what's weird?" Caroline said. "Although I'm really sad about Cathy, it kind of feels like her death brought us together last night."

Janie nodded as she sat up straight. "Strange, isn't it?"

"And I have to say, it's been very cool being with you guys," Marley said. "Kinda like old times."

"Old, old times." Caroline chuckled. "I mean, think about it: We've known each other for close to five decades. Doesn't that seem crazy? Are we really that old?"

"And yet being with you three makes me feel younger." Abby smiled. "I can't even explain it, because earlier today I was thinking of how you all seem younger than me, but then I'm with you and I start to feel younger and happier. Well, except when I think about Cathy. That kind of takes the happy away."

"I wish we lived closer together," Marley said sadly, "and that we could spend more time together."

"I'll be here a few more days," Janie told them. "I have to check on my parents' house and get it ready to list with a realtor. But maybe we could do some things together as well."

"I have to stick around too," Caroline said, "to help with my mom and figure some things out for her care. But I'd love to get together with you guys."

"I have to leave tomorrow," Marley admitted.

"We'll just enjoy what time we have," Caroline said. "And after seeing my mom and how she's deteriorated since the last time I was here, well, here's to youth." She held up her glass for a toast, and the rest of them followed suit.

"So are you going to put your mom into some kind of assisted living?" asked Abby.

"I'm not sure." Caroline frowned. "She's confused about a lot of things, but she's still determined not to leave her house. I feel bad trying to uproot her. I mean, I wonder how I'd feel if I were in her shoes. Who am I to say she can't live out her last days in her own house?"

"That sounds like my mom," Abby told her. "Fortunately she's still in good health both mentally and physically. Paul's parents are too. We're lucky in that area."

Marley wondered what area Abby was not lucky in. Perfect house, perfect marriage, perfect parents … Abby's kids were probably perfect too. Marley didn't want to go there. She wasn't going to give in to the envy.

"Still," Abby continued, "I don't look forward to the day when our parents do start to fail. It seems inevitable."

"At least you'll have Paul to help carry the load." Caroline shook her head. "I thought my brother would help more, but he's just checked out. The way he lives, I won't be surprised if he's not the one needing care before long. Anyway, I'm pretty much on my own when it comes to my mom."

"I can't get over the irony of it," Janie said. "I was barely finished caring for my own kids, and suddenly I was caring for my parents. Of course, they're gone now. But it seemed weird."

"I heard someone on *Oprah* say that your fifties is a time when you need to take really good care of yourself," Abby told them. "A lot of us have been in the habit of neglecting ourselves to care for others, whether it's our kids or parents or grandkids. But if we keep that up, we might suffer the consequences."

"And end up like Cathy?" ventured Janie.

"She didn't have kids," Abby said. "But I know she'd been helping care for her elderly parents, and she was a workaholic to boot."

"I know I've been guilty of putting things off," Marley admitted. "Things like regular checkups, and a social life, and doing what I want to do. Like painting. I have to agree with you, Abby. It's time to put ourselves back on the list."

"Here, here." Caroline held up her margarita glass to make another toast. "Here's to putting ourselves back on the list."

"And here's to renewing old friendships," added Marley.

"And here's to taking better care of ourselves." Abby held up her glass.

"And here's to living the life that you really want," Janie said. They all drank to these toasts, and then it grew quiet with just the background sound of surf and the occasional seagull.

"So what is the life that *you* really want?" Caroline asked Janie.

Janie sighed. "I'm not even sure."

"But you're not happy doing what you're doing?" Caroline persisted.

"Not really." Janie shook her head sadly. "Or maybe I'm just unhappy about life in general. It's hard to tell."

"How about you?" Marley asked Caroline. "Are you happy about your LA life?"

Caroline just laughed. "Are you kidding?"

They all looked at Caroline with surprised expressions.

"You seem happy," Janie pointed out.

Caroline just waved her hand. "Oh, I'm pretty much an optimist, and I'm so used to acting cheerful. I'm sure I appear much happier than I feel."

"Then why not make a change?" suggested Marley.

"And do what?"

Marley shrugged. "Whatever makes you happy."

"I almost did that. Back when I was going through cancer treatment, I promised myself to make some changes if I survived. I was even ready to chuck the LA lifestyle and start over somewhere totally different. But then I got well, and life went on. I guess I sort of fell back into my old ways. And because the cancer would be a preexisting condition, I was afraid to give up my job and lose my health coverage. The restaurant I work for has a really comprehensive plan."

"You work for a restaurant?" Abby looked surprised.

"Yes." Caroline nodded. "The secret is out. I'm a waitress."

It seemed that no one knew what to say.

"Oh, don't feel sorry for me," she said. "It's one of the classiest restaurants in Beverly Hills, and I see famous people almost daily, and the tips are great."

"That actually sounds kind of fun," Abby said.

"But it's hard work." Caroline held up a tanned foot with a great pedicure. "It's not easy being on your feet all day. I can't imagine doing this into my sixties." She gasped. "Did I just say *sixties?*"

"It'll be here sooner than you think," Marley said wryly. "It's like the older we get, the faster the hands on the clock seem to move. Before you know it ..."

"That reminds me of Cathy again." Janie spoke slowly. "It makes me wonder: Do you think she wishes she'd lived her life differently?"

No one responded to this. And Marley decided it was time to change the subject. "So we should plan our next get-together," she said suddenly. "When do we have the next Four Lindas reunion? And where?"

"That's a great idea." Abby's eyes lit up. "You're welcome to have it here."

And suddenly they were all offering their own towns as possibilities—LA, New York, Seattle—but Marley sensed the hesitation in everyone when it came to nailing down something specific.

They all probably suspected it wasn't really going to happen. As fun as this had been, and as much as they'd enjoyed each other, they would probably all go home, get pulled back into their busy everyday lives, and put a Four Lindas reunion at the bottom of their to-do lists.

"I think I hear the golfers coming in." Abby glanced at her watch. "Can you believe it's almost two? The others, if there are others, should be arriving soon. I better go check on the food."

"And I need to freshen up." Caroline was already on her feet.

"And I need to freshen up my drink," Marley joked.

"And I need to simply sit here and soak up this view." Janie sighed and leaned back. "Because I know I'll be missing this place when I'm back in the city next week."

Marley knew she'd be missing it too, even sooner than Janie, because Marley was leaving tomorrow. Not that Seattle wasn't a great place to live, and it did have some of the most gorgeous views on the planet. But it wasn't only the natural beauty of the seascape that Marley would miss. It was the whole small-town experience. She'd enjoyed those laid-back shopkeepers and the friendly folks at the coffee house as much as the leisurely walk on the beach. She would miss it all. But mostly she'd miss her three friends and the comforting company of the Four Lindas.

As she waited for the bartender to freshen her margarita, Marley considered extending her stay like Janie and Caroline were doing, but she knew it couldn't work for her. She was expected back in the gallery Tuesday morning at ten. And there was a big show to prepare for the following weekend. No. For her, time and responsibilities marched on. Whether she liked it or not, she had to march along with them.

=Chapter 6=

CAROLINE

As Caroline touched up her makeup in Abby's powder room, she was well aware that her looks no longer turned heads like they used to, back when she was younger. At least not down in LA, where pretty young things were a dime a dozen. But up here in Clifden, with a bunch of fifty-something classmates, she was treated differently. She'd be a liar to say she hadn't enjoyed the attention she received last night.

As she fluffed her hair and freshened her lip gloss, she remembered the training ground of her childhood. Her father had been a hard man—hard working, hard talking, hard drinking, and hard on her mom. So early on, Caroline discovered the need for softening him. She learned to turn on her sunshine and light in order to thaw her father's cold heart. Call it codependency or enabling; often it worked. The habit stayed with her.

Exiting the powder room and feeling relatively pretty, Caroline turned on the charm. Shamelessly ego tripping, she worked the room, relishing the attention of her male classmates, moths to her flame. Then, noticing that more guys were outside, she headed out there. She knew it was pathetic to be so greedy for this kind of male attention, but it wasn't entirely selfish. She always repaid them with exactly what they wanted to hear.

"No, I don't think bald men are unattractive," she assured Tom Barnes as she ran her hand over his pale, shiny head. "What about all these young athletes who shave their heads? It's very cool." The guys standing around her chuckled like they weren't buying this.

"It won't be cool if that cue ball of yours gets sunburned." His wife sneaked up from behind him and smacked him on his head. "For heaven's sake, put your hat on, Tom!"

Caroline laughed. "Now listen to your wife, Tom."

"Speaking of wives, did you guys get a look at Ron Smith's new wife?" Keith Arnold's voice still held the same sleazy edge it had in high school. "She's one hot babe. My guess is she's young enough to be his daughter."

"What happened to his last wife?" asked Caroline.

"Guess he got tired of the old model." Keith chuckled. "When you've got the bucks that Ron's got, you can afford to be choosy about your wrist candy." He nudged Caroline with a sly grin. "But, hey, I'd be perfectly happy with someone like you for my trophy wife."

"Oh, that's so generous of you," she said sarcastically. "But if you'll excuse me, I need to find someone." She broke away from her pack of beer-guzzling worshippers and went back inside the house. Her purpose was twofold: For one, she wanted to check out Ron Smith's new wife, but she also wanted to see if that handsome Victor had come.

"There you are," Abby said as Caroline came into the den, where several old classmates were gathered.

"We were just reminiscing about Cathy," Rob Jenson told her. "It's hard to believe she's really gone."

Abby patted the spot next to her, signaling Caroline to join her on the leather sofa. "Do you remember when she tried out for cheerleading?"

"Not until just now." Caroline sat next to her. "But yeah, I do remember. I was so shocked when she tried out for varsity even though she'd never been a cheerleader before. And then she tried out by herself. No one ever went solo. I actually thought it was very brave of her."

"Well, she sure had spirit," Rob said sadly.

"But not too much coordination." Abby shook her head. "I still can't believe she's gone."

"I couldn't sleep much last night," Rob told them. "I kept thinking it should've been me to have the heart problem." He patted his large belly. "I'm overweight and my cholesterol is sky-high. Cathy was in great shape."

"She was training for a marathon," Abby told them. "Jim Stuart just mentioned that she was signed up for one in September."

"Well, I'll tell you what this has done for me," Rob said with determination. "I am going to start walking the beach again. My goal is to walk for one hour every day. I'll do it in honor of Cathy."

"What a great idea," Abby agreed. "I should do that too."

Caroline heard laughter coming from the living room, and although she felt guilty for not staying and memorializing Cathy, this group was kind of a downer. She stood. "So have you guys seen Ron Smith's new wife yet?" she asked quietly.

Rob nodded eagerly. "Oh yeah, I saw her."

"She's really young." Abby lowered her voice. "And she looks like she could be a swimsuit model, or maybe one of those Victoria's Secret angels. Not that I think they're so angelic."

"I heard he met her in Vegas," Rob told them. "Maybe she was a showgirl."

Caroline laughed. "I want to get a peek at her."

"Sizing up the competition?" teased Abby.

Caroline shrugged. "Just curious." She gave them a dainty finger wave. "Later, kids."

Caroline resisted the urge to fluff her hair again as she went into the great room. Instead she glanced around in what she hoped was a nonchalant way until she spotted Ron Smith and the attractive young woman who was obviously his wife. Oddly enough, the girl seemed to be deep into a conversation with Marley. Caroline went over for a better look, and Marley introduced them.

Caroline smiled brightly as they shook hands. "Nice to meet you, Cleo."

"Cleo is an artist too," Marley told Caroline.

"Really?" Caroline was surprised. Perhaps this girl was more than just wrist candy.

"She does green sculpture."

"Green sculpture?"

Cleo chuckled. "Yes, I usually have to explain it. I recycle old junk to create new pieces of art. Mostly metal, but sometimes glass and wood, too."

"Interesting."

She nodded. "It was something I'd always wanted to do, but I never had the time before I married Ron."

He turned from the conversation he was having with a couple of classmates and grinned. "Yeah, did Cleo tell you girls I support the arts?"

"And maybe someday the arts will support you," Cleo tossed back at him.

"Anyway, it keeps her out of trouble." Ron winked at Caroline. "Speaking of trouble, how are you doing these days?"

"Trouble?" Cleo's brow creased. "What kind of trouble?"

"Oh, Caroline and I used to get into all kinds of trouble, didn't we?" he teased.

Caroline nodded. "Remember when we TP'd Mr. Brimson's yard?"

"Or how about the time we kidnapped South Shore's mascot?"

"It was a bulldog," Caroline explained to Cleo. "We dressed him in a pink tutu, then let him loose on the football field right before the game."

"But no animals were harmed in the making of our prank," Ron assured her.

"Of course, the poor bulldog was in therapy for years," Marley joked. "I heard he had gender-identity issues."

They all laughed. Caroline glimpsed the back of Janie's head a few yards off and noticed that she was talking to Victor. Caroline elbowed Marley. "Did you see who Janie's with?" She nodded toward the kitchen, where the two were standing by themselves.

Marley glanced over and smiled. "So he decided to come after all."

"Should we go say hi?" asked Caroline.

"Why not?"

They excused themselves from Cleo and wandered over to where Janie and Victor were visiting. "Nice to see you made it," Marley told Victor.

"I guess it's not as bad as I expected." He smiled at both of them.

"I was just telling him that if no one talked to us, we could always take off and have our own little misfits reunion somewhere else," Janie told them.

"Then you better take me along too," joked Marley.

"Besides, *we're* talking to you now," Caroline said.

"Hopefully it's not just a mercy visit." Victor chuckled.

"So, Victor, I'm curious," Marley began. "You said you moved back to Clifden recently."

"Last spring."

"What brought you back?"

"Several things really." With a thoughtful expression he rubbed his whiskered chin. "For one thing, I was tired of the corporate rat race."

"Who isn't?" said Marley.

"I was at a place where I could make some changes in my life, so I sat down and asked myself what I wanted to do when I grew up."

"How did you answer yourself?" Caroline inquired. "What did you want to do?"

"I wanted to walk on the beach and fly fish and kayak and basically just take it easy."

"Yeah." Marley sighed. "Who wouldn't?"

"Does that mean you're retired?" Caroline asked.

"Semi. I still do some consulting."

"He worked in marketing," Janie explained. "In Chicago."

"Which I don't miss at all."

"Not even things like restaurants or the arts?" queried Janie.

"Not yet."

"And I'm guessing you won't miss the weather," Marley pointed out.

"So you're a man of leisure." Caroline guessed that meant he was independently wealthy, too. So far no one had mentioned his marital status, and she had already noticed the absence of a wedding ring. But she wasn't about to ask.

"Oh, I have some ideas for business projects I might like to try," he said. "That is, if I get bored with my current laid-back lifestyle, which doesn't seem terribly likely."

"He's considering organizing a farmers' market," Janie told them. "To make more local produce available to people in Clifden."

"My motives are selfish," he admitted. "I'd like to have local produce, and I can't seem to talk anyone into running with my idea. So maybe I'll have to run with it myself."

"I think it's a brilliant idea," Marley said. "Kind of like Pike Place Market in Seattle."

He laughed. "Only on a much smaller scale."

"Where would you locate the farmers' market?" Caroline asked.

"Somewhere down by the docks," he told them. "That way the fishermen could get in on it too."

"So it really could be like a mini Pike's Place," Marley said. "Really smart!"

"Victor was always smart," Janie told them.

"Yeah, the academic geek who made good."

Caroline couldn't stand the suspense any longer. "Do you have family here in Clifden?"

"My parents moved to Florida quite some time ago."

"No kids? Or wife?" Caroline persisted. She knew she was being obvious now, but she decided she didn't care. This guy was good-looking, intelligent, probably well-off, and perhaps even available.

"My wife and I split up about ten years ago. My fault mostly. I was an incurable workaholic back then, and she found someone with more time for her. But we have two grown sons. The oldest recently graduated from Northwestern. The younger one is in his second year at Lewis & Clark."

"Was that part of your motivation to move back here?" Janie asked. "To be closer to your younger son?"

He nodded. "To be honest, it was a pretty big part. I was pleased when Ben chose my alma mater for college. I thought it would be nice to be nearby. In fact he's stayed with me for most of the summer. He's turned out to be a pretty good surfer too."

"He surfs in this cold water?" Caroline questioned.

"He wears a full wet suit. He's even gotten me out there a few times. It's pretty invigorating."

"I used to surf," Caroline told him. "But never in Oregon. And never in a wet suit."

"You should give it a try."

"Is there a place to rent boards?" she asked. Not that she was seriously interested. Not in surfing anyway.

"We have a couple extra boards," Victor told her. "You could borrow one if you like."

"What about the wet suit?"

He sort of sized her up, then smiled. "We've got some of those, too, but they're designed for a more masculine figure."

Caroline wondered how far she was willing to go with this. "I wonder if there's a place in town."

"They have them at the Outdoorsman Shop," he told her.

"And you'd really let me borrow a board?"

He grinned. "Why not?"

Caroline tried not to imagine herself wiped out with broken bones and a bad case of hypothermia. "Why not?" she said. "Especially in light of what happened to Cathy last night. Why not live life to the fullest while we still can, right?"

He nodded. "My sentiments exactly."

"So you're really going surfing?" Marley looked slightly skeptical. "This I'd like to see."

"So would I." Janie wore a hard-to-read expression, and Caroline hoped it wasn't jealousy. She knew she had the capacity to bring that out in her female friends, and there was a time when she hadn't cared. But for some reason, she really didn't want to turn Janie, or any of the Lindas, against her.

"Why don't you all come out to my house?" Victor offered. "You can all go surfing if you want."

"Not me." Marley firmly shook her head. "I'm not crazy like some people. Besides, I have to go home tomorrow."

"I'll pass too." Janie's eyes twinkled now. "Although I wouldn't mind watching Caroline take the plunge."

"Hopefully I won't take the plunge too hard," Caroline told her.

They continued to talk about surfing and living life to the fullest, and Caroline sensed some good-spirited rivalry going on between her and Janie. But Janie seemed to be up for it, like she was able to hold her own. In a way, that was kind of fun. However, it was slightly unnerving for Caroline to realize she was actually going head-to-head with a woman who had previously been one of the homeliest girls in high school. And they seemed to be competing over the guy who'd once been the class geek. Wasn't life interesting?

=Chapter 7=

ABBY

"You're crying?" Paul said when he found Abby in the bedroom that evening. "Are you feeling sad about Cathy again?"

Abby sniffed and shook her head. "No, I wish I could say that was it."

"What then?"

"I'm feeling sad for myself."

"Why?" He sat down on the bed next to her, putting his arm around her shoulders. "Did I do something?"

She considered this. To be honest, she wasn't too pleased with how friendly he'd been to Ron's new wife, Cleo, but then maybe that was just Abby being paranoid. "No," she told him. "It's not you."

"Should I be relieved or worried?"

"I'm just so sad to see my friends all leaving."

"All your high-school friends?"

"Not all of them. Good grief, I'm relieved to see most of them gone."

"You mean the other Lindas?"

She nodded and sniffed again.

"It was odd how close you girls seemed to get." He stood and stretched his back. "But don't you think that had to do with Cathy's, uh, her sudden death?"

"That was the catalyst," she admitted. "But there was something more. Something about being in your fifties and wondering about what's important in life. It makes me value friends more, and it reminds me that I don't have that many. Not really good ones anyway." She started crying again.

"Do you think this could be a hormonal thing?"

That made her really want to throw something at him, but she controlled herself. "No, I do not think it's hormonal—but thank you for asking!"

"Well, you know how you're always telling me about menopause and—"

"And you know what MEN-o-PAUSE really is?"

"Huh?"

"It means give me a break—a pause—from men. Time to take a 'men a *pause*.'"

He chuckled but wisely backed away. "Fine. I'll give you a break. Some of the guys are getting together at Mike's Place to play pool."

She peered curiously at him. "Mike's Place?" That musty old pool hall had never been one of Paul's favorite hangouts.

"For old time's sake. You know, 'Remember the good ol' days.'"

"Have fun," she said curtly. "I'm sure you'll enjoy the escape from hormone hell. And Mike's Place is probably just dripping in testosterone."

He frowned. "Hope you feel better."

Abby turned away from him, folding her arms across her chest like her granddaughter sometimes did. Then she listened as he left the room, left the house, and finally started up his Corvette. The car had been his fiftieth birthday present to himself a few years ago, and he babied it more than he'd ever babied any of his children or his wife. If the car got wet, although he rarely drove "her" in the rain, Paul would use a special chamois cloth to wipe it down. He probably kissed her good night, too. Abby had gotten him snob plates, with the initials MMLCC, which stood for My Mid-Life Crisis Car. She'd only driven the car once and that was with Paul sitting nervously in the passenger seat, acting as if Abby intentionally planned to total it.

As she heard the Corvette engine roaring down their street, she felt guilty for pushing Paul away like that. Especially since he was trying, in his own way, to be understanding. But any more comments about hormones or menopause would only take them down a very bumpy road. Really, men could be so dense sometimes. Even if she was hormonal, which she was sure she wasn't, she was still genuinely bummed to realize that three of her best friends all lived so far away. In fact the circumstance reminded her, in a way, of her three daughters. She loved them all so much. They'd had so many good times together while growing up, and yet she rarely saw them anymore. Now she'd reunited with these three friends only to say good-bye again. It just seemed so unfair. It was as if God was punishing her for something. But what? What had she done to deserve this?

Abby got up and looked at her bedraggled image in the mirror. With her flushed, tear-streaked cheeks and red, puffy eyes, she looked worse than usual. And old. Really, really old. Why was it that when she peered into the mirror these days, she didn't see Abby looking back? Instead she looked more like her mother, and sometimes it seemed that her mother looked more youthful than Abby. Why was that? Of course, her mother had interests. And friends. That probably kept her young.

Abby sighed as she looked around her picture-perfect bedroom: old fir floors, oriental carpets, antique furniture, and a gorgeous pastel quilt that she had made herself while the house was being built. Yes, she lived in a lovely world, one she had helped to create, but it just wasn't enough. And yes, she had her hobbies—quilting and gardening and cooking—to occupy her time, although the truth was she'd been doing less and less of these things the past couple of years. Those activities were satisfying on some levels, but it was not the same as talking and laughing and sharing good times with good friends. Domestic hobbies were not enough to fill a life. Suddenly she wondered why she had settled for so little.

"Hello in the house!" called an all-too-familiar voice. For some reason Abby's mother had a problem with knocking before entering. Paul said she had boundary issues, but Abby suspected she was simply hoping to catch someone off guard, possibly doing something embarrassing or interesting. Like the time she'd walked in on Nicole and a boyfriend, which Abby had actually appreciated, since they had been getting carried away.

"I'm in here, Mom," she called as she reached for a tissue to blow her nose.

"What are you doing in here?" Mom asked as she came into the bedroom. As usual, she had on her baggy jeans topped with an oversized plaid flannel shirt, like she thought she was part of a rapper band.

Abby just shrugged.

"Where is everyone? Where's Paul? I thought you were having some big shindig here today."

"We were. We did. They went home and Paul is at Mike's Place."

"Mike's Place?" her mother looked confused. "Why?"

"He's hanging with his old high-school buds—remembering the good old days."

Her mom chuckled. "Oh, I get it." Now she peered curiously at Abby. "What's wrong with you? Have you been crying?"

Abby wondered why it wasn't possible to have a good cry without half the world invading her bedroom to investigate. "As a matter of fact, yes."

"But why?" Her mom's expression was one of genuine sympathy now—a sure way to get Abby to unload on her. Maybe that wasn't such a bad idea.

"I think I'm depressed, Mom." Abby went to the pair of pale blue club chairs flanking the big window and sank into one. She pulled the pillow out from where it was wedged behind her and stuck it in her lap, then punched it.

Her mom sat in the other chair and kicked off her Earth sandals, putting her feet up on the oversized ottoman between them. "What makes you think you're depressed?"

So Abby told her about Cathy's unexpected death and how the Four Lindas were reunited and how great that had been. "And now it's over."

Her mom sighed. "I heard about Cathy's death. Very sudden, and sad. I can see how that might have you feeling low."

Abby nodded, swallowing against the lump that was still in her throat.

"But I think it's wonderful that you've been spending time with the other Lindas." She laughed. "I always did like those girls. And it was so clever how you created your club like that. I felt badly when it disintegrated."

"But now they're all leaving."

"Yes. Life goes on."

"But I don't even have a life, Mom!"

She chuckled. "Of course you have a life. You have Paul and your girls and your home and your hobbies and friends and—"

"No." Abby shook her head stubbornly. "I do not. It might look like I have those things, but it's just an illusion."

"An illusion?" Her mom's faded brown eyes looked concerned. "What do you mean?"

"I mean, I sort of have Paul. But Paul has, well, all kinds of friends and interests that don't necessarily include me. You know that. And the girls, well, they're off living their own lives. And Nicole is so far away."

"But she'll be home by fall."

"As for my hobbies, I don't really do them much anymore. Not really."

"I noticed you've given up gardening since you moved into the new house. And I haven't seen any new quilts in the works. But you still love to cook."

"And eat." Abby frowned. "All that does is pile on the pounds."

"Well, you need to get out and walk." Mom nodded out to the wide-open beach. "And it's not that you're lacking a place to do that."

"I know." Suddenly Abby felt like a spoiled brat. Really, she had so much. Why should she sit here complaining and feeling sorry for herself? Of course, that only made her feel worse. Quiet tears began streaking down her cheeks again.

"Oh, Abby." Her mom looked sad. "I hate to see you like this."

Abby blotted her nose and tears with her crumpled tissue. "Me, too."

"I understand how you must feel. You've enjoyed your old friends, and now they're leaving. But do you know what I think that means?"

"No." But Abby was sure she was about to find out. Some people thought her mom had a special gift—a way of knowing things but Abby had never really appreciated it much. In fact it felt intrusive.

"I think the old Lindas are supposed to be a reminder to you."

"A reminder?"

"That you need friends in your life."

"Oh."

"And I know that you've always been a homebody, and that your girls took a lot of your time. But I think you've neglected to build any really good friendships."

"There was Michele." Abby got up and went for the tissue box. If she was going to talk about Michele, her old best friend, she would need a lot of Kleenex.

"Yes, there was Michele."

"She was always there for me, the whole time our kids were growing up. Whenever I needed to talk or vent or laugh or cry or do play dates or volunteer for PTA. She was always there with me."

"I know." Mom nodded. "And you were a good friend to her too. Right down to the end."

Michele had suffered a rare form of stomach cancer when she was only forty. She'd undergone treatments but eventually passed away almost ten years ago. The hole she'd left in Abby's life remained empty. "I still miss her."

"I know you do, honey. We all do."

"It's just never been easy for me. I mean, making new friends. Really good friends. I have a number of casual, sort-of friends. The kind you can chat with at the grocery store."

"Maybe within that group of friends, there's someone who needs to have a close friend, Abby. Someone like you."

Abby just shrugged. "I don't know."

"But you do know that you need friends, don't you?"

"I guess."

"Because I think the Four Lindas getting back together, even if it was only briefly, was meant to be a wake-up call. Sometimes that's how God works."

"Maybe."

"I also know that as we get older, we need a strong support unit around us." Mom smiled. "I am so thankful for my friends."

"But you've had them forever, Mom." Abby felt a rush of jealousy as she considered her mom's tight circle of friends. They were so close—closer than sisters—that sometimes Abby felt left out, almost as if her mother didn't need her. At least not the way Abby seemed to need her own daughters. It was frustrating. And yet she was glad for her mother, especially after Abby's father died. Without her supportive friends Mom would have suffered greatly.

"Speaking of friends," her mom said, "that's why I dropped by. I'm having everyone over for lunch tomorrow, and I wanted to borrow your ice-cream maker. I got a bunch of lovely blackberries and I thought they'd be great with some homemade ice cream."

Abby pushed herself up from her chair. "I just hope I can find it. Paul helped me put things away when we moved, and it's still a challenge to figure it all out."

"You're welcome to join us tomorrow if you like," Mom offered as they hunted through the kitchen cabinets. "I'm sure the girls would love to see you."

Abby knew her mom was just feeling sorry for her. She also knew, from experience, that she did not fit in with her mother's friends. They were nice enough, and interesting, too. But they were also *old*. Old enough to be Abby's mother. After spending time with them, she usually came away feeling even older than she normally felt. "No thanks, Mom." She spied the ice-cream maker in the back of the pantry and pulled it out. "I was thinking I might try to get together with Caroline and Janie, if they're not too busy. Marley will be heading back to Seattle. But the other two are here for a few days. Janie's putting her folks' home on the market. And Caroline is helping her mom."

"Poor Mrs. McCann." Mom shook her head sadly. "I saw her a few weeks ago, and she looked terrible."

"Terrible?"

"Like she's not in her right mind. She didn't even know me, and when I tried to explain who I was, she got frightened."

"Caroline said she's got Alzheimer's or something." Abby dampened a paper towel and used it to remove the dust from the top of the ice-cream maker.

"Well, I hope I never wind up like that. If I do, I think I shall simply go for a nice long swim in the ocean. Due west."

"What?" Abby was shocked. "Are you kidding?"

"It would be similar to what they do in Alaska. Old people go sit on an iceberg until they fall asleep. And that's the end of it."

"Mother!" Abby frowned at her. "And you, a good churchgoing woman!"

"Which is exactly why I have no fear of the afterlife. I know where I am going."

"You'd take your own life?"

"I merely said I'd take a swim in the ocean. A nice, long swim."

"Oh, Mother, really!"

"Well, think about it," she said as she picked up the ice-cream maker. "How would you like to be in Mrs. McCann's shoes? Confused and crazy, probably about to be locked up in some loony-bin nursing-care home, where someone changes your Depend diapers, and you're fed mushy peas and pudding and—"

"Good grief, Mother, it sounds as if you've given this plenty of thought."

Mom just laughed. "At my age you have to consider these things."

"Well, don't think too hard about it."

"I'm just saying, Abby." Mom headed for the door. "If I ever start losing it, you know, heading in that direction, I might seek another alternative."

Abby just shook her head as she followed her mom outside. Why should this even surprise her? Really, her mother had always been a little offbeat about a lot of things. Paul said it came with the artistic temperament, but Abby always thought maybe she just wanted attention.

"So if I hear about the Coast Guard dragging some waterlogged old lady out of the ocean some day, I should probably call and make sure it's not you?"

Mom laughed loudly. "Thanks for the ice-cream maker, sweetie." She waved as she got into her old Willys Jeep, then drove away.

Abby went back inside, but before she could close the oversized front door, a breeze blew threw the great room and, catching the heavy, solid door, slammed it with a loud bang that echoed throughout the quiet house. For some reason Abby heard a feeling of finality in that sound, like what it might be to have a prison door shut behind her after they'd locked her up and thrown away the key. Her picture-perfect house. Her prison. And here she was, crying again.

=Chapter 8=

JANIE

"I'm so glad you called." Abby sounded genuinely happy to hear Janie's voice, which made Janie wonder once again if Abby was a bit lonely, although that seemed impossible considering her happy marriage, her hometown life, and her nearby family.

Janie quickly explained her need to do something with her parents' home. "It seems the simplest solution would be to just sell it. But that could be a challenge from New York. I need a good realtor that I can really trust."

"I know the perfect person for you. Her name is Lois Schuler, and she's worked in real estate for at least twenty years. She knows everyone in town."

"I thought you'd have a good recommendation." Janie slid her feet into her loafers as she gazed out the window. Her hotel suite overlooked the wharf, and from what she could see, Monday was going to be another gorgeous day on the Oregon coast.

"Lois has her own office," Abby continued, "just a few doors down from Clifden Coffee Company. Schuler Realty. There's a model of a big wooden lighthouse right next to the entrance."

"Oh yes, I've seen that."

"If you like, I could meet you in town for coffee, then introduce you to Lois. I'm guessing she won't be in before nine."

"You don't mind? I don't want to take up too much of your—"

"I'd love to come. Give me about twenty minutes, okay?"

"Sounds perfect."

"I wonder if Caroline would like to join us too." Abby sounded hopeful.

"I can check and find out."

"I'm sure Marley must be on the road by now."

"Yes. She planned to leave early this morning."

"Anyway, I'll see you in a few."

They both hung up and Janie, out of habit, dug out her laptop and turned it on. She was supposed to be on vacation, but everyone in her firm knew there really was no such thing. And everyone knew never to go off and leave themselves disconnected.

"No rest for the wicked," Phil used to say when they'd try to plan a quiet little getaway. But sometimes the constant need to be in touch did get old.

Not surprisingly she had a few "urgent" e-mails. She handled one of them herself, delegated another to an underling, and flagged the last one for later. Then it was time to meet Abby. Of course, as she was leaving her room, she remembered Caroline. Abby had wanted to invite her. For some reason Janie had blocked that out of her mind when she hung up the phone. Probably Freudian.

In truth she was feeling a bit jealous of Caroline and the way she'd so smoothly arranged to have a surfing date with Victor

Zilkowski. Although Janie had no interest in surfing. The last time she'd attempted such a feat was in Hawaii when her kids were preteens and Phil had insisted they all take a lesson. A few nasty wipeouts later, Janie had bowed out and opted for a warm strip of sand instead. No, she had no intentions of squeezing into a smelly wet suit and attacking the Oregon surf. But she might like to watch.

In the hotel lobby she dialed Caroline's cell phone, and when Caroline answered, Janie explained her plan. "Would you like to join us?"

"Sure," Caroline said cheerfully. "But I can't stay long. I need to do a little shopping before I head over to Victor's."

"Oh, right." Janie fibbed. "I forgot about your surfing date."

Caroline laughed. "Oh, it's not a date. Just good fun. Do you want to come?"

Feeling a little coy, Janie said she'd think about it, then told Caroline they could catch up at the coffee place. As she walked through town, Janie wondered what kinds of things Caroline would need to shop for before a surfing expedition. A bikini perhaps? Janie snickered at the idea of a fifty-something woman in a bikini. She couldn't remember the last time she'd worn a bikini, but it was definitely BC—before children. After two cesarean births, Janie's midsection was not fit for public viewing.

But Caroline had never had kids. Not only that, she was tan and fit and had those implants, too. No doubt she would look great in a bikini and probably would show a lot of skin today. Even as Janie thought this, she felt utterly foolish. What difference did it make what Caroline wore or did? For all Janie cared, Caroline could go in the buff. Really, what was it to Janie? And why was she acting like an adolescent, obsessing over the silliest of trivialities?

"Hey there," called Abby as they arrived simultaneously. "Good timing."

"Yes." Janie smiled.

"You seemed deep in thought," Abby said as they went inside. "I hope nothing's wrong."

"No." Janie shook her head. "Just thinking."

They both ordered coffee, then found a table. "I took the liberty of giving Lois a jingle before I left home," Abby told her. "I know your time in town is short, and I thought we might want to make sure we caught her."

"Oh, I appreciate that."

"Anyway, she said she'd pop over and meet us here for coffee." Abby smiled in an apologetic way. "I hope that's okay."

"That's fine. And Caroline should be coming too." Janie explained about Caroline's need to do some shopping before the big surfing date.

"Is it really a date?" Abby looked surprised.

"No, not really. In fact Caroline sort of invited herself."

Abby's brow creased slightly. "Do you think Caroline is interested in Victor? I mean romantically?"

Janie just shrugged. "Maybe. I don't see why not. He's a nice guy and he seems to be pretty comfortable. Caroline might think he's a good catch." Janie felt like she was being catty. "But I'm not suggesting that Caroline is out fishing for men."

"She might be." Abby nodded. "I happen to know she's not that happy in her work and she—" She stopped herself, then waved. "There she is."

Their conversation shifted gears, and by the time Caroline joined them with her coffee, they were discussing real estate. "The market's been pretty much like everywhere—pretty slow," Abby was saying. "Except our prices haven't dropped quite as much, but I think that has to do with the location. Coastal real estate holds its value better than some places."

"So even if I list my parents' house this week, I might be waiting a while to see it sell?"

"Lois can give you a better idea about that. But I'm guessing it will take some time."

"Maybe I should talk to her about listing my mom's house," Caroline said.

"You're really going to move her, then?" asked Abby.

Caroline frowned. "I'm not sure. But I have until Thursday to figure it out. I don't know how I'll manage to get it all done by then."

"I'm surprised you wanted to take the time to go surfing today," Janie said. "I mean, if you have so much to do."

Caroline just smiled. "You know what they say about all work and no play."

Abby nodded in agreement. "Yes, and when I think about poor Cathy Gardener, I think we all need to take more time to enjoy life."

Janie considered this. "You're probably right. It just doesn't come easily to me."

Caroline made a sympathetic face. "I don't know how you do it, Janie. Being a New York lawyer and all that responsibility and everything. It must be exhausting."

Janie softened toward Caroline now. "Yes. Sometimes it really is. Even this week. I'm supposed to be on vacation, and yet this morning I opened my laptop and started to work."

"You need to give yourself a break," Caroline told her. "Especially considering all that you've been through the past several years. Why don't you just take a month or so off? Rent yourself a little beach house in some nice sunny place like the Bahamas."

Janie sighed. "I wish."

"I'd be happy to join you there," offered Caroline. "I could be your cook and housekeeper."

Janie laughed. "You make it tempting."

"I want to come too," said Abby. "We could all run away."

"And we should invite Marley, too," joked Janie. "Four Lindas on the lam."

"Can anyone join this party?" said a tall, dark-haired woman in a taupe business suit. Abby introduced Janie and Caroline to Lois Schuler, and she joined them with her coffee.

"I'm not a hundred percent sure I want to sell my parents' house," Janie admitted. "I need to figure out how much I'll lose in taxes and all that. Also, I need to see what the market's like and whether I might be better off turning it into a rental property."

"Those are all good questions." Lois nodded as she made some notes. "My company also handles income properties as well as vacation rentals. Depending on the location and condition of your house, you might want to consider renting it as a vacation cabin."

"It's close to the beach," Caroline pointed out.

"But it doesn't have an ocean view," Janie explained to Lois. "Still, you can walk there in about five minutes."

"And you can walk to town in about five minutes too," Caroline added. "As I recall, it was really a cool little house."

Janie told Lois the address, and the realtor nodded as she noted it. "That's one of those old neighborhoods that's becoming desirable again."

"I noticed a lot of houses have been fixed up in there," Janie said. "Unfortunately my parents' house isn't one of them."

"You should see my mom's house." Caroline shook her head. "Actually I don't want anyone to see it, although I know it'll be necessary. But I'm thinking it might be best to have it torn down so I can sell the lot."

"You never know," Lois told her. "A lot of people are looking for fixers these days."

"Well, it's a fixer, all right." Caroline rolled her eyes. "It would help if my mother could be coaxed to throw anything away. Really, it's a fire trap. I should probably call someone with some authority to come and look at it."

Lois wrote down a name and phone number for Caroline. "Why don't you give her a call? I think she could help you to locate some resources."

"Thanks!" Caroline glanced at her watch. "Well, I hate to drink and run, but I've got a busy day ahead. Nice meeting you, Lois. Will I see you over at Victor's, Janie?"

Janie laughed. "I'm not sure."

"You should come too, Abby," Caroline urged. "Maybe we can have a picnic lunch on the beach—kind of like we used to do as kids."

Abby looked interested. "Sure, that sounds fun. Maybe I could fix something and bring it over."

"All right." Caroline nodded as she hooked the strap of her oversized bag over a tan shoulder. "See you later!"

"She's sure a perky one," Lois said as Caroline left.

"She's always been like that," Abby told her.

"So you've known each other for a while?"

"Since first grade," Abby said. "Can you believe it?"

"You're all the same age?" Lois looked surprised.

"That's right." Janie nodded.

"I know what you're thinking," Abby said to Lois. "I look like I'm at least ten years older than both of them."

"No, no. That's not what I—"

"You're right." Abby frowned. "I know it's true. I've really let myself go these past few years. But I plan to start doing something about it now. I really, really do. I just don't know what."

They laughed.

"Just take care of yourself," Janie told her. "Remember what we were saying? You need to put yourself back on the list."

"That's right," Lois agreed.

They finished up their coffee, and after Abby left, Lois offered to drive Janie over to walk through her parents' house. "It's a place to begin," she told her. "What you do from there is entirely up to you."

"It's pretty run-down," Janie admitted as they pulled up in front of the small ranch-style house. The overgrown yard was weedy and brown, and blackberry bushes had swallowed what was left of a rotten fence. "I spoke to a landscape service about getting someone over here on a regular basis. I should've done it a long time ago, but life's been busy."

"And New York is a world away from Clifden."

"You got that right."

Janie unlocked and opened the door. As always, walking into the musty-smelling old house brought back all kinds of memories. But nothing particularly happy. "It's pretty much cleared out," Janie told Lois. "Between Goodwill, Salvation Army, and a storage unit, I've been trying to get it ready to be sold. But I haven't had anyone come in to clean or anything yet."

"At a minimum you should consider getting it painted in here," Lois said as they walked through the dingy living room. "Just a nice, clean neutral color."

"There are hardwood floors underneath this horrid carpeting. I'm guessing they might be in pretty good shape."

"These single-pane windows need replacing," observed Lois. "If anyone wanted to buy it with a conventional loan. But I did notice that the roof looks sound."

"Yes, I paid to have it replaced about five years ago."

"And be thankful that it's on a foundation. That's important. A lot of houses around here aren't."

"Oh."

Lois went into the kitchen and just shook her head. "Not much updating in here, I see."

Janie laughed. "Nothing in here has changed since when I was a kid. I tried and tried to talk my mom into a dishwasher, but she was so set in her ways. She honestly believed that dishwashers couldn't get things really clean."

Lois looked at the old aqua-blue appliances and smiled. "These might actually be collectable, although I hate to think of how much energy they use. Is this fridge running?"

Janie nodded. "I'm afraid so."

"You might as well unplug it and have it removed. No sense in throwing your money away on electricity."

"Right."

Lois was peeking in the half bathroom now. "This old tile looks like it's in nearly perfect condition," she said wryly. "And the fixtures, too. Now, if you can find a buyer who's into fifties retro and mint green, you'll be set."

"But hasn't Mid-Century Modern been popular?"

Lois laughed. "That's true, but I'm afraid most of those people are thinking more along the lines of Frank Lloyd Wright. They don't necessarily appreciate Pepto-Bismol pink plumbing fixtures."

Suddenly Janie was seeing her parents' house with different eyes. "What if this place was stripped clean? I mean what if I removed all the old horrible cabinets and fixtures, and the nasty carpeting— and replaced the windows? And I'd put in some sleek Mid-Century Modern touches and good paint colors. I wonder what a place like this could sell for."

"I can do some comps for you if you like," offered Lois. "Put it side by side with homes in this neighborhood that have been renovated."

"Yes." Janie nodded. "I'd like that."

"Well, I have an appointment for a showing at ten thirty." Lois glanced at her watch. "I should be going."

Janie smiled and shook her hand. "I'm going to stick around here for a bit," she said. "I can walk back to town. Thanks for your help. I'll be in touch." After Lois left, Janie continued to walk around her parents' house. No, she told herself, this wasn't her parents' house anymore. It was Janie's house. And she could do what she liked to it.

She imagined sleek maple cabinets, granite countertops, and state-of-the-art stainless appliances in the kitchen. With glossy hardwood floors and modern furniture, this sleepy old ranch house could get a new life. Maybe she could too. The strangest part of her imaginings was that she thought she might actually be able to live here.

That was pure craziness.

"No way," she quietly told herself as she locked up the house and stepped away from the door. "I must be losing it. There's no way I could live here and be happy. No, I was delusional. The sea air must've messed with my mind." She turned her back and walked away, saying, "No way. No way. No way." Really, there was no way. Or was there?

==Chapter 9==

MARLEY

Marley switched over to the fast lane again. It was her best method for remaining alert and awake and safe. Stay in the fast lane. Focus, concentrate, don't be distracted, and don't get a speeding ticket. Her insurance had already gone up twice. Since her divorce she'd become careless about driving and had racked up one fender-bender and three speeding citations. Any more unfortunate traffic troubles, and she'd have to store her car and start using mass transit or biking to work.

Biking actually sounded like fun. Once upon a time she'd been an avid bicyclist and one of her goals was to do the coast highway from the Oregon-Washington border down to California and maybe farther. But John always balked at the idea. "It would take too long. It's too dangerous. Why not just drive?" Not that they ever had driven it. Perhaps she'd go dig her bike out of the storage unit and get it tuned up. She could imagine herself biking around Seattle. It would be fun. Except for those cold rainy days that could pop up any time of year. That might not be so fun. Plus she'd have several

challenging hills to climb just to get back and forth from work, and
navigating city traffic might be frightening, not to mention slightly
suicidal. No, her best course of action might be to avoid any more
traffic tickets. So she made her way from the fast lane over to the slow
one. Really, wasn't that kind of how her life felt anyway? Like she was
stuck in the slow lane?

To distract herself from thinking—make that lamenting—over
the metaphorical speed of her life, she turned on some music, crank-
ing it up high. A Carly Simon CD was in the player, and before long
Marley was rocking out to the old "Mockingbird" song. But then
she felt depressed as she wondered, not for the first time, why Carly
Simon and James Taylor (two of music's most talented people) were
unable to make their marriage last. Of course, she hadn't done any
better with hers. But still.

As she was singing along to "Haven't Got Time for the Pain,"
the lyrics hit her in a slightly painful way. Driving the speed limit,
heading north on I-5, Marley began to weep. First she thought her
grief was aimed at Cathy Gardener—she no longer had time for the
pain either. Not after Saturday night.

But then Marley realized she was crying for herself just as much
as she was crying for Cathy. Marley was tired of the pain too. She
didn't need any more pain, didn't have time for it. Who did? But
for some reason, it felt like pain was all she had left. Just plain old,
wearisome pain. Pain over her failed marriage. Pain for her failed
(make that never-really-started) art career, and pain over her loneli-
ness. Pain for the fact that she'd never have grandchildren. Usually
she didn't even notice these aches. What was wrong with her today?
Maybe it was just hormones talking.

Really, she just needed to get home. That was all. Once she was snuggled into her cozy little apartment, back to her old routines, life would be fine. Maybe she'd even splurge and get a cat. She'd been considering that for the past year. Yes, home and a cat. That would put things back to right. Then, imagining Dorothy clicking her ruby red slippers together three times, Marley said, "There's no place like home. There's no place like home. There's no place like home."

But when Carly began to sing "So Far Away," Marley became melancholic again. She asked herself what her definition of *home* was and if there even was such a thing. When had she ever felt truly at home anywhere? Certainly not in the old suburban house that she'd shared with John all those years, at least not when he was around making life miserable. Perhaps when John was doing the international flights and she and Ashton were home alone, she'd felt at ease. But her son had grown up, her marriage had disintegrated, and she'd moved on. Although she was relatively happy in her city apartment, it had never quite felt like home. If anything, it had seemed a temporary abode, a place where she could hide out and lick her wounds until something better came along. She'd been there for several years now, and nothing better ever showed up.

Marley continued on down memory lane, thinking back to when she was a girl in her parents' home. Her childhood had been relatively painless. Her parents had been in love with each other and were happy with life in general. They gave Marley her space and independence and, from an early age, treated her as an adult. In fact, as unlikely as it seemed, some of her fondest memories were during adolescence. She let her hair grow clear past her waist and started doing things like tie-dye and macramé and beading and painting, fancying herself to be a real hippie. She remembered how she and Tommy Tortelli (her first serious boyfriend) would play guitar together, and how she wrote antiwar poetry and went to various hippie fairs and rock concerts. She also remembered the mutt that she and Tommy rescued from the surf one windy afternoon. She'd tied a red bandana around his neck and named him Harvey. When no one bothered to claim the little black dog, she adopted him. They were almost inseparable until she left home for college, but then her parents took over, and Harvey enjoyed a long, happy life.

Marley wondered what had happened to that girl—that fun-loving creative spirit who had such grand plans for her life. What had persuaded her to give up her dreams? Of course, she knew exactly what had derailed her and why. But she still had to scratch her head over it. The only real explanation was young love and infatuation.

Despite the fact that he was not her type and they were polar opposites, John Phelps had swept her off her feet. It made no sense then and even less sense now. He'd actually been in uniform when they met on campus. It was one of those magical autumn days in mid-October, and Marley had felt like she was on top of the world. Their paths crossed in front of the ROTC building, and she made some sassy remark about how it was better to make love not war, and they plunged into an argument.

She was wearing her usual hippie garb: a well-worn embroidered denim skirt, a lacey handmade top, and a pair of tall leather boots she'd gotten in Italy the previous summer. It wasn't long before the heated argument shifted gears into heated flirting session. There was no denying that John was strikingly handsome back then, even if his hair was too short. So when he invited her to continue their debate after his ROTC meeting, she couldn't say no. Later that night, after a few beers, she still couldn't say no. And after a couple months of turbulent romance, Marley discovered she was pregnant. And suddenly the rules all changed.

She had considered exercising "a woman's right to choose" by aborting the baby, but John begged her not to. On Valentine's Day he surprised her with a ring that had been in his family for several generations and, in a moment of weakness, she accepted. They were married in Reno during spring break. A few months later John was deployed to an air force base in Ramstein, Germany, where their already rocky relationship was shaken. After a couple of months there, Marley begged to return to the States to have the baby, and John happily agreed.

It wasn't until years later that she discovered why he'd been so amicable about his wife living stateside. It turned out that John, like a number of his young pilot buddies, was participating in a twisted game they liked to call Rack 'Em Up, where the philanderers kept tally of their sexual encounters outside of their marriages. Of course, by the time Marley discovered this, John was retired from the air force and flying commercially. He claimed that he had simply suffered from a case of wild oats and youth, although she was never entirely convinced that his adventures were over.

Worse than being cheated on (and that was bad enough), Marley suffered the most damage to her self-esteem through his unpredictable rages and verbal abuse. Always walking on eggshells, she never knew what the mood of the day might be. If she'd had the strength (and the money), she would've left him a lot sooner.

Still, as she drove through southern Washington, where the

morning fog had still not burned off, she wondered why she was torturing herself with this crazy sentimental journey. *Oh yeah,* she remembered, *I'm trying to unravel what has become of the old Marley.* How could she tap into the Marley who had shown up during the reunion? Where could she find the Marley who seemed to come back to life in the company of her old friends—the other Lindas? Who was that girl, and where did she live? And how could Marley manage to bring her back for good?

As she continued to drive, though, Marley felt as if she was being gently lulled back into the same-old, same-old. Sucked back into a life that wasn't really a life. Tugged back to a job that wasn't anything more than just a job. Pulled back to an apartment that would never really feel like a home.

One thing she knew for sure: She would not be getting that cat after all!

==Chapter 10==

CAROLINE

Caroline knew it was a waste of good money to purchase a wet suit, and yet she couldn't stop herself. For some reason—as crazy as it sounded—a wet suit felt like her ticket to freedom. Or perhaps an investment in her future.

"Anything else I can get for you, young lady?" Orville Hornsby had been the owner of the Outdoorsman Shop since forever. His hearing was patchy, and he was pretty slow on his feet, but his eyes were kind and he seemed to mean well. She figured he must be in his eighties by now. He'd already told her, a couple of times, that his son really ran the store, but sometimes he came in to help out. She actually remembered him from her childhood, when she had occasionally come in here with her father for fishing bait.

"That's all for now," she said cheerfully.

"No flippers or goggles?" he asked. She'd already told him a couple of times that, no, she wasn't going snorkeling, but surfing. Just the same, he'd told her about some of the local boys who went diving for mussels and such on a regular basis. Apparently they sold the shellfish to the restaurants and managed to make a few bucks while having some fun.

"Here you go," he said as he held a little blue booklet out for her. "The tide tables. To make sure you don't get swept out to sea." He chuckled like that was a good one. "Complimentary. It was the son's idea. A way to advertise and such."

"Thank you." She tucked the booklet into her bag.

"You be careful out there. And don't forget about the undertow!" he called as she exited the store.

As she got into the rental car, Caroline felt a stab of guilt that had something to do with being in that old store. Maybe it was the musty smell of canvas and rubber. But it got her to remembering how her dad used to bicker with Orville about whether the worms were fresh or not, and for some reason that made her start thinking about her mother. She glanced at her watch and realized she still had plenty of time to go check on Mom before heading to Victor's house. She would pick up a cheeseburger (Mom's favorite) and try to entice her to eat something besides the horrible canned beans that she seemed determined to survive on. At least it was worth a try.

———

Caroline pasted on her most cheerful smile as she rang her mother's doorbell, waiting with a hot cheeseburger and fries in hand. She could let herself in, since she had a key, but the last time she'd done that, her mother had nearly gone into a cardiac arrest. For several minutes she believed that Caroline was a stranger—and even worse, that she was from the IRS.

The door cracked open as wide as the old chain lock would allow, and her mother's voice rattled. "Who is it?"

"It's me, Mom."

"What do you want?"

"It's *me*, Mom. Caroline."

"Caroline who?"

"Caroline, your daughter. Let me in."

Her mother spent about a minute fiddling with the chain and finally opened the door wider. "Who are you again?" she asked a bit more softly.

"Caroline, your daughter." She held the McDonald's bag beneath her mom's nose. "I brought you lunch."

Recognition flashed through her mother's faded blue eyes. Whether it was the smell of fast food or the sight of her daughter's face, Caroline couldn't be sure. At least her mom wasn't getting ready to call the cops.

Caroline followed her mom, picking her way past tall stacks of old newspapers and magazines, boxes of glass jars, and all other sorts of dusty, smelly, useless items that her mother, for some reason, could not part with. By now Caroline knew the trails through the house and understood the wisdom of sticking to them.

Eventually they reached the kitchen, which was also piled high with all manner of junk. Her mother had quit having garbage picked up years ago. She might have been one of the first trash-conscious environmentalists, although for the life of her, Caroline could not understand how storing one's garbage in one's home was any better than having it hauled to a refuse center. After all, trash was trash.

In the kitchen her mother pushed aside a pile of junk mail

to clear about one square foot of table space. Caroline watched as her mother set the paper bag on what was once a white "marbled" Formica-topped table, but it now looked yellow. Then she pushed some miscellaneous clothing items off the one chair and sat down.

"I was on my way to the beach," Caroline told her, "but I saw McDonald's and remembered how you used to love their food. So I stopped."

Her mother was already unwrapping the cheeseburger. She carefully unfolded the paper, examining it closely and even smelling it, as if to make sure it was safe to eat. Ironic, considering the present condition of her kitchen. Caroline could only imagine what a health inspector might say about it. The whole house might be condemned. And perhaps that would be a good thing. Then Caroline would have a good excuse for forcing her mom to live someplace decent, in some kind of home where she could have assistance and supervision.

"I'm going to go surfing today," Caroline said as she watched her mother take small, cautious bites of the burger.

Her mother looked up with a creased brow. "Surfing?" she repeated with food still in her mouth.

Caroline handed her a napkin and nodded. "Yes. It's been a while. I hope I remember how to do it."

"Surfing?" she said again, as if trying to grasp what that might entail.

"There are fries in there too." Caroline tapped the paper bag.

"Fries?"

"You know, french fries. And ketchup, too."

"Ketchup." She nodded with a thoughtful expression.

Caroline looked around for something to sit on and finally

decided on a plastic crate that looked semisturdy. She scooted it over by her mother and sat down. "How would you like to have someone fix all your food for you?" she asked cautiously. "Breakfast, lunch, and dinner."

Her mom nodded as if this seemed a good idea.

"And someone to do your laundry and housecleaning."

Now her mom looked puzzled.

"You know," Caroline said, "to keep things clean and neat. So you don't have to. Wouldn't that be nice?"

"Wouldn't that be nice," she echoed as she reached for a fry. "Nice."

"And you could have friends, too," Caroline continued.

"Friends?"

"People your age to do things with." Caroline smiled. "Remember how you used to like to play cards?"

Her mom brightened. "Cards?" Now she stood up and pushed the chair back. It screeched on the floor. "Cards. I have cards." She started digging around in the piles of junk.

"You can get the cards later," Caroline told her. She picked up the half-eaten burger and held it under her mom's nose. Almost as if leading a dog, she used the food to lure her mother back to the table. "Go ahead and eat now."

Her mom nodded, then sat back down.

It took about thirty minutes for her mom to finish her "fast food," but Caroline wanted to make sure she really ate it. Her mom was already so thin, so much more fragile than the last time Caroline had seen her. Literally skin and bones.

Caroline went over to the refrigerator, opening it to reveal the cans of Ensure and other nonperishable foods she'd bought a few days ago. "Don't forget you have more things to eat here," Caroline said. She wished that Meals on Wheels would continue to deliver, but thanks to her mom's unpredictable reception of their services, they had removed her from their list. Caroline tried to talk them into putting her back, but they simply told Caroline that if she really cared about her mother, she'd get her into an assisted-care facility—and soon!

Unfortunately that was easier said than done. Although Caroline had put her mom's name on some waiting lists, there was still the matter of convincing Mom to go. Even if she was offered a room, which sounded likely at Sandy Cove, Caroline wasn't sure how to pry her mother out of the only home she'd known for more than fifty years.

"I have to go now," Caroline finally told her mom. "But I'll be back later tonight to check on you."

"You're going?" her mom said sadly. "Don't go." Tears welled in her eyes. This happened every time Caroline left, whether she had been there for five minutes or five hours. Her mother never seemed ready to say good-bye.

"I'll be back soon," Caroline promised.

Her mother started to cry, and part of Caroline wanted to sit down and cry with her. "Don't go."

"I promise, I'll be back in a few hours."

Caroline led her mother into the living room and helped her to sit down in her old stained rocker recliner. Then she picked up the remote, which she'd spent more than an hour locating yesterday. She turned the TV on and handed the remote to her mom. "Here, watch TV until I come back, okay?"

Her mother frowned at the old TV screen as if she were looking at a space alien.

"See the dog?" Caroline said hopefully as a dog-food ad began. Of course it featured a golden lab. Caroline stared at the TV with longing.

"Dog." Her mom nodded with realization.

"I'll be back," Caroline called as she left the house. By the time she was outside, her eyes were filled with tears too. Honestly, it was brutal to grow old like that. Confused and befuddled and frightened, her mom seemed to get absolutely no pleasure out of life. Really, what was the point? Caroline wished she had some answers, but when it came to aging and her mother, she was at a complete loss. In some ways it would be a relief if her mom quietly passed away in her sleep.

Caroline thought about Cathy Gardener again, and about being knocked down like that in the prime of life. It seemed so unjust and senseless compared to the circumstances of Caroline's poor old mother, who continued to linger on, miserable, lonely, and pathetic. Really, where was the fairness in that?

Caroline had always believed in God. She believed that God really did care about everyone equally. But sometimes the way he worked mystified her. Sometimes it more than mystified her; it irked her. Yet she knew that God was God, and he could do as he pleased. So who was she to complain? Just the same, she wouldn't mind if he shone a little more light on her mom's situation. As well as Caroline's. More than ever, Caroline felt that she was stumbling around in the dark, fumbling to figure things out, and often making even more messes as she went.

"I am not going to think about this now," she told herself as she turned down Sea Perch Lane. Instead she focused on the new housing development out here. She'd never seen it before, but it was nice. Not in the upscale way that Abby's neighborhood was nice, but in a more casual, beachy sort of way. There were only about a dozen homes out here, and they all seemed to be situated on larger lots, all of which appeared to have beach access.

She drove all the way down the street and found Victor's house on the end. Like the other homes, it had cedar-shingle siding that was faded to a nice warm gray, and the trim was painted in a crisp, clean white. An SUV and small pickup were parked in front, and the garage door was opened to reveal what appeared to be a nice selection of surfboards lining the back wall.

"Hello?" she called as she got out of her car and approached the garage. "Anyone home?"

"Back here," called a masculine voice. When she wandered into the garage, she encountered a young guy working on a surfboard.

"You must be Victor's son," she said, sticking out her hand. "I'm Caroline McCann."

"I'm Ben." He smiled with what seemed approval. "Dad said he had some lady friend coming over to surf today, but I thought for sure he was pulling my leg."

She laughed. "Well, hopefully I'll be able to surf. It's been a while. I'm guessing I might be a little rusty."

"Hey, it's like riding a bike," he assured her.

"That might be true at your age," she tossed back. "But I think those rules change some later on in life."

"Oh, you can't be that much older than me," he told her.

She reached over and ruffled his sandy brown hair with her fingers. "Oh, I like you already, Ben. So is your dad around?"

"In the house," he said. "Go ahead and let yourself in. I'm going to finish up this board."

She knocked on the door to the house, then went inside. "Hello?" she called as she glanced around the spacious modern kitchen. Unlike Abby's house, with its Tuscany touches and faux vintage charm, this house was sleek and classic looking. The espresso brown leather sectional and low, heavy coffee table gave it a masculine feel, and yet the creamy shag area rug made it seem friendly and inviting, too.

"Hello?" she called out again as she went over to check out the view. The house was positioned to take full advantage of the ocean's beauty. Caroline sighed. She could be so at home in a house like this.

"Hello there."

She jumped to hear Victor's voice from behind her. "Oh!" She turned quickly. "I hope you don't mind. Ben told me to come in."

"Not a problem." He smiled warmly. "Can I get you something to drink? A soda or some iced tea?"

"Water would be nice."

He nodded. "It's always good to hydrate before you hit the waves."

"I love your house," she told him as she followed him to the kitchen.

"Thanks. I can't take too much of the credit. I bought it furnished."

"Well, it's perfect." She sat down on one of the metal barstools and waited as he poured two glasses of ice water.

"That's what I thought too. Not over-the-top by any means, but comfortable."

"And the view ..." She sighed. "It's awesome."

"Can't complain about that." He set the water in front of her, then took a sip of his own. "I considered myself pretty lucky to find this place. Or maybe I should say blessed."

"Blessed?" She peered curiously at him.

He chuckled. "Well, *lucky* works too. But I do believe that God has been generous to me. And I want to be grateful for that. So maybe I should say blessed. It sounds more intentional."

"That's so funny," she said, "I was actually thinking about God as I drove out here."

"How so?"

"To be honest, I wasn't feeling exactly grateful. In fact I was feeling more perturbed than anything else. I've just been to see my mom and, well, she's so old and miserable and not even in her right mind. I feel so sorry for her. I was wondering why God lets someone like Cathy Gardener kick the bucket when she's got so much life left to live, but meanwhile, he allows someone like my mom, who has pretty much nothing, to keep hanging on." Caroline felt embarrassed. "I'm sure that came out all wrong. It's not that I want my mother to die, I really don't. But I just hate seeing her suffer. I'd really like to move her to a care facility, but she is so darn stubborn." Caroline was on the verge of tears. "Oh, I don't know why I'm rambling on and on like this. I'm sorry. I must sound like a basket case."

"You sound frustrated."

She nodded, then took a long, cool sip of water. "I am."

"Well, I'm no expert on God, but I do know from experience that he has his own way of doing things. When I'm patient, things usually work out for the best in the end."

"Patience." She considered this. "That's never been my strong suit."

"Hey, Dad," called Ben from the garage. "You got some more lady friends here. Should I send them in?"

"Of course."

Janie and Abby came in, and although Caroline was glad to see them, she was a little disappointed, too. Things had been going well between her and Victor, but now she was forced to share him.

"We brought a picnic," Abby was saying. "Enough food to feed an army, I'm sure."

"Are you going to surf too?" Victor directed this more to Janie.

"Not on your life," she told him. "We are here to be spectators only."

Ben called into the house. "We better get going if we want to catch the tide at its best."

"My wet suit's in the car," Caroline told Victor.

"Go and get it," he said. "You can change in the bedroom down that hallway to your right."

Caroline jogged out to the car, wondering what on earth she was getting herself into and yet not really caring. At least she was alive and doing something. If nothing else, it would get her mind off of her mother. That was worth something!

She grabbed her wet suit and bag and hurried back to the house. After locating what appeared to be a spare bedroom, she slipped into the swimsuit she'd found at a beach shop just that morning. It was a one-piece cut low enough to reveal her cleavage and high enough to make her already long legs appear even longer. As she admired herself in the full-length closet mirror, she thought it really was a shame to cover all that up with a wet suit. On the other hand, she didn't want to freeze her buns off. Perhaps she'd have time afterward to sun herself and get warm without the aid of the wet suit.

"Ready to do this thing?" Victor asked as she emerged from the bedroom.

"I think so." She smiled with uncertainty.

"Good for you. Ben's got your board out there already, and the girls are setting up a picnic site on the beach. I'm just going to grab some folding chairs for them. I'll meet you out there."

Before long they took the plunge. As they walked into the surf, Caroline couldn't believe how cold the water felt to her exposed skin, and she was extremely thankful for the wet suit.

"You going to be okay?" Victor asked when they were about waist deep. "You look a little chilly."

"I'm getting used to it." She forced what she hoped was a brave smile. "I think my toes are numb."

"Once you start moving, you'll warm up," Ben told her from the other side. "Let's rock and roll!" Then he shot out on his board, swimming on out toward the waves.

"I'll wait for you," Victor told her. "Feel free to take your time if you need—"

"That's okay," she said quickly. "I think Ben's got the right idea." And so, she imitated Ben, throwing herself on the board and shooting out toward the deeper water. But the next thing she knew, a big wave slapped her right across the face. She went one way and the board went the other. So much for her carefully applied makeup.

Victor helped to reconnect her and her board. "You sure you're okay?"

"I'm okay," she said with chattering teeth. "I just needed to get used to the water."

He chuckled. "That's one way to do it."

On the second attempt she managed to stay on the board and made it through the surf without being tumbled. Then she slowly paddled out to where Ben was already positioned, straddling his board and looking behind him for a wave.

"You made it," he shouted.

"Barely," she admitted as she struggled to get herself upright on her board. She did not want to plunge into the water again. Not yet anyway.

Soon the three of them were all ready and waiting for a wave. "Here she comes," yelled Ben. "Get ready, boys and girls."

So, trying to remember the procedure, Caroline paddled to what seemed the right spot in the wave, then attempted to get her feet beneath her as the board began to move faster. But, just like that, the board went one way and she went the other. Only this time she swallowed what felt like a gallon of seawater. She came up sputtering and breathless.

Victor's face was a mixture of amusement and concern. "You sure you want to do this?"

Caroline looked longingly at the sunny beach, then shook her head. "Maybe it's not such a good idea."

"At least you tried."

She attempted a smile, but was shivering so hard it wasn't easy. "If the water was a little warmer."

"Oregon surfing's not for everyone."

"You go ahead and have fun," she told him. "I'll join the spectators."

He nodded. "Yeah, I'd like to catch a few waves with Ben. He's getting ready to head back to school this week. So this might be our last chance for a while."

She held up her fist. "Cowabunga!"

He laughed and then turned to paddle out toward his son. She went as fast as her frozen feet could take her toward shore, lugging the surfboard along with her. She couldn't remember when she'd been so happy to see dry land. It was all she could do not to bend down and kiss the warm sand.

"Not as much fun as you expected?" ventured Janie with what looked like a suppressed smile.

"That water is freezing!" she exclaimed as she clumsily unzipped and peeled off her wet suit, grabbing up a towel to wrap around her goose-pimpled flesh. So much for showing off skin today.

"Can you believe we used to swim in it as kids?" Abby said.

"We must've been stark-raving nuts." Caroline held out a foot. "Look, my toes turned blue!"

"The sun will warm you up in no time," Janie patted the dark blue chair next to her. "Sit here, it's nice and toasty."

"I'll admit it was a little bit of an adrenaline rush at first." Caroline sat down in the sun-warmed chair and sighed. "But I'm guessing that might be my last attempt at surfing—even if the ocean turned to bathwater. I swear I must've swallowed a gallon of seawater."

"I have to give you credit for trying," Abby told her.

"And for coming back in one piece," Janie added.

Caroline looked out across the water. "It's hard getting old."

"We're not old," Janie said defensively.

"No. I didn't mean us," Caroline explained. "I was thinking about my mom."

======Chapter 11======

ABBY

"You could be a professional caterer," Janie told Abby as they were putting away the remnants of their beach picnic.

"You really could," Caroline agreed. "That Greek salad was awesome."

"Oh, it wasn't much." Abby waved her hand but took secret pleasure in the praise as she snapped a lid onto the remaining coleslaw. Food might be the way to a man's heart, but compliments on her cooking went straight to hers.

"Everything was great," Ben told her. "Seriously, that was the best chicken I ever tasted." He glanced at Victor. "Sorry, Dad."

Victor laughed. "I attempted to make chicken parmigiana a couple of nights ago. Complete disaster. It looked like a burnt offering."

"Neither of my parents can cook," Ben told the women in a confidential tone. "Makes me wonder how my brother and I survived."

"You poor thing." Abby closed the picnic basket. "Maybe you won't mind if I leave the leftovers with you, then."

"All right!"

"But you might want to get them into a fridge," she warned, "before anything goes bad in this sun."

Ben picked up the basket. "Not a problem."

"Janie made a good point," Victor told Abby. "If you ever decide to start a catering business, count me in as a customer."

Abby was beaming. "You know, I've considered catering before. But Paul is really opposed to the idea."

"Why?" asked Caroline.

"He just thinks it won't work, that it'll be a waste of time and money." She sighed. "He's probably right."

"But if it's something you really want to do," Janie persisted, "why not do some investigating? Gather some evidence to convince Paul otherwise."

Abby grinned at her. "You sound just like an attorney."

"Don't remind me." Janie frowned. "I've been ignoring my email all day."

"Good for you," Victor told her. "You're supposed to be on vacation."

"Unfortunately the firm doesn't seem to have gotten that same memo yet."

"Do you know how long it's been since I've had a real vacation?" Caroline mused. "I mean, more than just a few days snatched here and there. I can't even remember."

"I know what you mean." Janie shook her head.

"I *used* to know what you mean." Victor leaned back in his chair, exhaling loudly.

Abby felt a conflicting mix of guilt and envy. On one hand some people might think her life was nothing more than one big, long vacation. She could sleep in as late as she liked, walk on the beach whenever she wanted. Really, she had a life of relative leisure. The problem was, she didn't want it. More than ever, she had the desire to be doing something useful and challenging and maybe even profitable. Was it ridiculous for a fifty-three-year-old woman to want a career? She wasn't sure.

"Like I keep telling myself," Caroline continued, "I'm on vacation now. Just relax and have fun. But at the same time, I know I really need to use this time to help my mother get settled into a better place. In fact I should probably go right now. I only have a couple more days to figure this thing out. So far it's like hitting my head against a brick wall."

"Are you going to call that woman Lois told you about?" asked Abby.

"That's at the top of my list." Caroline stood and stretched. "Although I'd really rather go take a nap."

"The ocean air and exercise does that," Victor told her.

She looped the handle of her big bag over one shoulder, then bent to pick up the surfboard.

"Just leave the board." Victor stood. "Ben and I can take care of that."

"And you just stay put," she told him. "At least someone should be enjoying this gorgeous day." She waved and told everyone goodbye, then took off.

"Poor Caroline," Janie said after she was gone. "She's really in a tough spot with her mom. I hope she can figure something out."

"It sure makes me thankful for my mom," Abby told them. "I mean, sometimes she gets on my nerves. But I'm so glad her mind is sharp and she stays active. She's got this really great circle of women friends. It makes such a difference."

"Here's to growing old in style like your mom," Janie said as she held up the last of her drink. "I want to be like her someday."

It was hard to admit, but Abby did too. Only she didn't want to wait until she was her mother's age. "I have a confession to make," she said.

"What is it?" asked Janie.

Abby regretted opening her mouth. "Oh, it's really silly."

"Come on," urged Victor. "They say confession is good for the soul."

Abby took in a deep breath. "Well, here it is, then: The truth is, I really don't have any good friends. I mean, I have friends. But no really close, good friends. And I have to admit it's a bummer."

"But I'm your friend," Janie told her.

Abby nodded sadly. "Yes, but you live so far away. It'll probably be ages before I see you again."

"You're probably not in the market for guy friends," Victor said apologetically. "But I'm still trying to get to know people in town, and if you want—"

"Of course I consider you a friend." Abby reached over and took his hand, giving it a squeeze. "And I'd like you to get better acquainted with Paul, too."

"Great. He seems like a good guy."

They talked a while longer, but Janie was looking at her watch now. "As much as I hate to break up the party, I really need to get some things done today. I'm trying to make some decisions on my parents' house."

"What kind of decisions?" Victor asked as they gathered up chairs and things.

"Like whether to list it for sale yet. I can sell it as is, but it's so run-down and dated that I know I'll be leaving a lot of money on the table. And yet, realistically, do I have time to do much else?" She turned to Abby. "I'll bet Paul could recommend someone to help me fix it up."

"Do you want to fix it up?" Abby asked as they trudged through the sand toward Victor's house.

"Well, I was in it today." Janie brightened. "And I could imagine that sad old house with new windows and new cabinets and new countertops and the old hardwood floors refinished, and I got this, well, kind of a rush of excitement." She looked embarrassed. "I probably sound like I've lost my mind."

"You actually sounded happy," Victor told her.

"That's true," Abby agreed. "You did sound happy."

"Happy as in, I must be living in La-La Land. Really, there's no way I can manage a renovation project like that from Manhattan."

Abby stopped walking and turned toward Janie. "I could help you!"

"Really?" Janie looked hopeful. "How?"

"Well, I know the building industry pretty well," Abby began. "I know most of the contractors in town, who's good and who's not. And I picked out a lot of things for our new house. In fact I still have a lot of catalogs. And I know the Web sites, and I know the products. Oh, Janie, I really *could* help with your house."

"You would do that for me?" Janie looked incredulous.

"I would so love to do that." Abby nodded eagerly. "I've been wishing for something to do. I need a project—something to get me out of bed in the morning."

"I would pay you for your—"

"No." Abby firmly shook her head. "I can't let you pay me. That would be too much pressure. I could only do this if you let me be a friend helping a friend."

"Well, your house is beautiful," Janie told her. "So it's obvious that you know what you're doing. Although our tastes are different."

"Which is as it should be. I wouldn't want to help you recreate my house. You need to make your house the way you think it should be, but keep in mind that you want it to appeal to home buyers, too. You don't want it to be too taste specific."

"It sounds like you really know what you're talking about," Janie said as they set the beach chairs in Victor's garage, and then followed him into his house.

"Thanks to Paul, I pay attention to the building industry. We never miss a home-and-garden show, and I watch the home-improvement channels on TV."

"Oh, Abby," said Janie happily. "You're really giving me hope."

"Sounds like you girls are a match made in heaven." Victor tossed some used towels toward what looked like a laundry room.

"So what kind of style do you like?" Abby asked.

Janie looked around Victor's house. "Actually I like this. Kind of classic contemporary."

"Why, thank you." Victor did a faux bow. "I wish I could take the credit and say I designed this myself. At least I had the good sense to buy it."

Abby patted him on the back. "Yes, you are a smart consumer."

"And I could see maple cabinets in the kitchen," Janie continued dreamily. "Kind of like these, only in lighter tones. The house isn't as bright as this one." She ran her hand over Victor's dark granite countertop. "And granite, too, maybe a little lighter than this. Of course, stainless appliances."

"Those would all be good choices for that neighborhood," Abby told her. "Already I'm getting ideas."

"Have you considered holding on to that house?" Victor asked Janie. "As an investment? Or perhaps a place to retire to someday? That is, if you ever decide to quit working."

Janie got a thoughtful expression. "I suppose I should think about that."

"Yes!" Abby said eagerly. "And you should fix the house in a way that you could live there if you wanted to. Just in case."

Janie nodded. "Yes, you're probably right." She turned to Victor. "Thank you for your hospitality."

"Yes," Abby said. "Thank you, Victor."

"Hey, you're the ones who brought lunch," he said. "Thank you!"

"Well, thanks for sharing your beach, then," Janie said. "I wish we could stay longer. It's really lovely here."

"Anytime." He smiled at Janie in a way that made Abby wonder if he was flirting. *"Mi casa es su casa."*

Janie laughed. "Well, I've already admitted that I really like your house. You might want to be careful with an offer like that."

Abby blinked in surprise. Was Janie flirting back?

"I'd like to see you again," Victor said as he walked them to the door. "Before you leave for New York. If you have time."

"Sure." Janie nodded. "Maybe we should all get together one

more time. I'm not sure about Caroline, but my flight home is on Thursday."

"How about Wednesday, then?" Victor suggested.

"That reminds me," Abby said. "Wednesday is Cathy's memorial service. At three o'clock at New Hope Church."

"So a dinner get-together might be a good follow-up," Janie suggested.

"I'd be happy to have everyone here," Victor said, "but you already know that I can't cook to save my life."

"I'll cook," declared Abby.

"And I'll help," offered Janie.

"If you want to have it here, I'll clean it up and get everything ready."

"Sounds like a date," Abby told him. As she and Janie headed out to her car, she started planning the menu in her head.

"Victor's such a nice guy," Abby said as she drove them back toward town. "I get the feeling he likes you."

Janie laughed. "He likes you, too, Abby. And Caroline as well."

"No, not like that. I mean I think he's *interested* in you."

"And I think you're imagining things. Besides, he knows that I'm going back to New York. Really, what would be the point?"

"Yes." Abby nodded sadly. "I suppose you're right."

"Besides," Janie continued. "I think Caroline is *interested* in him. And it probably makes sense for her."

"Makes sense?" Abby frowned. "Are we talking about potential romance or a business deal here?"

Janie chuckled. "Sorry. I didn't mean to sound so clinical. I simply meant that Caroline seems genuinely unhappy with her life in LA. Plus she has her mother to think about. Really, it wouldn't surprise me at all if she decided to move back to town."

"Seriously?" Abby felt strangely hopeful. "You think she'd come back here for good?"

"Why not? She's fairly free to do what she wants. Working in a restaurant isn't the sort of thing to tie one down. Why wouldn't she want to move back home?"

"That actually makes a lot of sense." Abby nodded. "She could help with her mother and maybe slow down a little. Enjoy life more. Who knows? Maybe she and Victor would get together in time." Abby glanced at Janie in time to see her jaw clench ever so slightly. Perhaps Janie was more interested in Victor than she let on.

"So are you really serious about helping with my house?" Janie asked.

"Absolutely. In fact I was about to suggest we stop by and do a walk-through. I'd like to know what I might be getting myself into."

"I'll warn you, it's not pretty."

"Not yet anyway." Abby chuckled. "But when we're done, well, you just make sure you get some good 'before' photos so I can show it off afterward."

"You know, Abby, if you're really good at this kind of thing, like I suspect you are, you might consider doing it professionally. It might be easier than catering. Plus you have Paul in your back pocket. You guys could be quite a team."

Abby considered this. "Well, before I start running ads in the paper, I'd better make sure I can deliver."

"And make sure you really like doing it." Janie pulled her BlackBerry out of her purse. "Because sometimes we get into a career for all the wrong reasons, and by the time we figure things out, it's too late."

"Too late?"

"Oh, you know. You're invested in something and you can't just quit because you're tired of it."

"Oh." Abby wondered if Janie was talking about herself.

"At our age—I'm not saying we're old—but at this stage of the game, who wants to get into something that's not right for them?"

"I see your point." Abby did see it, but that only made her more determined to work on Janie's house. Because more than anything, Abby wanted to do something with her life—something beyond making beds, shopping for groceries, and sitting around feeling sorry for herself or guilty about something that was beyond her control. Yes, Abby decided, she was ready for more. It remained to be seen whether that something would be Janie's house, but Abby was done with frittering away her time. Finished, through, kaput!

Chapter 12

JANIE

"Oh, Janie," gushed Abby, "this is such fun!"

"You honestly think so?" Janie pushed a strand of hair away from her face, then took another energetic swing at the last of the kitchen's old upper cabinet. The sledgehammer caught it solidly this time, and the whole thing came crashing down with a loud boom, erupting a volcano of dust. Debris, grime, and shattered remnants of what once had been "home" were everywhere, and Janie was getting worried that she and Abby might be in over their heads. But it was too late to back out now.

To be fair, it was Janie's fault. She'd been the one to start pulling up the carpet last night. But it felt good to see the wood floors again. It made this project seem possible. Then Abby had met her here this morning, arranging for Paul to stop by and drop off tools as well as some advice.

"Oh, I know it's not going to be easy," Abby assured her as she pushed the broom across the kitchen floor to create a trail. "And if we don't get done, we can always have Paul send a crew in. But you have to admit it's a hoot tearing things up."

"It's actually been kind of therapeutic, like I'm in control of the situation." Janie laughed as she kicked a wooden drawer with the toe of what had been a top-notch running shoe. "But I'm afraid the feeling is rather delusional."

"You *are* in control, Janie. It's your house and you're doing what you want with it."

"You mean tearing it down." Janie frowned up at the decrepit light fixture hanging over the sink. It wasn't just ugly, but probably a fire hazard, too.

"And don't forget, you're saving money by doing the demolition yourself."

"Yes. Saving money is good. We'll need to be disciplined to stay on budget." Janie and Abby had gone over finances last night, and already Janie was feeling a little worried. This renovation was definitely going to stretch her for a while. But she hoped the project would be completed in a couple of months and the house would be sold before the holidays.

At least Abby thought it was possible. Paul had been a little skeptical, and Janie knew that was something of a red flag. Still, she was trying to be optimistic. Besides, Abby was right. Taking the place apart was kind of fun. Already they'd had the appliances and plumbing fixtures removed by some of Paul's guys, who'd known to turn off the water first and shown Janie how to work the electrical panel so that no one got electrocuted. Abby's goal was to have the whole place gutted before Janie left town on Thursday. After that the subcontractors could start coming in and putting things back together. Really, it sounded fairly simple. But Tuesday was nearly over, and so far Abby and Janie had only managed to pull out the carpets and tear down the kitchen cabinets.

"Hello, ladies?" called a voice that sounded like Paul.

"In here," Abby called back.

"How's the demo crew holding up?" He looked around the kitchen with a hard-to-read expression.

"We're okay," Janie told him. "Does this look like we're doing it right?"

He stuck his hand into one of the holes that had popped open in the wall when a cabinet came down. "You'll need to do some Sheetrock repairs."

"Sheetrock repairs?" Janie frowned.

"Drywall." He picked up a chunk of the wall, crumbling it so that white plaster dust splattered his jeans. "But I can send some of my boys in here to help with it."

"Oh." Again, Janie wondered what she'd gotten herself into.

"I forgot to ask you last night," he continued. "Are you going to change the footprint of the house?"

"Footprint? I didn't even know my house had feet."

He chuckled. "Are you going to take out any walls, make any additions, change anything from the original design?"

"No." Janie glanced at Abby to see she looked blank. "I don't think so."

"Good. That'll save you from having to pull permits. As long as you leave your plumbing and electric where they are."

"And if I want to move a light or something small?"

"It'll probably be okay. Just don't start changing *everything*," he warned. "That will really send your expenses climbing."

"Okay." Janie tried to absorb all this.

"I see that your Dumpster's been dropped." He tossed the

chunk of Sheetrock to the floor. "Looks like you'll be needing it."

"Let's get this cleaned up and call it a day," Abby told Janie.

"How about if I get my wheelbarrow for you to use?" Paul offered. "It's in my truck anyway."

"How about if you roll up your sleeves and help us?" Abby asked.

But Paul just laughed. "Sorry, ladies, but it'll be a cold day in you know where before I go back to doing grunt work again."

"Real nice," Abby said as she picked up the sledgehammer and gave a whack to the last cabinet.

"That's right," Janie told her. "Take out your aggressions if you like."

It was nearly six by the time they hauled all the junk out of the house, and both women were exhausted. Janie couldn't remember when she'd ever been so dirty. "Oh, Abby," she said as she examined her ruined nails, "have we lost our blooming minds?"

Abby laughed in a tired way. "Maybe. But I do think we could finish the bathrooms tomorrow."

"No." Janie shook her head. "I think we need to call it quits and let the professionals take it from here. Tomorrow is Cathy's memorial service, and we promised to cook dinner at Victor's. I'm so beat now that I can't even imagine how sore I'll be by then."

Abby sighed. "Yes, I'm afraid you're right. I'm going home to soak in the tub."

"I wish the hotel had a tub. That sounds good."

"They have a hot tub by the pool."

Janie didn't normally like the idea of public hot tubs, but today she was willing to make an exception. "That sounds great, except I didn't pack a swimsuit."

"I'll bet they have some in the hotel gift shop." Abby was digging her purse out from beneath a pile of dust.

"Thanks so much for your hard work," Janie said as Abby headed out. "I'll see you tomorrow."

"Don't worry about how bad things look right now," Abby called back. "It's all going to fall into place. You'll see."

Janie walked around the empty, ravaged house, and she wondered if she'd made a mistake. Really, wouldn't it have been much simpler to just sell the house as is, or even rented it? Who would possibly want it now? And what if something went wrong during the renovations? She would be so far away. What could she do? She wondered what Phil would say about this. He was always so sensible, and yet he'd also been more of a risk-taker than she. Perhaps he would think this was a great adventure. Janie didn't want to consider how her parents would've reacted to what she'd done. If they hadn't already passed on, Janie was certain they'd both fall down dead if they could see their house now. But it wasn't their house anymore. It was Janie's. This great big mess belonged to her.

Outside, the yard looked as dismal as the interior. She locked the door, not that there seemed much sense in locking it now. Really, why would anyone want to go in there? And what could they possibly take? She attempted to brush off her dirty jeans before getting into the rental car, but her effort seemed useless. If the pants hadn't been expensive and a perfect fit, she would probably just throw them out. As for her running shoes, they were history.

Feeling like a battle-fatigued soldier, Janie drove back to the hotel, parked the car, and slowly walked up to the door. She hoped that she'd packed some Advil.

"What happened to you?"

Janie turned to see Caroline coming from behind her.

"Don't ask." Janie just shook her head.

"Seriously, you look like you've been in a train wreck." Caroline peered curiously at Janie's hair. "What happened?"

So Janie gave her a quick rundown on the renovation. "It's not for the faint of heart," she said as they walked through the lobby.

"I've decided that the only hope for my mom's house is probably a bulldozer," Caroline said. "Or a well-timed fire." She chuckled. "Mind you, I'm not into arson, I'm really not."

"No, you wouldn't want to do time for arson." Janie was heading for the elevator. She usually took the stairs, but now she could barely put one foot in front of the other. "Oh, I just remembered, I was going to see if the gift shop has swimsuits."

"Swimsuits?"

Janie nodded. "So I can soak in the hot tub."

"Oh, don't waste your money on their ugly suits," Caroline said as she pushed the up button. "I can loan you one."

"Really?"

"Sure. In fact I'll join you in a soak. I'm still feeling sore from my failed surfing attempt yesterday."

Janie sighed as they went into the elevator. "Isn't aging fun?"

"I'll change and then bring the suit by your room," Caroline said before getting out.

"Thanks, I'll grab a shower first." Janie touched her filth-encrusted hair and cringed. "I'm sure the maintenance people will appreciate it." As Janie went into her room and began peeling off her grimy clothes, she felt conflicted about Caroline again. On the one hand she wanted to dislike Caroline immensely. She wanted to believe that the woman was shallow and selfish and just plain silly, like she'd been back in high school.

And yet Janie was continually surprised to discover that Caroline seemed to be kind and thoughtful and refreshingly genuine. Besides that, she was cheerful and fun. So why was Janie feeling disturbed? As she showered and scrubbed, Janie pondered this. Was it because Janie suspected it might all be a very good act? After all, Caroline had gone to Hollywood to pursue a career in acting. What if she was good at it?

Well, what if? Why should Janie care one way or the other?

As she toweled dry, she wondered if her concerns were related to Victor. No, that seemed ridiculous. What difference was it to Janie if Caroline wanted to pursue a relationship with Victor? If anything, Janie should encourage her. *Quit acting like you're in middle school!*

"Hello?" called Caroline from the hallway as she knocked on the door. "Anybody home?"

Janie tied the belt of the thick terry robe and went to answer it. "Come in," she told Caroline. "I'm almost ready."

Caroline wore her lime-colored swimsuit with a brightly colored sarong wrapped around like a skirt. "Here." She handed Janie a plastic bag. "I'm going to see if I can find us some refreshments." She winked. "Meet ya down there, okay?"

"Sure." Janie thanked her and closed the door. As she pulled on the sleek navy blue one piece, she wondered what kind of refreshments Caroline had in mind. It wasn't that she cared particularly. Mostly she just wanted to soak her tired muscles, then call it an early night.

Janie was relieved to see that no one was in the pool area, and the hot tub wasn't being used either. She sighed and closed her eyes as she eased herself down into the hot churning water. Bliss.

After a few minutes she heard Caroline giggling. "I got treats," she said as she set two plastic cups with little paper umbrellas and lime wedges on the edge of the hot tub. Then she pulled two bottles of water from her bag and set them there as well. "In case we get dehydrated."

Janie peeked into one of the plastic cups and saw something pale and icy inside. "What is it?" she ventured.

"Piña coladas. The bartender made them special."

Soon Caroline was in the hot tub and they were both sipping piña coladas, and Janie could imagine that before long she'd be feeling no pain.

"Is this the life or what?" Caroline said happily.

"Uh-huh." Janie took a sip of water and sighed.

"I wish we'd been better friends in high school," Caroline said unexpectedly.

"Better friends?" Janie peered through the steam at her. "We weren't friends at all."

"Oh, I know we didn't hang out together, but I still thought of you as a friend."

"Seriously?"

"Sure. Don't you remember I used to say hi to you?"

Janie shrugged, then sank deeper into the water. "I probably thought you were just trying to make popularity points. I mean, you were always running for something. Homecoming queen, prom queen, cheerleader queen. Good grief, Caroline, how many crowns do you have anyway?"

Caroline laughed. "Oh yeah, I'm just buried in crowns. The problem is, I don't have a kingdom. Or even a king."

Something buzzed Janie's memory now. "Didn't you get married once?"

Caroline nodded. "Once and briefly."

"Why didn't it last?"

Caroline set her piña colada aside and pushed her bangs back. "There were a few reasons."

"You don't have to tell me if you—"

"No, that's not it. I just don't want to tell it falsely. You know, I've told that story for so long that the truth is a little blurry."

"Oh."

"I was pushing thirty when Max and I met. He was about ten years older and had never been married. Kind of a confirmed bachelor, you know?"

"Uh-huh."

"Well, I really wanted this guy. I mean he was everything I'd ever hoped for. He was a director and had a great car and a house in Malibu. But besides that, I was in love with him. It was actually pretty magical."

"And?"

"We got married and we were deliriously happy for a while. But his dream had always been to have kids. He'd put off marriage and family for his career, but his career was taking off and he was ready."

"But you weren't?"

"No. I was ready too. I wanted kids. At least four."

"So what happened?"

"I just couldn't get pregnant. It wasn't for lack of trying."

"Oh."

"We spent a lot of money on infertility treatments, and my obstetrician kept trying to give me hope."

"But …"

"But nothing worked. I finally went to a gynecologist who told it to me straight." Caroline downed the last of her piña colada. "She said I'd never be able to have children because of an abortion I'd had about ten years earlier."

"Oh, Caroline." Janie could see that Caroline was crying. "I'm so sorry."

She sniffed. "Yeah, so was I."

"But what about adoption?"

"Max is pretty traditional. Not to mention Jewish. He really wanted his own kids. So when I told him about the abortion, well, it was pretty upsetting to him. Like I hadn't come clean." She wiped her nose with the back of her hand. "It's not that I was trying to hide anything from him. More like I wanted to forget it."

"That's understandable."

"If I'd had that first baby …" Caroline cried harder. "He … or she … would be thirty-two by now. Can you believe it?"

To Janie's surprise, she was crying too. Whether it was weariness, the hot tub, the piña colada, or empathy for Caroline, she couldn't be sure, but she felt so sad for her friend. She reached out and hugged Caroline. "I'm so sorry," she said. "If it's any comfort, it hasn't been easy having children. I mean, I hate to complain, but my daughter, well, she's a mess. Drugs. Haven't heard from her in months. Not easy."

Now they were both crying, hugging each other and crying

loudly. Really, Janie thought in a moment of clarity, if someone walked in right now, they would surely wonder. But Janie didn't care. For once in her life, she couldn't care less what anyone thought.

===Chapter 13===

MARLEY

Marley was definitely not herself this week. Not on Monday afternoon, when she got home to her stuffy apartment and a pile of junk mail. And not on Tuesday, when she showed up for work and not one single customer darkened the door of the art gallery. And not on Wednesday, when she was decidedly in a snit.

She couldn't even blame the weather, because it was absolutely gorgeous, especially for Seattle. She'd been trying to distract herself from her emotions by focusing on work. She wanted to get everything absolutely picture perfect for the Georgia Martini showing this coming weekend. Like an obsessed woman, she fretted over every little detail, spot cleaning already spotless walls, vacuuming carpets that didn't need it, ordering wine and cheese and crackers like she thought that the president and his cabinet were going to unexpectedly show up, checking and rechecking the lighting—the works.

"Wow," Kevin Leonard, owner of the shop, said to her Wednesday afternoon when he caught her polishing the doorknob to the bathroom. "You're like the Energizer Bunny. That minivacation must've really agreed with you."

She turned and glared at him. "Are you complaining?"

"No." He held up his hands and backed off. "It was a compliment."

"Because if you'd like me to slack off, I'd be—"

"Not at all, Marley. I love that you care about the gallery."

"And you're right. It was a *mini*vacation. Make that micro-mini. I really should've taken a few more days." She sniffed indignantly. "In fact, a good friend of mine is being buried today. And I didn't even stay long enough to pay my respects."

He placed a hand on her shoulder. "I'm sorry, Marley. You should've told me."

She softened a bit. "Well, I knew you had the big show."

He nodded. "But I could've gotten Warren to come in."

"Warren?" Marley narrowed her eyes at him. Warren was Kevin's domestic partner and, although she liked him, he was probably the most extreme homebody Marley had ever met. She'd always suspected he had some kind of social phobia or OCD going on, and it was hard to believe Warren would agree to work at the gallery. "Are you kidding?"

Kevin nodded. "Yes, he's been seeing a new shrink. And she tells him he needs to face his fears and get out there. I even think he'll come over this weekend to help with the show."

Now Marley not only felt unnecessary but indignant as well. "Why didn't you tell me that sooner?"

"I didn't know it was an—"

"It's called communication," she told him sharply. "My exhusband was really bad at it too."

He put a hand on her shoulder. "Marley, I can tell you're out of sorts and I'm sorry. Is it too late to catch a flight and attend your friend's funeral?"

She looked at her watch. "Of course it's too late."

"Well, why don't you take the rest of the afternoon off?" He smiled. "The place is spotless, and if a customer comes in, I'll be here."

"Are you serious?" Normally Marley would jump at any unexpected time off. But this time she wasn't so sure.

"Yes, yes." He gently nudged her toward the back room. "I'm sure we'll both be happier."

"Okay." She opened a storage cabinet and retrieved her bag, peering curiously at him. "You're not firing me, are you?"

He laughed nervously. "Are you kidding?"

"Okay. If you're sure." She tucked her purse under her arm and, feeling slightly off balance, went out the back exit and got into her car. Although she knew it was absurd, she could've sworn that he really was firing her. For all she knew, he was happy to be rid of her. Perhaps he had planned it that way from the start. Warren the social-phobe was going to replace her.

Marley felt lost and old and useless as she drove through town to her apartment. Any normal person would take full advantage of time off on a day like this. But all she wanted was to crawl into bed and pull the covers over her head. No, to be honest, she wanted something else, too. She wanted to be in Clifden. She wanted to be with her old friends. She even wanted to be at Cathy's memorial service, which was an impossibility. The service was supposed to start at three, and it was nearly two now. Even so, before she went inside her apartment, she dialed Abby's phone number.

"It's so good to hear your voice," Marley told Abby after they said hello. "I feel so sad that I'll miss Cathy's service. I wondered, if I sent a check, could you put my name on some flowers?"

"Of course."

"Thanks." Marley sat down on the bench outside her front door. The sun was baking the cedar deck, and she noticed that her favorite red geranium was nearly dead from lack of water.

"How are you doing?" Abby's voice sounded so warm and compassionate that Marley felt even worse.

"Do you really want to know?" She picked off the dead blooms, tossing them over the railing to the overgrown shrubbery below.

"Of course!"

"Well, not so good."

"Really?" Abby sounded concerned. "Is it your health?"

"No, it's more my spirits. Sagging. Definitely sagging."

"Why?"

Marley considered this. "I'm not even sure."

"I hate to say it, but at our age, it can sometimes be a hormonal imbalance."

"That's occurred to me."

"Paul's gotten pretty good at figuring out when to cut me a wide berth." Abby chuckled. "Not sure what I'll use as an excuse once perimenopause ends."

"You think it'll ever end?"

Abby laughed louder now. "Well, it did for my mom."

"I was thinking about your mom," Marley admitted.

"My mom? Why on earth were you thinking about her?"

"I was wishing I had her life."

"What?" Abby sounded stunned. "Are you serious?"

"I wouldn't mind having a little cabin on the beach like hers. The freedom to do art whenever I want. Friends to gather around me. Honestly, it sounds perfectly idyllic. And pathetic, right? Being jealous of an octogenarian!"

"Oh."

"You probably think I'm nuts." Marley sighed. "And you wouldn't be alone in that department. I think my boss is ready to give me the boot."

"Not really?"

"He gave me the day off."

"But that sounds like a good thing."

"Except for the look in his eye. Like maybe he'd be relieved if I never came back."

"Well, maybe you just needed a break." Abby began cheerfully talking about other things, mostly the goings-on at Clifden. She probably thought it was a good distraction for Marley's sagging spirits, but it only drove Marley deeper into the dark funk that engulfed her. Hearing about how Abby was helping Janie with house renovations, how they were all attending Cathy's memorial service, and how they were cooking dinner at Victor's beautiful beach house tonight all just made Marley want to throw a temper tantrum. Why couldn't she be there too? She felt so left out.

"Well, I really should get going," Abby said finally. "We need to get over to the church for Cathy's service. I have some photos to put up."

"I wish I were there too."

"You're here in spirit."

"Right." Marley just shook her head. "In spirit."

They said good-bye and hung up, and Marley continued to sit

there on the bench, sweating in the afternoon sun and wondering just what was wrong with her. Who—or what—had stepped in and derailed her life like this? She picked the last of the dry leaves from the geranium and moved its heavy pot into a shaded corner, reminding herself to water it before the day was done.

"And get a life," she said as she stood up and dug her keys out of her bag. "And get real." She continued to berate herself as she unlocked her front door. What was wrong with her? She was acting like a four-year-old, having a pity party like this. Good grief, she'd been through harder times and come out just fine. What if she were in Cathy's place right now? What if she'd been the one to check out at the reunion last weekend?

Even that gloomy notion didn't make her feel much better as she went into her cluttered apartment, which felt even stuffier than yesterday. At least Cathy had been doing what she loved. She'd been living in Clifden, working in a job where she was appreciated, using her energy to make the town a better place for everyone. Besides that, she had died dancing! What a way to go.

Marley tossed her purse onto a chair and looked at the clock above the tiny kitchen table. It was nearly three. The church would be filled with mourners, all there to honor the fond memory of Cathy Gardener, all sad to know that she was really gone. Because Cathy, both during school days and well beyond, had always been loved.

Tears dampened Marley's cheeks again. She wished her melancholy was purely for Cathy, but her sorrow was almost entirely selfish. As incredible as it seemed, she felt slightly envious of Cathy. At least Cathy was surrounded by friends. It felt as if Marley had no one. Not even a cat.

====Chapter 14====

CAROLINE

Caroline dropped by her mom's house before the memorial service. Once again she took a cheeseburger and fries. It wasn't exactly health food, but it was better than nothing. Now more than ever, it seemed that her mother survived on little more than air—and it wasn't even fresh air at that! Caroline's plan was to "warm up" her mother before the social worker Lois Schuler had recommended, Beverly Miller, paid a visit.

But when Beverly arrived to do her evaluation, Caroline's mother became very childlike and uncooperative. Caroline tried to coax her into answering the questions, but that only made things worse. Not only did her mother want Beverly to leave, she wanted Caroline to go as well. "Get out of my house," she said over and over, waving her hands as if shooing a bad dog.

Caroline apologized profusely to Beverly, suggesting that perhaps another time might be better, although Caroline knew that wasn't true. Her mother's social skills seemed to deteriorate daily. Still, Beverly didn't seem a bit deterred. Apparently she'd been down this road with the elderly before. Instead of trying to engage the stubborn old woman, who was glaring at both of them, Beverly simply walked around, making benign comments about pictures or lamps or whatever. Finally Caroline's mother grew weary of the game and retreated to her bedroom. When she was safely out of the picture, Caroline gave Beverly the full tour, going into great detail to show exactly how her mother was living and why she was worried.

"I unplugged the stove," Caroline said quietly, "after I found an element left on high. And then I told her it was broken."

"That's wise."

"So she can use the microwave, but even that's a little scary. There's no telling what she might put in there." Caroline felt close to tears. "Honestly, I expect her to do something crazy and burn the whole house down, with her in it."

"More likely she'll fall down and break something. That's usually how it goes."

Caroline wasn't sure whether to be relieved or worried.

"She refuses to get rid of her trash." Caroline opened the garage door to reveal what looked like a dump site. "It's disgusting."

"And unhealthy."

"I'll say." Caroline held her breath as she closed and locked the door. "It's not that she can't afford a trash service. She's just afraid that there's something valuable in there. Something she'll need someday. It's nuts."

"What are you going to do?"

Caroline shrugged. "What can I do? I live in LA. I can't run herd on Mom every day, even if she would let me. Sometimes she doesn't even know who I am. If I don't have a cheeseburger in hand, sometimes she won't even let me in the house."

"Has she been in for a physical exam lately?"

"Are you kidding? She's certain that her doctor is a quack."

Beverly was making notes. "You know she needs assisted care."

"I know, but she refuses to leave her house, and I don't see how I can force her, not without a straightjacket. I'm sure not going there."

"Is it possible that you could hire someone to come and—"

"I've tried that." Caroline held up her hands in a helpless gesture. "In the first place, who would want to work, let alone live, in this trash heap? A few applicants have seen the conditions and withdrawn. One time I thought I'd hit the jackpot with this sweet Latino lady. I suspect she was an illegal alien, but she was willing to live here, and she told me she loved doing housework and laundry, so I didn't really care. But my mother threw so many fits that after just a few days, the poor woman couldn't take it anymore. I just don't know what to do."

Beverly put her hand on Caroline's shoulder. "If it's any consolation, you're not alone. There are a lot of people in this same situation."

"I just feel so helpless. Like there's nothing I can do for her. And I'm worried she's going to starve to death or …" Caroline was crying.

"We do have a support group in town."

"But I don't live in town." Caroline tore off a paper towel and used it to wipe her tears.

"Yes, I realize that."

"I'm afraid that Mom's not going to make it. I have to go back home on Friday. I worry it'll be the last time I see her."

"I'm sure that's a possibility."

"I just don't know what else to do."

"I'm assuming it's not possible for you to move back here, to help manage things for her?"

Caroline sighed. "I wasn't planning on it. But now I'm wondering if I shouldn't be more open to the idea. I mean, who else does she have?" Caroline thought of her shiftless brother, Michael. If he didn't have such a drinking problem, she'd put some pressure on him. As it was, that would be like adding fuel to his fire.

"It's just that people like—well, like your mother—they need an advocate. A guardian of sorts. There's a lot of paperwork and things to be done. The state could step in and take over, but I'm not sure you'd like that. If there's any way you can take some time off from work and stick around, the whole transition would probably go a lot smoother, and I think you'd feel better about it in the end. Of course, that might not be possible for you. I don't know your situation."

Caroline considered this. What would happen if she quit her job and moved back here? Really, there were worse things. In some ways it almost seemed as if life—or maybe God—was already pulling her in this direction, as if it was something she couldn't put off any longer. "Maybe I should just do it," she told Beverly. "Maybe I should quit my job, sell my condo, and relocate back here. Maybe that's the answer."

Beverly looked surprised. "Oh, I wouldn't be too hasty. It might not be necessary to do all that. Perhaps you could take a few weeks' leave of absence. Just long enough to get her settled in somewhere."

"No." Caroline firmly shook her head. "I am going to do this.

My decision is made." When she said this, she felt as if a load had been lifted from her mind.

Beverly retrieved a folder of papers from her briefcase, then handed them to Caroline. "You'll need to start working on these things, filling out these forms, filing for guardianship and whatnot. It's all in there. You can call me if you have any questions."

"I'll get right to it." Caroline looked at the closed bedroom door, imagining her mother hunched up against the other side, trying to eavesdrop. "I just want to be sure that Mom will get the kind of care she needs, whether it's here or someplace else."

"Your mother is lucky to have you."

Caroline wasn't so sure about that, but she walked Beverly outside, thanking her and promising to be in touch. Then she went back into the house and told her mom it was safe to come out.

"Is that woman gone?" Her mother glanced around.

"Yes." Caroline pushed a strand of dingy gray hair away from her mother's eyes. The woman needed a haircut. Of course, she wouldn't let anyone near her with scissors.

"Did she steal anything?"

Caroline was tempted to say something sarcastic but knew from experience it would only backfire. "No, Mom, I watched her carefully. She didn't steal anything."

"Good." Her mom shuffled around the stacks of papers and things, poking here and there until she finally seemed satisfied that all was well and nothing was missing. How she could even know was a mystery. "You never know what people will do."

"No." Caroline sighed to think of the work ahead for her as she echoed her mother's words. "You never know what people will do."

Later that afternoon, as Caroline sat with her friends at Cathy Gardener's memorial service, she kept thinking about her mother and what seemed a hopeless situation. She wondered how she'd feel right now if this was her mother's service instead of Cathy's. While Caroline would be very sad and probably regret all the things she'd never said or done—as well as many of the things she had—she felt that, in a way, her mother had already left this life. Sometimes it seemed that she was "dearly departed," except that her body hadn't figured this out yet.

"What can I do to help with tonight's dinner?" Caroline asked Abby.

"Just be there to lend a hand. I've got everything covered."

"But can't I bring something? A bottle of wine perhaps?"

"Sure." Abby smiled. "That'd be great."

Caroline had some time to kill and so, after stopping by the wine shop, she decided she would attempt to tell her mother her plans. Not that the confused old woman would understand. But Caroline wanted her mom to know that she was going to be sticking around. For some reason it felt important. So for the second time today, she swung by McDonald's and ordered a cheeseburger and fries and, taking a chance, she ordered a vanilla milkshake as well. Her mother used to like vanilla ice cream. So maybe …

"What do you want?" her mother growled from behind the chain lock. "Why don't you leave me alone?"

"I brought you a cheeseburger," Caroline said. The door opened at the magic words.

As usual Caroline went into the kitchen, cleared a space on the cluttered table, and arranged her mother's food. "Here you go."

Her mother groaned as she eased herself onto the kitchen chair. "What's that?" She pointed to the milkshake with suspicion.

"A vanilla milkshake," Caroline said patiently. "You used to like vanilla."

"Vanilla?" She said the word as if it were foreign. "I don't like vanilla."

Caroline cleared off the old crate and sat down across from her mother, wondering what she could possibly say to soften this woman up. She opened the straw and stuck it into the shake, then took a sip. "Umm, this is good," she said.

"Why are you eating my food?" her mother demanded. "Where's your food? How come you never eat?"

Caroline put the shake back in front of her mom. "Would you like me to eat with you?"

Her mom just grunted and shrugged, taking another bite of the burger.

"Tonight I'm having dinner with friends."

"Friends?" Mom looked suspiciously at her.

"From school. Remember when I was little and I went to school?"

Her mom's face was cloudy, as if she was trying to remember.

"I lived here in this house with you and Dad and Michael."

"Michael?" The clouds seemed to part a little. "Where is Michael?"

Caroline frowned. "I'm not sure."

"Does he live here?" She looked confused again.

"No. He lives far away, Mom."

"Far away." She shook her head sadly.

"Try the shake, Mom," Caroline encouraged her. "Or I'll drink it."

That seemed to do the trick, because her mom took a hesitant sip. At first she looked angry, like someone had played a trick on her.

"It's cold," Caroline said. "Ice cream."

Her mom nodded as if she got this. "Cold." Then she took another sip and actually smiled.

"Do you like it?" Caroline felt happy.

She nodded and took another eager sip on the straw, and then another long one. Then she slammed the paper cup to the table, closed her eyes tightly, and clutched her forehead.

"Oh, no," Caroline said. "If you drink too fast, you'll get a headache."

Her mom moaned with both hands on her head.

"It'll go away," Caroline said apologetically.

"You go away!" her mother screamed. "You go away!"

Caroline knew the pain and confusion was talking, but she just couldn't bear it. It hurt too much to have her own mother yelling at her, hating her, and treating her like the enemy when all she wanted to do was help. Without saying a word, Caroline got up and walked out. Maybe selling her condo and moving to Clifden was not such a good idea for either of them.

———

"Abby's not here yet," Victor said when he opened the door to see Caroline standing there with the bag from the wine store.

"I'm sorry," Caroline said. "Am I too early?"

"No." He motioned her in. "You're fine. Come on in. Is everything okay? You seem a little upset."

"I just left my mother's house." She followed him to the kitchen, setting the bag on the counter with a thud.

"Oh." He nodded with a knowing look as he opened the bag and removed a bottle of wine. He examined the label. "Pinot noir." He nodded and set it down, then removed the other one. "Pinot gris." He chuckled. "Looks like you're covering your bases."

"I wasn't sure if Abby wanted red or white."

"I'll put the pinot gris in to chill, but it looks like you could use a bit of the noir now."

She sat down on the barstool and nodded. "I'm so frustrated, Victor," she confessed. "And hurt." She told him about Beverly's visit and Caroline's subsequent decision to quit her job and sell her condo and return home to help her mom. "I mean, I was willing to give up everything, and I was actually feeling kind of good about it." She explained about the milkshake and the brain freeze and how her mom turned on her. "I know she doesn't realize what she's saying or doing, but it hurts just the same. It's like trying to help someone and being slapped in the face."

He set the glass of red wine in front of her. "I guess I'm lucky to have both my parents healthy and in their right minds."

"You have no idea." She took a sip of wine, then sighed.

The doorbell rang. "That will be Janie," he told her. "She offered to come early to help me get things ready."

Caroline just nodded, sitting there like a dummy as Victor answered the door, greeted Janie, and told her that Caroline was already here. "I just opened a bottle of pinot noir," he said as he and Janie came into the kitchen. "Can I pour you some?"

"I'll wait for dinner." Janie set down her purse then looked at Caroline with a hard-to-read expression. Caroline suspected that Janie wondered why she was here early, and why she was drinking wine with Victor. Caroline just didn't have the energy to explain. Instead she sat there staring at the dark red wine.

"Are you okay?" Janie asked.

Caroline shrugged. "I was at my mom's ... and ..."

"She's feeling a little blue," Victor explained.

Caroline told Janie about her decision to make the big move back to Clifden. "It just seemed like the right thing to do. Especially after I talked to the social-services lady. It's like suddenly I was ready, and I wanted to do it. But then my mom, well, she was just being her charming self as usual. And my got feelings hurt. Now I'm questioning the whole thing. Maybe it's not so brilliant to move back."

"You could be setting yourself up for a lot of pain," Janie warned.

"Maybe. But I feel guilty being so far away. She has no one."

"But if she's rejecting you anyway"—Janie held up her hands— "what good will it do if you're here?"

Caroline sadly shook her head. "I don't know."

"And to turn your life upside down like that ..." Janie continued. "What if you cut all your ties and it turns out to be a mistake?"

"I've thought of that too."

"Your mom won't be around forever." Janie softened. "I don't mean to be harsh, but once the dementia sets in, people don't usually last long. What if you get all situated here, and suddenly your mom's gone?"

Caroline didn't know how to answer that. On the one hand she might be relieved. On the other hand, well, she just didn't know. How did people make big decisions like this? "I've been in LA for so long." She took another sip. "I don't know. I might feel lost without it." She looked at Victor. "How did you make that big decision? I mean, to give up your life in Chicago and just do"—she waved her hands—"this?"

"It was more like I couldn't *not* do it. I felt like there was a giant magnet pulling me toward the Pacific, and once I let go, I just had to come along." He smiled. "I think God had something to do with it too. I had this deep sense of peace. And of course I wanted to be near Ben. It just seemed right. It still does."

"Speaking of Ben," Janie said, "did he go back to school?"

Victor nodded sadly. "Just this morning. I miss him already."

"I know what you mean," Janie said. "I had a long chat with Matthew just before I came over. It was so good to hear his voice. I'd been hoping he'd come to New York for a quick visit before he goes back to school, but he doesn't think he'll have time." She turned to the sink and wiped down what already looked like a clean countertop.

"So we're all feeling a little blue," Caroline said. "I guess I came to the right place."

Victor laughed. "Hopefully we can cheer each other up."

"And say our good-byes too," Janie said as she turned around. "I leave tomorrow, and don't you leave on Friday, Caroline?"

Caroline nodded. "Now the big question is, do I go home to get ready to come back, or not?"

"You're the only one who can answer that," Victor told her. The doorbell rang again, and Abby and Paul came in, and the preparations for dinner began. As Caroline took dishes out of the cupboard, she thought the moment was nice: friends fixing food together, visiting and enjoying each other. Too bad it was all about to come to an end.

=Chapter 15==

ABBY

Abby tore off a long sheet of foil. "So how's everyone doing?" she asked Janie. Caroline was outside setting the table, and the guys were fiddling with the grill. Abby had sensed a little tension in the air but couldn't pinpoint the cause.

"Fine." Janie continued to toss the salad that Abby had brought from home.

"Caroline seemed a little upset."

"Oh yes. She's just been with her mother. Pretty stressful."

"Yes, it's been hard on her. Poor thing." Abby sighed as she arranged the salmon on the foil, then opened the jar of glaze she'd made earlier. "Paul's friend Ray caught this gorgeous salmon yesterday."

"What's in that glaze?" Janie asked as Abby started coating the fish.

"Just some orange marmalade, butter, garlic, ginger, white wine. And a few other secret ingredients. If I told you, I'd have to kill you." She chuckled. "Not really."

"Smells lovely."

"Caroline is really stuck between a rock and a hard place where her mother is concerned."

"Apparently she was all ready to leave LA for good and move back home."

"Really?" Abby put the jar in the sink and looked at Janie hopefully.

"But her mother rained on her parade, and now she's not sure it's a good idea."

"It might be easier to take care of things if she's up here," Abby said as she poured a bag of small golden potatoes into a stainless-steel pot. "It might even take some of the pressure off Caroline."

"I don't know. She seemed pretty stressed out from being with her mom. I'm worried she might relocate and give up her life, then be sorry." Janie lowered her voice. "What if Caroline went to all that trouble and her mother became even more hostile? Or worse, what if she died?"

"At least Caroline would have no regrets."

"No regrets? What about her job and her friends and everything she'd be leaving behind in LA?"

"From what I've heard, she doesn't have much of a life down there anyway."

"Maybe not, but it's probably a lot more than she'd have up here." Janie glanced outside. Caroline was talking to the guys, telling them what must be an entertaining story, judging by their interested expressions. "I'm sure you've noticed that Caroline is usually the life of the party. She's had fun with all her old friends around, but I can't imagine her enjoying herself after the party's over and her friends have gone home."

"Oh, I don't know."

"Think about it, Abby. Like, say, in the dead of winter. I think Caroline would be bored silly."

Abby frowned at her. "Are you saying Clifden isn't a nice place to live?"

"No, no. I didn't mean that. And I realize that you enjoy things like quilting and cooking, plus you have your beautiful home and Paul for company. But someone like Caroline, well, she's used to the city life and the sunshine. It's hard to imagine her being happy in a sleepy little town like this."

"I can imagine her being happy here." Abby turned back to the stove and tried to conceal how irritated she felt by Janie's condescending attitude. She couldn't believe that Janie was acting so snooty, as if Clifden were some nasty little hole-in-the wall where no one in her right mind would want to live.

"How does this salad look?" Janie asked.

Abby glanced at the salad. "It's fine. Why don't you take the salmon out and tell Paul to put it on in about five minutes."

With the kitchen to herself, Abby sulked. She continued getting dinner ready, but she was not happy about Janie's comments. In fact she would have resented her offer to help Janie renovate her house, except she was really looking forward to the project. She'd already torn out some magazine pages and begun putting together a notebook that she planned to copy and send to Janie.

As Abby began slicing a loaf of freshly baked rosemary bread, she was hit with a perfectly splendid idea. If Caroline really did decide to move back home, and if she sold her condo, maybe she would want to buy Janie's newly renovated house. It should be fairly well priced and would be big enough for Caroline to keep her mother with her if she liked. By the time Abby finished with it, the home would be absolutely delightful. Besides that, hadn't Caroline mentioned how she liked the contemporary style of Victor's home?

Really, the circumstances seemed almost providential. Thanks to her new, optimistic plan, she forgave Janie for being so negative about Clifden. Perhaps Janie had simply been describing how it would be for *her* to relocate from Manhattan to Clifden. Of course, Abby thought as she arranged the bread slices in a metal bread basket, that had to be it. Abby knew firsthand how easy it was to empathize with others, substituting her own emotions for theirs. Her therapist had warned her that this was one of her weaknesses. Could Janie have the same problem?

Maybe there was more to Janie's remarks than Abby could see. Perhaps Janie really did think it would be nice to live in Clifden. She'd said something to that effect already. Abby looked out to where Victor, Paul, Caroline, and Janie were visiting, and she noticed that Janie seemed to be focused in on Victor. Her eyes seemed warm and lit up as she listened to him. That's when it occurred to Abby that Janie's overreaction to Caroline's interest in Clifden might have more to do with Victor than anything else. Maybe she was jealous.

If that was the trouble, Abby felt genuinely sorry for Janie. It would be horrible to be trapped in a lifestyle that she didn't really want, especially if it forced her to forfeit a promising relationship. Would Janie really sacrifice all that just to live in New York City? That seemed crazy to Abby.

Before long Caroline and Janie came back to help take things out to the table. Naturally Abby kept her thoughts to herself. Really, she felt sorry for both Janie, seemingly stuck in her dead-end New York life, and Caroline, who had to decide whether to give up LA.

"What a gorgeous evening," Janie said happily as they sat down to eat. "And this meal looks amazing, Abby. You're making it very hard for me to say good-bye and get on that flight to New York tomorrow."

"Then don't," Victor told her as he filled wine glasses.

She laughed. "That's easier said than done."

"Sometimes you have to just go for what you want," he said seriously. "Take the risk in order to get the reward."

"Easy for you to say," Caroline chimed in. "You've already made the leap."

He chuckled. "Then I should know what I'm talking about. I've jumped in, and I'm telling you, the water's fine."

Caroline nodded. "I'm starting to feel convinced."

"You should feel convinced," Abby told her. "Clifden is a great place to live." She looked at her husband. "Right, Paul?"

"Absolutely." He smiled, then held up his wine glass. "Here's to Clifden, the best little sea town I know."

They all lifted their glasses.

"And here's to living your best life," Abby quoted Oprah, "and to going wherever that takes you."

After the toast Victor asked if they would mind him asking a blessing. No one objected. So they all bowed their heads, and he thanked God for their food and their friendship, and he invited God to lead everyone at the table. "Guide us along the path that you know is best for us, even if that means making changes or taking risks. And even if it doesn't. Amen."

Everyone echoed, "Amen," and then they began to eat. Conversation flowed freely among them, as if they'd been gathering like this for years. But as the sun was setting and they finished up, Abby noticed that Janie seemed unusually quiet. Was she feeling sad to know that she was leaving tomorrow? Or was she troubled at how easily Caroline seemed to be getting along with Victor? Caroline seemed to be feeling more confident about making this big move.

"This has been so wonderful," Janie said as they cleared the outdoor table. "As much as I'd love to stay for dessert, I think I need to make it an early night. I have to get up at four in the morning to make it back to Portland in time for my flight."

"Yikes." Abby looked at the clock. "You're not getting much sleep tonight."

Janie nodded, then hugged her. "You got that right." She went around and hugged everyone, and when she left, there were tears in her eyes.

"I'm going to make a fire in the fire pit," Victor told them.

"You go out with him," Abby instructed Paul. "I'll get dessert."

"And I'll make coffee," Caroline said.

"I set some decaf by the coffeemaker," Victor said as he and Paul went back outside.

After the guys were out, Abby turned to Caroline. "I don't want to tell you how to live your life," she began, "but I've been thinking about your situation with your mom. And I have a crazy idea."

"A crazy idea?" Caroline giggled. "That sounds just my style."

Abby told her about Janie's house and the renovations in process. "It's going to be beautiful when it's done." She gestured toward Victor's furnishings. "A lot like this house."

"How does that relate to me and your crazy idea?"

"Well, I thought if you sold your condo you might be interested in—"

"I could buy Janie's house!" cried Caroline.

Abby nodded. "Exactly. And if we knew you were going to buy it, maybe you could be involved in picking things like granite and paint colors and whatnot."

Caroline's eyes lit up. "Oh, do you know how cool that would be?"

Abby was getting excited. "It would be so fun to have you living in town."

"I wonder if I could afford it." Caroline frowned.

"If you sold your mom's place, you could put that money toward the house too. With three bedrooms you'd have enough room to have your mom with you if you liked."

"That's true." Caroline looked truly happy about the possibilities. "This feels as if it's meant to be. I can't believe it. I'm ready to move up here right now. How soon will the house be done?"

"It's hard to say. We've barely begun. But maybe while it's getting finished, you could live with Paul and me. We have a spare room."

"Seriously?" Caroline's eyes were wide with wonder. "You'd do that for me? You'd really let me crash with you?"

Abby chuckled. "Should you get obnoxious or demanding, we might be motivated to get the house done more quickly."

Caroline laughed as she threw her arms around Abby. "You are the best! Truly the best!"

All Abby had to do was break the news to Paul. This wouldn't be easy, since he could sometimes get territorial over his personal turf. Of course, she didn't need to tell him about this tonight, especially not when he seemed to be having a really good time getting to know Victor. Why spoil things?

Chapter 16

JANIE

For several hours Janie tossed and turned in the overly firm hotel bed. Finally she gave up on sleep altogether, gathered her things, and quietly checked out. It was barely three in the morning when she drove out of town. She was thankful for the darkness as well as the fog, because it was better not to see what she was leaving behind. Better not to think about it too.

To distract herself, as well as to stay awake, she turned on the radio and found a prerecorded talk show where "relationship expert" Dr. Karen was taking calls on the topic of lost loves. Janie almost switched the station, but the woman who'd called in sounded so desperate that Janie became intrigued.

"I can't seem to move on with my life," the woman was saying. "I try to do things to help me forget him, but it's impossible."

"What kind of things are you doing?"

"Oh, you know. Like shopping and—"

"Word of warning here: You might want to nix the shopping. I've seen brokenhearted women going into debt over a guy and, trust me, it's not worth it."

"Right. Sometimes I meet my single girlfriends for drinks, and before I know it, we're all getting down about how we've been hurt."

"Friends can be therapeutic sometimes. And an occasional pity party never hurt anyone, but on a regular basis, not so much. Keep in mind that some friends—you know the ones I mean, the kind who drag you down and make you feel hopeless—they can be toxic." Dr. Karen chuckled. "Not only that, but how appealing do you think a bunch of unhappy women appear to a guy who might be casually checking them out?"

"Not so much?"

"You got that right."

"So what should I do?"

"I know it sounds trite to say time heals all wounds, and that's not always true, anyway. Tell me, how long has it been since you broke up?"

"Six years next month."

"Oh." Dr. Karen sounded quite concerned now. "That's a pretty long time to be feeling so blue. Have you dated anyone at all since the breakup?"

"No."

"Well, maybe that's what you need to do. Just get back into the game."

"But how? How can I do that when all I can think about is, uh, my ex?"

"For starters you just need to jump in. And you need to give yourself permission to go out with a guy who might not even be that interesting. Don't sit around and wait for Mr. Perfect, if you know what I mean."

"I don't even know any Mr. Perfect. Well, except for—"

"Yes, I know, your ex. But you need to understand something. If your ex was really Mr. Perfect, you would still be together. In other words, he was *not* Mr. Perfect. Not for you anyway. And while we're on the subject, there really is no Mr. Perfect. For all you women out there listening, you know who you are, you think you're waiting for Mr. Perfect to come along, perhaps even on a white horse." She laughed. "Well, you might want to think again."

"I suppose." But she didn't sound convinced.

"Think about it, you've let six years slip by, and I don't know your age, but six years is six years, and you've been sitting around waiting for what?"

"For him to come back to me?"

"Which you know is not going to happen. You already told me he's engaged to someone else."

"Right."

"So six years have passed and—"

"Almost six years."

"Fine. Almost six years. Now I hate to be the bearer of bad news, but six years is a good-sized chunk of your life, and if you're like me and everyone else, you're not getting any younger."

"I know." The poor woman sounded really depressed. Janie wondered why Dr. Karen was being so hard on her.

"The question is, do you really want a relationship or not?"

"I do. That's why I called you."

"But you want a relationship with someone who's not in the game anymore. I want to know if you're willing to try a relationship with someone else."

"If it was the right someone. I think so."

"Well, if you're not out there dating, how will you find out if the right someone is even around?"

"I don't know."

"It's possible you've already let the right someone walk right past you."

"Oh, no. I don't think so."

"But you don't know, do you?"

"I guess not."

"You've got to get back in there." Dr. Karen sounded like she was wrapping this up. "You've got to start dating again. Meet guys and take risks by getting to know them. Otherwise you'll be sitting there six years from now, and you'll be more stuck than ever. And, trust me, the next six years will go by even faster than the last six."

"Okay."

"So you're going to do it?"

"I guess so."

Janie turned off the radio. Her guess, judging by the woman's voice, was that she wasn't going to take Dr. Karen's advice. As obnoxious as the relationship doctor sounded, she might've been right. Janie didn't see herself in that same situation, but if she was—if she allowed six years to pass without dating a single guy—well, perhaps it would simply be because she decided to remain single.

Janie had believed that she would remain single after Phil died. She had even told him as much, many times, in the late stages of his illness.

"No," he'd told her. "You will find someone eventually. You're not the kind of woman who should live out her life alone."

"Why not?" She'd been indignant. "Are you saying I'm not independent?"

"Not at all. You are absolutely independent, darling. You always have been. Stubborn, smart, independent. All reasons why you should have a man in your life. But he needs to be the right kind of man."

"You mean someone like you," she had teased. "Well, we all know that God broke the mold after he made you."

"Not someone just like me," he'd told her. "But someone who's patient and kind. A good man."

Too choked up, she had been unable to respond after that. Phil was all of those things and more. He was patient and kind and understanding and wise. He was truly a good man. Everyone who knew him said so. She knew now as she knew then that there would never be another one like him.

She turned the radio back on. This time she wanted a music station, so she searched around until she found one that played the oldies. She'd never been into music as a teen. Most geeks probably weren't. But she wished she knew the lyrics to some of these old tunes. It would be fun to sing more than just the chorus to "American Pie." During the reunion she'd heard Caroline and some of the others breaking out into old songs that everyone seemed to know, and yet Janie had just sat there like a dummy.

Really, she told herself as she turned on cruise control, she had never fit into that crowd of kids. Not back in high school and not now. This past week it had been fun imagining that she was finally accepted for who she was, although her designer clothes and fancy shoes had probably helped even more than she realized. But she wasn't really one of them. Despite this cloak of sadness that seemed to be going with her, it was probably just as well that she was on her way home.

Once she got back into her routine at work and caught up on sleep, she would probably laugh at her silliness for feeling so blue just now. Maybe Matthew would find a way to visit her after all. And Lisa. Janie didn't really want to think about Lisa right now. That was too much sadness for one dark night.

Instead she cranked up the radio and tried to listen to the lyrics, attempting to imprint them on her mind, hoping that someday she might be able to sing along with them after all.

———

Janie turned in the rental car, checked her bags, got her boarding pass, and went through security with plenty of time to spare. To stretch her legs, she walked up and down the terminal and finally stopped long enough to eat not just a bagel, but some eggs as well. Abby would've been proud of her. Then as she was lingering over coffee, her cell phone rang. Expecting someone from work, she answered it without checking the caller ID. To her surprise, it was Victor.

"I hope I'm not bothering you," he said, "but I just wanted to make sure you made it to Portland okay."

"That's thoughtful of you." She closed the *New York Times* that she'd been attempting to focus on, then confessed to leaving even earlier than planned. "I just couldn't sleep, so I thought I might as well drive."

"That probably helped you to miss some of the traffic, too," he said.

"Yes. It was pretty quiet when I drove through the city."

"Are you happy to be on your way home?"

She paused to consider this. Rather than giving him a pat answer, she decided to be honest. "I'm not sure."

"Well, you'll probably think I sound crazy, but I miss you already."

She really didn't know what to say.

"I'm sorry, I shouldn't have said that."

"No, no, it's okay."

"Did you see the sunrise this morning?" he asked, as if to change the subject. "The sky was totally pink."

"Uh-oh." She made a *tsk-tsk* sound. "You know what that means. Red sky at night, sailor's delight, red sky at morning—"

"Sailor take warning," he finished. "But I've never been sure if that was a West Coast thing or an East Coast thing or both."

"Hmm. That's a good question. Maybe you should do some investigating."

He chuckled. "Yes, you're probably thinking that should be easy, since I don't have too much else to keep me busy."

"I didn't mean it like that."

"But I'll defend my position," he said in friendly banter. "Nothing wrong with taking time to figure out your life and make sure you really like where your life is going. I mean, it's better to do it now than when it's too late."

"Ooh, was that aimed at me?"

"If the shoe fits."

She looked down at her sensible Cole Haan black loafers, her favorite traveling shoes. "Right now I just need to figure out how

I'm going to get all the work done before next Wednesday's court case."

"Hey, am I keeping you from working?"

She looked down at her briefcase, where her laptop was still securely in her bag. And then she decided to lie. "Actually, yes."

"I'm sorry. You should've told me sooner."

"Well, it was nice hearing your voice."

"Yours, too. And I'm glad you made it to the airport all right. Travel safe, okay?"

"Thanks." Then, as soon as she said good-bye, she reached for her laptop, opening it up with the intention of making her unexplainable lie at least partially true. For some reason she did not like knowing that she'd lied to him. Victor was a good man. And the fact that he was bothered her.

Chapter 17

MARLEY

"Are you okay, Mom?" Ashton sounded concerned.

Marley pushed some clutter from her sofa and sat down. "I guess so." Now she questioned herself—why had she called her son like this? What did she really expect he was going to tell her?

"You don't sound okay."

"I suppose I'm a little down." She put her feet on the coffee table and leaned back.

"Was it your reunion?" he asked gently. "Did something bad happen?"

So she told him about Cathy's sudden death on the dance floor.

"Oh-mi-gosh!"

"It was shocking and sad."

"Good grief, no wonder you're depressed. I'm sorry, Mom."

"But it was more than that."

"What?" he sounded curious. "Let me guess, you ran into an old boyfriend, and not only is he happily married, but his wife is drop-dead gorgeous?"

She tried to laugh. "Not exactly."

"An old girlfriend who confessed that she's always been in love with you?"

This time her laugh was genuine. "That's closer."

"Seriously?"

She told him about the Four Lindas and how great it had been to be with them. "Not that there was anything romantic going on. But thanks for asking."

He chuckled. "That's wild, Mom. I never heard you mention other friends named Linda before."

"Because I haven't been in touch with them for decades."

"But I don't get why that's making you sad."

"I guess I was sad to say good-bye."

"Oh yeah, I get it."

"And then I came home to Seattle, and I just feel all out of sorts. Like something is wrong with my life. And even though we're having a big show this weekend at the gallery, I honestly couldn't care less."

"That is bad. Which artist?"

"Georgia Martini." Her voice was void of enthusiasm.

"And you're not excited? Georgia's art is fabulous. I can't believe Kevin finally lured her in."

"Speaking of Kevin. I think he'd like to lure me out."

"Oh, Mom, you know Kevin loves you. He's like family."

It was true that she'd known Kevin forever. In fact, at one time John had blamed Kevin for Ashton's coming out of the closet. She'd even agreed for a time, although she knew now that their emotions at the time had nothing to do with Kevin. But for a while, and to her current shame, she followed John's lead by treating Kevin pretty much like an infidel. It wasn't until Ashton assured her that he'd felt "different" since early childhood, and that Kevin had absolutely nothing to do with it, that Marley was able to let go of her suspicions. And after the divorce, who was the first old friend to reach out to her and offer a job? Kevin, of course.

"Yes," she admitted. "You're right, Ashton. I suppose I'm simply jealous of Warren."

"Warren?" Ashton chuckled. "Don't tell me you're crushing on Kevin now."

"No, that's not it. But apparently Warren has been getting help for his phobia stuff, and Kevin thinks he wants to come help out in the gallery."

"That would be good for him."

"Good for him. Maybe not so good for me."

"So is that why you sound so bummed?"

"I don't know." She sighed.

"Because, no offense, Mom, but I never thought that working in the gallery was going to be your final career choice."

"No. I took the job to buy time until I figured out what I wanted to be when I grow up."

"What about your art?"

She glanced at several finished but never-shown paintings leaning against the wall. Her art materials were gathering dust. "I'm uninspired."

"Maybe it's because you need a change. Maybe you need to shake things up."

She thought about this. About the mouths of babes. Well, at thirty, Ashton wasn't exactly a child anymore. "You might be right."

"Maybe it's time for your gig at the gallery to come to an end."

"You know what I'd really like to do?" she said.

"What?"

"I want to move back to Clifden."

"Seriously?"

"I know, it's crazy."

"No, not at all. Clifden is a great little town. And it's only about an hour from where I live. I think it's a very cool idea, Mom."

"I don't know. I've lived in Seattle for so long. And moving, well, it's probably—"

"Why are you always second-guessing yourself, Mom?" Ashton's voice was tinged with impatience.

"Good question." She sighed.

"I remember how you said your confidence was coming back. I mean after the divorce. You told me how you were going to reinvent your life and do art and all kinds of things. But you moved into that pathetic little apartment and went to work for Kevin. It's like you got stuck. No wonder you're depressed."

"You're right."

"I'm sorry to speak so bluntly, Mom, but maybe you need someone to call a spade a spade. Maybe that's why you called me—to tell it like it is."

"Thanks, Ashton. And I apologize for dumping on you like this. Really, I don't know what's wrong with me. I suppose I'm lonely." It was time to change the subject. "So tell me, how's Leo doing?"

"He's great. By the way we're doing a concert the Sunday of Labor Day weekend."

"Wish I could come."

"Why don't you?"

She considered this. Eugene was about a six-hour drive away, so it wasn't exactly convenient. "I'll think about it. And how's the business?" She still found it hard to believe that Ashton and Leo supported themselves by making drums, of all things.

"It's growing. Leo just got our Web site arranged so we can sell instruments online now. We think that's going to take us to the next level. We'll probably have to hire a couple more guys before long."

"Good for you."

"Speaking of work, Leo and I need to get moving. Thursday night is drum workshop night."

"Tell Leo hi for me."

"Tell Kevin and Warren hi. And have fun at the showing this weekend."

"Thanks."

"And think about what I said, Mom."

"I will, Ashton. Thanks."

———

That afternoon, Marley dressed carefully for the opening of the four-day show. Then, to bolster her spirits even more, she layered on the jewelry, including some beaded pieces that she had made herself. She took time with her hair and makeup, and when she left her apartment, she told herself that life was good, that this evening would be fun, and that lots of people would be thrilled to have her life.

Unfortunately, by nine o'clock, she no longer believed it. Not that the showing hadn't been successful; it had. Even more so than they'd expected.

"This has been great," Kevin told Marley as she freshened up a cheese platter in the back room.

"Really great!" She gave him the same pasted-on smile that she'd been wearing for about five hours now. In fact her cheeks were actually starting to hurt.

"Have you seen how well Warren is doing?" Kevin was twisting the corkscrew into a new bottle of chardonnay.

She nodded. "Like he's been selling art his whole life."

"He really does have a good grasp on it." Kevin glanced out the door to where Warren was speaking to an elderly couple. "I can't even tell you how fun it is seeing him enjoying himself like this."

"He should spend more time down here."

"That's just what I've been telling him." Kevin's eyes glowed with happiness as he popped the cork off.

"Which brings me to something I've been meaning to tell you, Kevin."

"Oh no," he feigned fear. "You're not hitting me up for a raise?"

She forced a laugh. "Not even close."

"What then?" He looked worried.

"I need to give you my notice."

"Your notice?" He looked genuinely shocked.

"I need to quit."

"But why?" He lowered his voice. "Is it Warren?"

"No, not at all. I've decided I want to move to Clifden."

He brightened. "That delightful little sea town you grew up in?"

This time her smile was real. "Yes. I know it seems sudden. But I was talking to Ashton this morning and … I can't even explain it, but I know it's right. And I'm going to start painting again!"

Kevin hugged her. "I'm so happy for you, Marley. This is going to be great. I can feel it in my bones."

She picked up the cheese tray. "It looks like we've got some more latecomers. I better get out there." She felt slightly shocked as she returned to the gallery. Had she really just quit her job? And yet she felt happy, too, and relieved, as if she'd just taken the first step into the rest of her life.

"Marley." Georgia Martini joined her at the refreshment table, refilling her wine glass with merlot. "I have been meaning to tell you all night that your jewelry is absolutely fabulous." She reached over and fingered the chunky beaded necklace. "Turquoise and coral and silver. Really lovely."

Marley was stunned. "Thank you!"

"Do you mind if I ask where you got it?"

Marley's cheeks warmed now. "Actually I made this piece myself."

"Seriously?" Georgia looked impressed. "I had no idea you were an artist."

"I've been on a bit of a sabbatical."

Georgia nodded. "Sometimes it's good to take a break. Just as long as you remember it's only a break."

"Which is why I've recently decided to quit the gallery and devote my attention to art."

Georgia patted her on the back. "Good for you. Congratulations."

"Thanks."

Marley felt like she was walking on clouds during the last hour of the show. She couldn't remember when she'd last felt so wonderful and light, as if a sack of rocks had been removed from her shoulders. It seemed that her mood was contagious, because in the last few minutes she sold two rather substantial pieces of art. But did that make her regret her decision to quit? Not for a second!

===*Chapter 18*===

CAROLINE

"So what do you think?" Abby asked Caroline after they finished their quick tour of Janie's gutted house Friday morning.

"Well …" Caroline wasn't sure how to respond. She didn't want to hurt Abby's feelings. Especially since she seemed so enthusiastic.

"You have to use your imagination."

Caroline frowned out the dingy kitchen window. The grass in the backyard was shaggy and brown, and the hedges were overgrown with blackberry bushes. "I guess I've never had much of an imagination."

"Okay, let me help you." Abby joined her by the window. "Imagine new contemporary maple cabinets topped with sleek granite along this wall." She used her hands to indicate where.

Caroline giggled. "You look like Vanna White."

"Well, thank you." Abby grinned and continued. "And a stainless gas stove will go there, and an island right here. We'll hang a pair of lights over it—something small and sleek and stainless. And we're thinking a soft sage green for the walls, but if you decide to buy it, you can choose whatever you like."

Caroline frowned. "I'm trying, Abby, but I just can't see it."

"Then trust me. It'll be gorgeous."

"Are you sure?"

"Absolutely."

Caroline didn't share her confidence. Plus the musty smell was starting to remind her of her mother's house. "I need some fresh air," she admitted. "And coffee."

"Good idea."

"This is just so hard," Caroline admitted.

"What?"

"Making a big decision like this. I mean, it seemed easy last night, when I imagined moving into a beautiful house. But this morning the place looks, well, a little scary."

"But it'll get better."

"I know. But I'm unsure. I mean, what if selling my condo is a mistake? What if I'm sorry? How does a person make a big decision like this? I know Victor's answer. And he seems to have no regrets. But I just don't know."

Abby nodded thoughtfully as she drove them through town. "I can understand your hesitation. I've never been great at big decisions either." Suddenly she was taking a detour.

"Where are you going?" Caroline asked.

"My old house."

"Where you grew up?" Caroline felt confused, because that house was on the other side of town.

"No, I mean the first house Paul and I bought more than thirty years ago, right after Jessie was born."

"Oh, that sweet old Victorian." Caroline nodded. "That was such a beautiful house."

Abby drove past the library, then parked across the street from the big white house on the corner. "I always loved that house."

"I was surprised you were willing to part with it."

"I wasn't."

"Huh?" Caroline let her window down to see it better. "Then why did you move?"

"That's a good question. I guess that's why I decided to drive by and look at it now."

Now Caroline was really confused.

"Sorry. I don't mean to sound so mysterious."

"So what are you saying?" Caroline waited.

"I didn't want to leave that house." Abby looked sadly across the street. "And the girls did not want us to leave that house. Jessie was furious at me. She insisted that was the house where Lucy needed to come visit her grandparents. And Laurie was hurt that she was losing her bedroom." Abby shook her head. "You know that house had six bedrooms?"

"Wow."

"Nicole was the only one who seemed okay with it. But then she's always been more of a free spirit. And she loved the beach location of the new house. Plus she knew she would still have a room there."

"The beach house is awfully nice." Caroline studied the perfectly landscaped yard. "And probably a lot less maintenance."

"Paul's thinking exactly."

"So you must've come around." Caroline turned back to look at Abby.

"To be honest, I didn't come around. I never wanted to leave my house. Even at the very end." Her eyes looked sad and tired now. "But I hid my feelings."

"You pretended you were okay with it?"

"I've never told anyone this, Caroline. And I have to swear you to secrecy."

"But why? I mean why did you agree to leave your house if you didn't want to?"

"Because Paul wanted it so badly."

"So you gave in to make him happy?"

"Our marriage was a little rocky."

"Oh."

Abby sighed. "I know you're probably thinking I'm a wimp."

"No, not at all. I think you were very generous to let Paul build his dream house if it wasn't what you really wanted."

"Generous maybe. But was it stupid?"

"I don't know." Honestly, Caroline didn't know. "But why are you telling me this?"

"Because I still worry that I might've made the wrong decision. I realize you're making a big decision right now, and I've been encouraging you to take this big leap. Then I remembered what I did, and how I'm still not happy with it." Now Abby had tears in her eyes.

"So you're telling me to really think about this. To look before I leap."

"Yes."

"So do you mind if I ask what it is that you miss most about your old house?"

Abby reached for a tissue. "So much." She wiped her eyes. "I miss my garden. My flowers. I miss my little quilting room on the third floor. I miss the room I fixed up for my granddaughter. We called it the Teddy Bear Room. I doubt that Lucy remembers it; she was so little. But I had imagined having her and other grandchildren running up and down the stairs of that big old house. I miss all the memories that were tied up in it. I miss all the antiques I had to let go because they wouldn't fit in our new house."

Caroline reached over and squeezed Abby's hand. She was crying pretty hard now. "I wonder why Paul was so set on giving that house up," Caroline mused out loud.

"He said he was tired of working on it. We'd remodeled and replaced things for years. And he said it was going to continue being a money pit."

"Right."

"I even suggested that we could turn it into a bed-and-breakfast. You know, kind of like Jackie's place."

"It would be a great B and B. Great location, too."

"Well, that idea might've been what pushed Paul right over the edge. He put his foot down. He said he would rather live in a tent on the beach than run a bed-and-breakfast."

"Oh. Well, I suppose it would be a lot of work."

"And he didn't want to be tied down. Part of the plan with the beach house was to have freedom to travel more. Although we haven't really done much."

"So in a way, you've given up everything. Your gardening, your antiques, your memories, and you never even wanted to."

"I know I should be thankful for my lovely home. You must think I'm a spoiled brat. I often feel that way myself. But it's been so hard. It's like I got lost in the process of moving to the new house, and I haven't really found myself again."

"But you have to realize that you're more than just a house, right?"

"I know you're right. But I still feel lost." Abby blew her nose loudly. "Although I have to admit that it's been good medicine to help Janie with her house."

"It seems like you're good at it." Caroline laughed. "And you seemed happy when you were doing your Vanna White act."

Abby smiled. "It's nice having something else to focus on. I mean, besides my own little life and feeling sorry for myself." She started the car again. "Now we really need to get some coffee."

"So if I understand you right," Caroline began carefully, "you're sort of warning me to be careful. Like maybe I really could regret selling my LA condo and buying Janie's house."

"That's right." Abby parked in front of the Coffee Company. "And I don't want to carry the guilt for encouraging you into something that's not really right. Janie even pointed out that you're the kind of person who enjoys an active social life and sunshine and probably lots of other things that you have down in LA. Things we don't have here."

Caroline thought about that as they went inside and ordered coffee. What Abby had just said was partially true. But it was also true that Caroline had been getting tired of the LA pace. To be honest, the bright lights and big city had lost a lot of its glimmer during her cancer treatments.

"Hello, ladies," said Victor as he lowered a newspaper and smiled up at them. "Care to join me?"

"I didn't even see you here," Abby said as they sat down.

"Oh, I'm a regular, but I got a late start today." He gave Caroline a puzzled look. "Hey, I thought you were on your way home today."

"It's an evening flight," she told him as she stirred her coffee. "I'll be heading out in an hour or so."

"I was just showing her Janie's house," Abby explained.

"What did you think?"

Caroline shrugged. "It needs work."

"It's basically gutted right now," Abby explained.

He chuckled. "A little too rustic for your taste?"

"I'm sure it will be nice when it's done," Caroline said. "I'm just not sure it's right for me."

"For you?" Victor looked confused.

"Caroline was considering buying it," Abby told him.

"*If* I decide to relocate up here, which is still up in the air." Caroline looked closely at him. "I'm envious of the way you were so sure about moving here. I wish I had that kind of confidence."

"Maybe it's a matter of timing."

She nodded. "Maybe."

"Anyway, I'm trying to remain neutral," Abby said. "At first I wanted to encourage Caroline to just do it, you know, take the plunge. But I realize it's a huge decision, though I selfishly wish she'd move back here." Abby reached over and clasped Caroline's hand. "She's such a sweet friend and I'd love to have her around. But I wouldn't want her here unless it was really right for her."

Caroline sighed. "Hearing that just makes me want to move here."

Abby laughed. "Honestly, I'm not trying to use reverse psychology."

"Well, this is what I've decided to do," Caroline announced. "I will go home and I will pray about it."

"Pray about it?" Abby looked surprised.

Caroline nodded toward Victor. "Something you said reminded me of a promise I made several years ago."

"A promise?" Victor leaned forward with interest.

"Yes. You see, I'm a cancer survivor. And I prayed a lot during my treatments. I told God that if I got well, I wanted to live my life differently. I wanted him to be in charge."

"Really?" Abby's eyes grew wide. "I didn't know about this."

"I don't usually talk about it." Caroline shook her head. "It's actually kind of embarrassing, because it seems like nothing much has really changed since I made that promise. Oh, I'm thankful every day to be alive and well. I go to church somewhat regularly. And it's not as if I'm doing anything bad. But I can't honestly say that much about my life is different."

"Sometimes things about us change and we don't even know it," Victor said quietly.

"That's right," Abby agreed. "In fact I have to admit that I thought you'd changed a lot when I first saw you at the reunion, Caroline."

"Really?" Caroline felt hopeful.

"You seemed a lot more sincere than I remembered. And friendlier. Even happier."

"Wow." Caroline nodded. "That's cool."

"See?" Victor grinned. "Maybe God's at work on you already."

"I hope so. Anyway, my plan is to go home and pray that God will show me what to do. I've made enough bad decisions already in my life. I don't need any more mistakes. I'd honestly rather stay put, even if I don't like it, than move up here and discover it's the wrong place for me."

"Very wise."

Abby nodded. "Yes. Very."

"Anyway, I haven't even checked out of the hotel yet." Caroline glanced at her watch. "And it's almost eleven. I better get moving. I'll just walk back to the hotel."

They all stood and hugged. Caroline thanked them both for their friendship. "Whether or not I move up here, it's nice to know I have friends in town. I'll have to come back before winter to help get my mom moved, so I know I'll see you guys again."

"Travel safely," Victor told her as she headed for the door.

"Call me." Abby made a phone sign with her hand.

Caroline smiled and waved and blew kisses to both of them as she exited the building. But once outside she felt sad and let down, like the party was over and it was time to go home. And yet she remembered her promise to God. She was going to trust that he knew what was best for her. So, as she walked the several blocks to the hotel, she prayed. She asked God to do something to show her what she needed to do. "It doesn't have to be anything huge," she said as she finally reached the hotel parking lot. "I don't expect lightning or a burning bush. Just something that makes me certain." As she said amen, she remembered what Victor had said about having a special kind of peace when he made his decision to uproot his former life. That was what she wanted more than anything—a peace like that. Then she'd be certain.

=Chapter 19=

ABBY

When Abby got home, she was pleased to see that Jessie had left her a message. "I know it's a lot to ask, Mom," she began, "but would you be willing to have Lucy this weekend?" Abby didn't even wait for the rest of the message before she was dialing Jessie's cell-phone number.

"Of course we'd love to have Lucy. When is she coming?"

"Did you even listen to my message?"

"Not all of it."

"Oh, well, I wondered if Brandon could bring her over in the morning. Or better yet, if you or Daddy would want to meet halfway. Otherwise Brandon will have to get Lucy up at like six in the morning to get back here in time."

"In time for what?"

"He got these great tickets to a preseason football game. We were going to drive up to Pullman to meet some friends, and it's a night game, so we thought we'd stay over. I know it's last-minute, but Brandon was so excited about being at his old school and I—"

"You don't need to explain, and if your dad's busy, I'll be happy to meet Brandon and our princess. Name the place and time and I'll be there."

"Thanks, Mom! Lucy will be thrilled. She's been begging to go to the beach."

"We'll be thrilled to have her."

"Brandon can call you with the details." Then Jessie explained she had to get to a meeting, and they hung up. Abby would've liked to talk longer, but she knew Jessie was busy. She was always busy. At least Abby would get to spend time with Lucy now. She would freshen up the guest room, then do some quick grocery shopping to be sure she had Lucy's favorite foods like string cheese and apple juice on hand. She might even pick up some crayons and things, just in case the weather changed and they were stuck inside.

Abby was making a list when the phone rang again. This time it was Janie, calling to check on the progress of her house. "I don't want to be a pest," she told Abby, "but it feels like it's been a week since I was there. Although I realize that's not really true."

"To be honest, nothing has changed since you left."

"Nothing?" she sounded really disappointed.

"Paul's got Sheetrock guys lined up for next week." Abby reached for the notebook she'd created. "And I've got some photos of cabinets and windows and things that I'll make copies of to send you."

"Oh, good!"

"But probably not until next week. I just found out my grand-daughter is coming to visit this weekend."

"That sounds fun."

"Oh, it is. Lucy is our little ray of sunshine."

"That must be nice." Again Janie's voice sounded sad, or maybe wistful.

"And don't worry about your house," Abby assured her. "These things go in fits and starts. But eventually they get done. In fact I actually showed the place to a potential buyer today." As soon as she said this, she wished she hadn't.

"A buyer?"

"Uh, yes, but I explained that it would be a while and—"

"Who was interested?"

"Actually it was Caroline."

"Caroline?" Janie sounded shocked.

"Well, it's very premature. She's not even positive she's moving back here."

"But she's seriously considering it?"

"She's going to pray about it."

"Pray about it?" Janie sounded bewildered.

"Yes, that's what she said this morning. She's going to ask God to show her what to do."

"Really?"

"Yes. She said that she'd made a promise to God back when she was being treated for breast cancer, and she means to keep it."

"What kind of promise?"

"Oh, you know, she wants to live her life differently. Something to that effect. I'm sure she could explain it better."

"I just never thought of Caroline as a praying sort of person."

"It turns out she is. I actually think Victor had something to do with it."

"Victor?"

"My guess is that he was an inspiration to her, since he's a praying kind of person too." Abby laughed uncomfortably. "I know I'm making it sound like I'm not a praying kind of person. I actually do believe in God, and Paul and I even go to church sometimes. But I've never been what I'd call strong in my faith. That would be my mother."

"Right."

"So anyway, I hope you don't mind that I showed Caroline your house."

"Of course not. Why should I mind?"

"Well, you know, it is your house. I don't want to overstep my bounds."

"Just don't go selling it yet," Janie said in a teasing tone.

"Oh no, I'll leave that to the realtor."

"Because who knows? Maybe I'll decide to keep it."

"Really?"

"Probably not. But I guess a girl can dream."

"Certainly," Abby said. "A girl can dream."

"Well, I better get back to work. Good talking to you. Tell, uh, the local folks hello for me."

Abby felt certain that Janie was referring to Victor, but also felt she shouldn't say so. "I'll do that."

"Enjoy that granddaughter."

"Oh, I will."

After they hung up, Abby felt slightly sorry for Janie. She wasn't even sure why. Perhaps it was simply that Abby would not want to be in her shoes. Although Janie did have beautiful shoes. Abby chuckled as she looked down at her comfy old sandals. Janie's fancy high-heeled designer shoes would probably cripple Abby within seconds.

————

"I already told Rob I'd play golf with him in the morning," Paul told Abby that night as they got ready for bed.

"That's fine. I can pick up Lucy." She squirted some lavender lotion into her hands and rubbed them together. "I kind of figured I'd have to anyway."

"Now you're mad at me."

"No, I'm not mad."

"But you think I'm being selfish again, don't you?"

"I did not say that, Paul."

"You didn't say it, but I can tell."

Abby stopped rubbing lotion into her elbows and looked at him. "Why are you trying to pick a fight with me?"

"I'm not the one picking a fight." He scowled, then left the bedroom.

Replaying their conversation in her head, she sat down and rubbed some lotion into her heels. It really did seem that he was trying to start an argument. But why? She considered finding him and demanding to know what was going on. If she did that, though, she'd likely be the one, as usual, to apologize and take the blame and do what she could to straighten things out.

She didn't really want to. She just didn't have the energy. Besides, he was probably in the den by now, lost in some stupid sports show or surfing the Internet. She just didn't care to put on her robe and slippers to go make peace. Really, why should she? Besides, she needed to get up early tomorrow in order to meet Brandon and Lucy. If Paul wanted to act like a juvenile, she'd let him.

Of course, once she was in bed, she felt slightly guilty. Maybe the episode really was her fault. Had she snapped at him without realizing it? Had she acted resentful about his golf game? Surely it wouldn't be the first time. But, even so, why was she the one who always ended up apologizing? Why couldn't he take the blame sometimes? She remembered her old house and the confession she'd made to Caroline. Maybe that part of her history with Paul was the whole problem. Maybe she had an attitude, like she really was mad at him. Maybe she still wasn't over it. Well, even if that was the case, she was not going to get out of bed, put on her robe and slippers, and go out there to apologize. Not tonight anyway.

―――――

"Where's Grampie?" Lucy asked cheerfully after Brandon helped to transfer her booster seat into the back of Abby's SUV and kissed his daughter good-bye.

"He's playing golf today."

"I want to play golf too."

Abby smiled as she adjusted her rearview mirror and pulled out into traffic. "I don't know, Lucy, you might be too little."

"I'm not too little."

Abby remembered an old croquet set in the garage. "Maybe you and I can play beach golf," she suggested.

"Yes!" Lucy rocked back and forth in her seat. "Beach golf!"

"Are you hungry, sweetheart?"

"Yes. I want a hot dog."

"A hot dog?" Abby considered this.

"And I want to see the octopus."

"The octopus."

"Yes. Don't you remember the octopus, Grammie?"

"Oh, you mean at the aquarium."

"Yes. The 'quarium."

Abby thought for a moment. The aquarium was the opposite direction of home, but only thirty minutes out of the way. Plus it was starting to cloud up outside. Maybe the aquarium was a better option than beach golf in the rain. And unless she was mistaken, they had hot dogs at the aquarium. "The aquarium it is," she said as she pulled into a grocery-store parking lot and turned around.

Lucy entertained them both by singing songs and pointing out sights, and before long they were nearly there. Abby was just about to turn onto the aquarium's street when she noticed a familiar car ahead. Of course she knew there were other shiny red Corvettes around, but they did tend to catch her eye. She was close enough to see the plates. MMLCC. At first she thought she was imagining it, but then she saw the back of Paul's head. And next to him was a head of long, wavy brunette hair. She blinked, then looked again.

"Grammie," cried Lucy, "there's the big whale. Turn. Turn."

"Oops," Abby said in a forced cheerful voice. "I missed it, but don't worry, I'll go up here and turn back."

Lucy continued to complain in the way a four-year-old does, but it went right over Abby's head as she followed the red Corvette with one car between them. Eventually the car turned left at an intersection, and Abby knew Paul would spot her if she continued following.

If she did follow, what would she say once they all came to a stop? What would she do? And what about Lucy?

With shaky hands and a heavy heart, she put on her right-turn signal, went down a side street, and eventually worked her way back to the aquarium. Then, as if on autopilot, she allowed Lucy to lead her around, listened as Lucy chattered away, somehow responded in ways that Lucy found acceptable, ate a hot dog, stopped by the gift shop, spent too much money, and eventually helped a very tired Lucy back into the car.

Lucy fell asleep, and Abby, still feeling robotic, drove home in silence. She told herself that she might be mistaken, that perhaps she'd read the plate wrong and only imagined she'd seen Paul with a strange woman. When she wasn't convinced, she told herself that maybe there was a logical reason for all this. Sometimes Paul met with clients who needed a remodel or wanted to build a custom home. He had worked up and down the coast for years. Surely that was the explanation.

"Are we home yet?" Lucy said unexpectedly.

"Oh!" Abby jumped. "You scared me."

"I scared you?" Lucy laughed. "Boo!"

Abby made a sound like laughter. "Yes, we're almost there."

"It's raining," observed Lucy.

"That's okay," Abby told her. "I got some fun things for us to do inside."

Soon they were in the house, and Lucy's energy was the perfect distraction to the painful hole that seemed to expand in Abby's heart. It was nearly three, and Paul was still not home. Lucy was happily coloring, so Abby checked the caller ID on their phone. Normally she never looked at this feature. In fact she was surprised she even knew how. But there was nothing unusual there. And why would there be? If Paul was seeing someone on the sly, he would certainly be using his cell phone.

What about his computer? She glanced toward the den. Had he left a trail on the desktop in there? She'd heard there were ways to check these things, but the truth was, Abby was pretty much hopeless on the computer. She barely knew how to go online. In fact that was one big reason she missed Nicole. Abby's daughter used to help her with the computer. Of course, Abby couldn't solicit her daughter's help in something like this. No, Abby was on her own.

Out of habit she began getting dinner ready. It was about four when Paul finally showed up. He went directly to Lucy, who was ecstatic to see him.

"Lucy Loo," he said as he hoisted her up to his shoulders. "How are you?"

"I want to play beach golf," she insisted.

"Beach golf?"

"Grammie said we could if it stopped raining." She pointed outside. The gray clouds had finally moved on. "And it did."

"But what's beach golf?" he looked helplessly at Abby.

She was peeling carrots in the kitchen, trying to look normal for Lucy's sake. "I thought we'd take the croquet set out to the beach to knock around some balls."

He grinned. "That's a great idea." He set Lucy down. "Your grammie always has great ideas, doesn't she?"

"Yes!" Lucy ran in to get Abby's hand. "Let's play beach golf."

"Why don't you and Grampie go play while I work on dinner?"

Abby suggested. And just like that, they were gone. Abby looked at Paul's jacket, which he'd draped over a chair in the dining room. It was quite possible his cell phone was in the pocket. But for some reason Abby didn't want to look. Maybe ignorance was bliss, or maybe she wasn't ready to find out anything for sure with her granddaughter here. Whatever was going on with Paul would have to wait.

She looked out the kitchen window to see Paul and Lucy taking turns whacking the big colorful balls. He even dug ball-sized holes in the sand, then stuck driftwood sticks nearby to resemble the flags on a real golf course. The twosome actually looked terribly sweet out there, almost like a postcard or water-color painting. Picture-perfect. Abby wondered how many parts of her life looked picture-perfect. "Your husband is such a dear," she'd been told many times over. "Your home is so lovely." And, "Your daughters are all so beautiful."

Abby knew that some people assumed Abby lived the perfect little life. She never did anything to change this perception. Not really. She wasn't even sure she would do anything now. And, really, wasn't Paul's philandering partially her fault? She was always pushing Paul away, saying she was too tired, or too moody, or too whatever—always putting him off, again and again. Who could blame him for looking elsewhere? It had been over a year since she'd been to her therapist. Of course things would fall apart. Why wouldn't they?

Chapter 20

JANIE

Sunday, the weather in New York was scrumptious. And as August was coming to an end, Janie knew she should get out and enjoy the sunshine. She remembered how she and Phil would sometimes take a ferry on a day like this, often with no specific destination in mind. The outings were adventures waiting to happen. She knew she wasn't going to do that today, though. She could go for a walk in the park, or a walk in her neighborhood. At the very least she could go down for coffee. She could sit at an outdoor table, read the paper, and people watch. And yet she knew she wouldn't. Janie rolled over and decided to go back to sleep. She didn't want to get up. Not today. Maybe not tomorrow either.

It was nearly two in the afternoon when she finally dragged herself out of bed. Her head throbbed, probably from a lack of caffeine. Unfortunately she was out of coffee, and she didn't want to dress and go out to get more. She looked at her frightening reflection in the mirror. Her unwashed hair was lifeless, and the circles beneath her eyes looked darker than usual, though she had slept more than twelve hours. She stuck out her tongue as if to see if she was sick.

Other than feeling like a horse had died in her mouth, she knew she wasn't sick. Not physically anyway.

She got herself a glass of water and, still in her wrinkled silk pajamas, sat down at her dining-room table and turned on her laptop. There was only one thing she could do in this pathetic state of mind: She could work. And why not? It was preferable to sitting around feeling sorry for herself. Besides, the best way to get past something was usually to simply do something else, right? The approach had served her well in the past.

The longer she sat there, however, staring at the sleeping screen, the more obvious it became that she was unable to work. It was as if her mind had shut down, and yet she had a trial next week—a trial she was completely unprepared for, and not because she didn't care about her client. She did. At the moment, though, she couldn't even remember his name. This was not good.

Janie stood up, went to the window, and looked out. Her view wasn't the most spectacular one in Manhattan, but if she stood in the right corner, she could spy Central Park. On a day like this, the park would be filled with life. Unfortunately she did not care.

"What do you want?" she asked herself. She walked around her apartment, taking in the sleek furnishings, hardwood floors, Oriental rugs—everything one would expect to find in the home of two successful New York attorneys. Some of the more expensive things had come from Phil's family, as had the apartment, which Phil's father gave to him when the senior Sorenson retired. "You kids need a nice place to entertain business associates and clients," he'd told them. Unfortunately these rooms had seen little of that in the last five years. For the most part these rooms had witnessed a man sicken and die.

They'd watched a young woman become addicted to drugs. They'd observed an older woman become addicted to work, and a young man who'd grown impatient to get away.

Janie felt sorry for Matthew. Really, what did she have to offer him if he did come for a visit, which no longer seemed likely? They might act as if they were having a good time. They might even take in dinner and a show. But it would all be filler, a space holder for a real life, for what had been taken from them. And Lisa. Well, Janie couldn't bear to think of her. The last she'd heard, Lisa was in the Southwest, begging Janie to send money. But the rehab counselors had warned her not to do this. "If you enable her, she'll never escape," they'd said over and over. All Janie was allowed to offer Lisa besides love, which she never took away, was more time in rehab. Each time she offered, though, Lisa insisted she didn't need it. She tried to convince her mother she was clean, just out of work. When Janie refused to send cash, offering airfare and a stint in rehab instead, Lisa would go into a rage. That was always what gave her away. The old Lisa hadn't been enraged all the time.

Janie returned to the big window again, leaning her head against the cool glass and wishing that she could turn back time and do this whole thing all over again. Even if that were possible, what would she do differently? How could she possibly change anything? It was ridiculous to think about that. Crazy. Maybe that was it. Maybe she was going crazy. As a child, Janie once heard about an aunt who had lost her mind and been sent to some sort of lockdown facility. Janie couldn't even remember the woman's name, or which side of the family she was from. But it seemed possible that some sort of insanity ran in her family.

The sound of her cell phone ringing brought her back to her

senses. She peeled her forehead off of the glass, leaving an ugly greasy spot behind, and searched for her phone. She found it in her purse, then fumbled to open it. She hoped it was Lisa, calling to say that she wanted to come home, that she wanted help.

"Hello?" she said eagerly, her voice raspy from lack of use.

"Janie?" The caller was male.

"Yes?" She didn't try to mask her irritation. If this was a solicitor, she would let him have it with both barrels.

"This is Victor. Sorry to bother you."

"Victor?" She felt strangely unfocused and slightly dizzy, perhaps from lack of food. But she sank onto the suede sectional, leaning her head between her knees.

"Are you okay?"

"I'm not sure," she whispered.

"Is something wrong?"

"I think so."

"What is it? Can I do something to help?"

"I just feel … sort of unwell."

"Do you need medical attention? Should I hang up and call for help?"

"No." She sat up now. The stars in her vision seemed to fade. "I think it's just low blood sugar. I get that sometimes."

"Have you eaten anything lately?" His voice was so concerned, which almost made it seem as if he were nearby, not on the other side of the country.

"Not lately."

"Well, why don't you go pour a glass of juice or something. I'll wait."

She slowly walked to the big stainless refrigerator, opening it to see the same contents it had held last night when she'd absently looked inside. Except for club soda, some old condiments, and moldy cheese (not the good kind of mold), it was empty.

"Are you getting some juice?" he asked hopefully. "Or a piece of fruit?"

"Uh, I need to get groceries."

"You don't have anything to eat in the house?"

She just shook her head as if he was watching her.

"Oh, Janie." Disappointment was in his voice. "How about your neighbors?"

She attempted a laugh. "I don't even know them. Not really. Not well enough to go begging."

"Will you go get some groceries, please?" he asked patiently. "But before you get groceries, go get some lunch? Will you?"

"You must think I'm nuts."

"I think you're sad."

She nodded now. Tears were burning her eyes.

"I wish I lived nearby," he said. "I'd bring you groceries and cook you some food."

"You'd do that?" Now the tears flowed.

"Absolutely."

"You know what I wish?"

"For pizza delivery?" he joked. "Hey, that's actually a good idea. Why don't you call for pizza delivery?"

"Yes. That's what I'll do."

"Do it right now, okay? I'll give you fifteen minutes, and then I'm calling back to check on you. Understand?"

"Yes."

"And then you have to tell me what it is you wish, okay?"

"Okay." Janie hung up, then went over to the drawer, where she kept a stack of menus. She flipped through them and found the closest pizza place that delivered. She called and ordered a small vegetarian pizza, then hung up and waited to see if Victor would really call back. When the phone rang exactly fifteen minutes later, she tried to sound more together when she answered.

"Pizza on the way?" he asked hopefully.

"On its way." With her purse in her lap, she sat in a chair near the door, ready for the delivery.

"So tell me, when did you last eat?"

"Really?"

"Yes, really."

"Lunch. Yesterday."

"Oh, Janie."

"I know. I'm pathetic."

"I think you're depressed."

"You think?" She actually sort of laughed.

"I think you're good at hiding it, but I do think you're depressed."

"Yes, I think you're right. Today I wasn't even able to work." She sighed. "And I have to admit, that scares me."

"Well, having low blood sugar can't be good for your brain."

"No, probably not."

"Why are you working on Sunday? Don't they give you any time off?"

"It was my choice."

"So, before your pizza arrives and I lose your interest, you were going to tell me what you wish."

Janie wasn't so sure she wanted to say it.

"Come on," he urged. "You promised you would."

"I promised?" She tried to remember.

"Sort of. You gave me your word. Your okay."

"Right."

"Come on. I won't tell anyone."

"Okay, if you promise."

"I promise."

"I wish I lived in Clifden."

"Then why don't you?"

"I don't know."

"What is there for you in New York?"

"My job?"

"You can practice law anywhere."

"What if I don't want to practice law?"

He laughed. "Well, you can do that anywhere too."

"I just don't know if I could really do it. I mean quit my job, sell my apartment ... just pack it up and move. I don't know if I have that kind of strength."

"I think you do."

"Really?" She felt a flicker of hope.

"Not only do I think you're that strong, I think you'll be even stronger once you do it."

"What makes you so sure?"

He chuckled. "Just a hunch."

"Hey, I hear someone coming down the hall," she told him. Then the doorbell rang. "My pizza has arrived."

"Good."

"Thank you, Victor." She was fumbling to open the door and her purse simultaneously. "I should go."

"Do you mind if I call you back later?" he asked.

"Sure, if you want."

"Bon appétit," he said cheerfully.

"Thanks!" She hung up, paid and tipped the delivery guy, then carried her pizza like precious gold to her dining-room table, where she sat down and slowly polished off the whole thing along with a glass of water. It was probably good that she'd only ordered a small. She was pretty sure she might've eaten more.

Feeling more like herself, she took a long shower and, as she got dressed, convinced herself that her problem had simply been fatigue and hunger. She was going out to get some fresh air, some sunshine, and some groceries—along with a taste of her beloved New York!

After a couple of hours, Janie began to feel flat again, as if the wind had been sucked right out of her sails. Had it even been there at all? She looked at the people moving around her—navigating the sidewalk, mingling, talking with street vendors—but it was as if she were watching a black-and-white movie in slow motion with mute on. Everything was meaningless and unrelated to her. She felt alone in a crowded place, on the verge of a panic attack.

Taking deep, calming breaths, she crossed the street and found a vacant table at a busy sidewalk café. She sat her purse on the sticky table and retrieved her cell phone, wondering why Victor hadn't called her yet. Perhaps she had missed his call. To her dismay, her phone was dead. She shoved it back into her bag and tried to catch the eye of a waiter. Naturally not one was anywhere to be seen, and yet the people

filling the other tables seemed perfectly happy and oblivious. Their
needs had already been met.

She waited about fifteen minutes, then, feeling slightly calmer
(if not more irritated), she gave up on ever getting service and hurried down the street to the grocery store nearest her apartment. Of
course, she'd forgotten to bring her shopping bag, and so she bought
a new canvas sack and filled it with her usual staples—orange juice,
whole-wheat bagels, coffee, and yogurt. She paid for her purchases,
then continued on to her apartment, where she immediately plugged
her phone into the charger.

Waiting for it to get enough power so she could dial into voice
mail, she put her groceries away and checked her landline. She was
surprised to see she had two messages. Both were from her sister-in-
law, Edith, inviting Janie to meet her and Ross for dinner at Zenon
Taverna. Ross was Phil's older brother as well as a senior partner in
the firm where Janie worked. As much as she didn't want to have
dinner with them, she knew she couldn't keep making excuses. She
called Edith and agreed to meet them at seven thirty. At least they had
chosen a restaurant that was handy for Janie. That was something.

"Wonderful," Edith said happily. "I already made reservations,
and I was not going to take no for an answer. See you then." Janie
thanked her, then hung up and checked her cell phone again. She
had two calls from Edith there as well, and one message from Victor.

"Hi, Janie. I hope your pizza hit the spot. You really didn't sound
too good there. I was worried. Maybe you could call me back just so
I'll know you're okay. Thanks."

So she went ahead and called, but she got his voice mail. "Hey,
Victor," she said in an intentionally cheerful tone. "Thanks again for

helping me out earlier. I'm feeling totally fine now. I think I had a bad case of jet lag, fatigue, and hunger. The pizza did the trick. I've been out and about, and I'm going out to dinner with my brother-in-law and his wife. Thanks again for your encouragement today. Please don't worry about me. I'm fine." Hoping that sounded convincing, she hung up. Then, feeling completely exhausted again, she poured a glass of orange juice and carried it to her bedroom, where she collapsed on the bed and hoped she'd wake in time for dinner.

As it turned out, she was late for dinner by fifteen minutes. Edith assured her it was all right. "You look lovely, Jane," she told her. "Your vacation on the Oregon coast must've agreed with you."

Janie put the napkin in her lap and wondered if Edith's compliment was genuine. Although, Janie had used a little more blush and lip color than usual, hoping it might add some life to her face. "It was wonderful. I forgot how much I like it there."

"All ready for the Brewster-McMillan case this week?" asked Ross.

"Ross," Edith warned him. "You know the rules."

He smiled sheepishly. "No business. Sorry." Now he glanced uncomfortably at his wife. "So who's going to tell her?"

Janie felt a rush of nerves now. "Tell me what?"

"Oh, Jane, I hope you won't get mad," Edith began, "but I invited an old friend of mine to join us tonight."

Janie smiled. "Oh, that's okay. Why would I be mad?"

"Because Edith thinks she's playing matchmaker," Ross said quietly.

"Matchmaker?" Janie stared at Ross in disbelief. She wasn't surprised that Edith would pull something like this, but it seemed out of character for Phil's older, sensible, dignified brother to stoop to this level.

He looked apologetic. "I told her not to do it, but she didn't listen."

"Because I just know you're going to like this guy, Jane." Edith smiled like a cat with canary feathers sticking out of her mouth. "His name is Adam Fletcher, and he's not a lawyer."

"Not a lawyer?" Janie frowned. "Is that supposed to be a good thing?"

Edith nodded. "Yes. I've always had a concern about married couples with the same profession."

"Oh." Janie glanced at Ross for support, but he was pretending to study the menu.

"Anyway, he should be here any minute," Edith said. "His wife died a few years ago, and he's been out of the dating scene too. He's got two grown children, a vacation house in Martha's Vineyard, and a studio in town. And he's an architect." Her eyes sparkled. "Doesn't that sound perfect?"

"Just perfect." Janie couldn't keep the disappointment out of her voice. It was bad enough that she was here against her better judgment, but to be subjected to an evening with a stranger who probably had as much interest in dating as she did was beyond comprehension.

"And there he is."

Janie braced herself, expecting the guy to be short, fat, and bald. Or worse, he would be stunningly handsome, full of himself, and arrogant. As it turned out, she was wrong on all accounts. He was nice looking, gracious, and interested in knowing her. The problem was that she was not interested in him. Not in the least. She was perfectly polite and loquacious, though, and hoped no one was aware of her real sentiments.

After dessert and coffee were finished, she thanked everyone, made apologies on the grounds that she was worn out and still had work to do, and excused herself to go home. As she walked the two blocks to her apartment, she couldn't help comparing Victor to her blind date. In some ways the two men weren't so much different. And in others, well, Janie didn't want to think about that right now.

=Chapter 21=

MARLEY

Monday afternoon, Marley could hardly believe what she'd done. Was she really going to follow through with her half-baked plan to leave Seattle? Certainly she was done at the gallery—there was no question about that. Kevin had told her that she could take her last day whenever she liked, because Warren was willing to step into her place until Kevin found a part-time person to share Marley's job. Not only would this save Kevin a few bucks, it would take some pressure off Warren.

The gallery was closed on Mondays, so Marley had planned to begin packing today. She'd made a good start on it too. She got up early, picked up some bundles of flat boxes from the moving store, then packed and filled a number of them until midafternoon, when she ran out of gas. She sat there in the midst of a sea of brown cardboard, wondering, *Is this nuts?* So she was moving to Clifden—but where did she plan to live? Had she even considered that?

She picked up her phone and called Abby. When Abby didn't answer her house phone, Marley tried the cell number.

"Oh, Abby," she said in relief after Abby finally answered. "You're just the one I need to talk to."

"Marley?"

"Yeah, it's me. Sorry. I'm in kind of a pickle."

"A pickle?"

Marley chuckled. "I quit my job at the gallery, and right now I'm packing up my apartment."

"You're moving?"

"Yes! To Clifden."

"Really? You're moving here?" Abby's voice brightened considerably.

"Yes. Is that crazy or what?"

"It's great. Did you say you're packing already?"

"It's my day off, so I thought I'd get an early start." Marley didn't confess that she worried she might not follow through if she didn't just jump in and get going.

"Wow, that's really good news."

"The question is, where will I live in Clifden?"

"Where will you live?"

"I have no idea."

So Abby gave Marley the name and number of Lois Schuler, the realtor who had helped Janie. Marley thanked Abby and immediately called Lois.

"Goodness," Lois said after Marley explained. "Abby should be working for the chamber."

"The chamber?"

"Of commerce. She's becoming the goodwill ambassador of Clifden. I think her plan is to move all her friends here."

Marley laughed. "Well, a lot of us started out in Clifden."

"So you know the town, then?"

"Absolutely."

"What do you think you're looking for?"

Marley considered this. "Ideally?"

"Why not?"

"Ideally I'd like a lovely beach house."

Lois cleared her throat. "Is money an object?"

"Of course money is an object."

Lois chuckled. "Sorry, but I had to ask. I just got this listing for a beautiful beach home."

"Really?" Marley's hopes soared. "How much?"

"Two point three million."

Marley gulped as her hopes plunged.

"A little out of your price range?"

"About two million out of my price range."

"Well, it never hurts to ask."

"So do you have anything a little more economical?" Marley's settlement from the divorce wouldn't buy a mansion, but she hoped it would be enough for something special—a place she could call home.

"Of course."

"Really?" Marley's hopes climbed up one rung on the ladder.

"It might not be a long list, but how about I start putting one together for you?"

"That would be fantastic." Two rungs now.

"So are you only interested in beachfront property, or are you open to something nearby?"

"I guess I'm open." Marley considered this. "But a house with a view, well, that would be so great. You see, I'm an artist—actually, an artist whose artistic life has been on hold. And I think the ocean view would be inspiring."

"I understand."

"Even if it's just a little shack."

"A shack?"

"Well, it needs to be habitable. But a small beach bungalow, even one that needs work, would be okay."

"Right. So a fixer maybe."

"Nothing that needs major help, of course, but I'm happy to paint walls and make small fix-ups."

"When do you plan to move here?"

Marley looked up at the calendar. "As soon as possible. Mid-September at the latest."

"Wow, that is soon. I better get busy."

"I suppose I could rent something at first." Marley didn't really want to rent. Renting sounded temporary. She wanted something permanent. Like an anchor, a place she could dig into and hold onto and live out the rest of her days.

Lois promised to do some looking and to call back by tomorrow morning. After she hung up, Marley returned to filling her boxes with renewed energy. As she packed, she imagined herself settling into a lovely beachside home. She hoped that it would have vaulted, open-beamed ceilings and a wall of windows that overlooked the ocean and good light for painting. As she carefully wound bubble wrap around a beloved old lamp of turquoise-blue hand-blown glass, she imagined herself filling this house with her treasures. It would be delightful to finally have room to spread things out and enjoy them.

By midweek Lois had found an assortment of properties for Marley to consider. Unfortunately none of them resembled her dream house even slightly. Not that she could afford her dream house. That much was clear. But as she skimmed the photos of houses for sale in Clifden, she began to form some strong opinions. First of all, she would not live in a mobile home. No way. Second of all, she decided that she simply had to have something with an ocean view. It could be as tiny as her apartment, but she needed the view. Unfortunately there was nothing like that available.

"All the beachfront properties are beyond your price limit," Lois explained once again. "Unless you think you can stretch yourself a bit financially."

"I'd settle for a smaller house," Marley pleaded. "I don't need a bunch of bedrooms and baths."

"I'll keep looking," Lois promised.

Marley's hopes dropped back down to the bottom rung of the ladder again. Make that the ground. Or maybe beneath the ground. She questioned her decision to make Friday her last day in the gallery. She couldn't back out, though; Kevin was throwing her a little "surprise" party after they closed. Oh, what had she gotten herself into?

Lois had assured Marley that there were apartments available in town. Not with ocean views, mind you, but it was possible that Marley could store her belongings and "camp" someplace until a desirable property magically appeared on the multiple listing. Marley did not want to "camp" anywhere, however. Perhaps she was being unrealistic or just plain stubborn. But she really wanted to move directly from her Seattle apartment into a real house. Was that too much to ask?

"Here's to a future so bright you will need sunglasses every day of the rest of your life," Warren said as he toasted Marley at her going-away party Friday night.

"Here's to needing sunglasses at all," added Tina. She was the gallery's accountant and had been complaining all day about the damp, gray weather.

"And here's to creating art that will one day be displayed right here in this gallery," Kevin told her.

She laughed. "Is that an invitation? Because I have witnesses."

"Time will tell," he assured her.

Of course, that response simply fed her old insecurities. As she drove home afterward, she was plagued with doubts. What if she really had no talent? Or not enough talent to buy groceries or pay the electric bill? What if she could find no one to purchase her pieces, no gallery willing to take a risk on someone unknown? What if she ended up peddling her wares on the street? She envisioned herself outside on a cold winter day, wearing a ragged overcoat, trading a painting for a loaf of bread.

She knew enough about art to have great respect for the "starving artist" stereotype. It was no joke. In fact she'd seen these pathetic characters on a regular basis while working at Kevin's gallery. At first she didn't recognize them. Back in her early days, she would suppose them to be patrons of the arts and potential customers because they lingered so long. Many times she'd been pleased by their willingness to hear her explain unusual techniques. They would be equally eager to share their opinions on why a particular piece did or did not work for them. And then—the ah-ha moment—they would nonchalantly inquire about commissions, about having their own art displayed in the gallery, or perhaps a special showing just for them.

At that point she would politely explain that the owner handled such arrangements himself, and that he was solidly booked for more than a year (which was partially true), and then she would ask the artist to leave a card that she would drop into an old coffee can in back, never to see Kevin or the light of day again.

Some artists would get belligerent at that point, demanding to see the owner or going into some kind of rant about why their art was superior to anything and everything in the gallery. Sometimes they would blame politics or pop culture or even the pope for their own obscurity—anything but themselves or their talent. Sometimes they would simply blame her and stomp away angry, slamming the door behind them and causing real customers to wonder.

Those were the easy ones to send packing. Others were not so easy—people with hungry eyes and shabby shoes. They had poignant stories about almost making it before being knocked down in defeat. They had tried and tried and were on the verge of giving up altogether. Marley didn't want to become one of them.

Marley didn't sleep well that night. Haunted by images of starving artists and broken dreams, she finally got up at six and decided to take a road trip. She maneuvered around her maze of boxes, gathered up a few things, including her dusty portfolio, then went out and began driving south. She was going to Clifden. It was time to do more than just dream (or suffer nightmares). It was time to do some honest-to-goodness research.

This time she skipped the hotel and drove straight to Jackie Day's bed-and-breakfast. To her relief Jackie had a room. "So what are you doing back in Clifden already?" Jackie asked cheerfully when Marley completed the registration form.

"Checking it out." Marley glanced around the lobby. Ocean-themed knickknacks cluttered every imaginable surface.

Jackie looked confused. "But you already know the town."

"I'm thinking about relocating here," Marley confessed. "But I just need to be sure. It's a big decision."

Jackie clapped her hands together. "Oh, how wonderful. Well, I hope you find exactly what you need. You know, Clifden is changing all the time. It just gets better and better."

"So tell me, what are your opinions on the galleries in town?"

She grew thoughtful. "Well, the One-Legged Seagull is quite popular with the younger crowd. And Dockside has been here for years. Then there's the Treasure Chest, my favorite since they've started carrying jewelry and gifts."

"Thanks." Marley smiled and reached for her overnight bag. "That's helpful."

"I hope you're comfortable here." Jackie handed her a brochure. "Breakfast is served between seven and nine. We have free Internet service and cable. And, well, it's all on the card."

Marley got settled in her room, which was also filled with ocean-themed stuff. It wasn't that Marley didn't like nautical décor, it's just that she liked authentic pieces more than the cutesy ceramic bric-a-brac that Jackie seemed to prefer. In fact, if Marley ever did move back here, and if she ever did get a house, she imagined using large pieces of coral or real glass floats as accents. Now that would be nice!

Marley had to purposely slow down her pace as she walked through town, reminding herself that she needed to observe and take things in. Once again, she was pleased by the easygoing feeling in this place. A couple of old men were sitting on a bench, contentedly looking out over the wharf. A trio of middle-aged female shoppers moseyed along the sidewalk, talking among themselves, pausing to smile at her. No hurries, no worries. Everyone seemed to be just taking their time. All in all, there was a refreshing feeling of relaxed congeniality in the air.

She stopped in a couple of the somewhat familiar galleries but could tell right off the bat that they weren't her style. Without even inquiring, she made her exits. Finally she came to the edge of town, close to the wharf, where the One-Legged Seagull was situated. She pushed open the door, walked in, and was met by good jazz music and the sweet smell of cedar. Not bad. The gallery wasn't bad either. Old wood floors and well-lit displays showed that someone here cared. Someone knew what he or she was doing. Marley appreciated this.

The paintings were a mix of modern, contemporary, and traditional styles in oil, acrylic, watercolor, and pastels. In her opinion some of it (not all, which was a relief) was quite good. Besides wall art, there were some metal and wood sculptures, as well as some glass and ceramic pieces. A little bit of everything. She slowly walked around for the second time, taking it all in, enjoying the sights and sounds and smells, thinking this truly was her kind of place.

"I'm sorry," said a man's voice from behind her. "I was so caught up in finishing this framing project that I didn't hear the bell ring."

She turned to see a gray-haired guy in a plaid shirt emerging from the back room. He was about her height and carried a framed picture in his hands.

"That's okay," she assured him. "I was just making myself at home."

His smile reached his warm brown eyes. "That's how it should be. Anything I can help you with?"

"Are you the owner?" she asked cautiously.

He laughed. "Is it that obvious?"

"No, of course not."

"But why else would an old codger like me be working here?"

"No, not at all. The truth is, I used to work for a gallery in Seattle. So I probably have good instincts."

He frowned slightly. "Oh, are you looking for a job?"

She laughed now. "Not at all."

He seemed to relax again. "Oh, good. I already have a pretty good staff. But I usually keep shop during the weekends. I like to give the others time with their families."

"That's nice."

"It also gives me a chance to catch up on framing." He set the painting, a nice seascape watercolor, on the counter, then looked back at her. "What's that under your arm there?"

"Oh, this?" She made an uncomfortable smile.

He chuckled now. "I know it's a portfolio."

"Well." She focused her attention on the watercolor. "I'm not really that crazy about watercolors in general," she admitted, "but this is quite good. Is it a local artist?"

"As a matter of fact, it is."

She nodded. "I like it."

"Why, thank you."

She was surprised. "Is it yours?"

"Guilty as charged. Yes, I'm one of those desperate artists who had to open his own gallery in order to sell his own art. Kind of like people who think they're writers and pay money to have their books published at those vanity presses." He shrugged. "I suppose this is my vanity gallery."

"Except that you're really an artist," she told him. "A good one."

He moved the watercolor aside and nodded toward her portfolio. "How about you? Are you a good one too? Let's see what you got."

She wasn't so sure she wanted to do this now. "Are you sure this is a good time? I could leave my portfolio with you and come back tomorrow."

"Would that make you feel better?"

A real customer entered the shop. "Yes," she said. "Immensely."

"Do you have a business card in here so that I can reach you?"

"No, I forgot."

He slid a pad of paper and pen toward her, and she wrote down her name and cell-phone number. He looked at it, then stuck out his hand. "Nice to meet you, Marley Phelps. I'm Jack Holland and I'll be in touch."

"Thanks." She self-consciously turned away and hurried out the door, wondering why anyone in her right mind willingly opened herself up for the kind of abuse she was asking for here. Oh, sure, Jack seemed like a kind person. He would probably be gentle in his rejection. But really, what was wrong with a person who went in search of new and clever ways to make herself feel inadequate?

==Chapter 22==

CAROLINE

Caroline almost never worked Sundays at the restaurant. That wasn't for church reasons, although she wanted to become more regular in her attendance. Once she'd established some clout with the managers, she refused Sundays because the business was lighter, and tips were lighter too. After she returned from her reunion, though, she found herself on the Sunday schedule and felt as if she'd been demoted.

"I'm getting too old for this," she had told Remo, the maître d', on her first day back at work. The truth was, she felt out of shape and slightly lazy, not to mention offended that she'd been reduced to the bottom of the restaurant's food chain.

"Then quit," he had said in a snooty tone, as if he really didn't care.

She'd stood straighter then, adjusting her apron and tucking one side of her neatly pressed white shirt into her slim-fitting black trousers. And then she walked away with her head held high. Remo was smoother than silk with patrons, but he wasn't known for his sensitivity toward the wait staff. Still, as she picked up an order for an elderly woman who was dining alone, she considered his advice. Just quit. He made it sound so simple. Maybe it was. After all, she'd been praying about this whole thing ever since leaving Clifden two days earlier. But still. She wasn't ready.

"Here you go," Caroline said pleasantly as she set the entrée in front of the woman, taking time to refill her water glass.

"I ordered it *medium-well*," the woman said curtly.

"It is medium-well," Caroline gently told her.

"This is *not* medium-well." The woman's voice got a bit louder.

"Can I have the chef put it on the grill for you again?" Caroline kept her tone friendly and warm. "It's really no trouble."

"Fine." The woman folded her arms in front of her. "I'll just wait."

"Would you like a complimentary side salad while you wait?" Caroline offered.

"If I had wanted a side salad, I would have ordered one."

"Yes." Caroline removed the plate and returned to the kitchen to explain the situation as tactfully as possible.

"If that filet mignon was any more well-done, we could offer it up to the gods of inedible food," he said.

"I'm sorry, but the woman insisted."

"Why do people like her come here in the first place?" he demanded as he stabbed the innocent steak with a meat fork, then flung it on the grill. He continued to complain and Caroline quietly exited, glancing at her watch and wishing that an earthquake would conveniently shake this day to an end. But as she stood there waiting for the chef to burn the poor steak, she seemed to see God's handwriting on the wall.

Q-U-I-T. Just like Remo had said. And quit she would. Her

decision was made. Before her shift ended that day, she would write a resignation letter and mark the end of an era.

"Your order's up." The chef had a mean twinkle in his eye. He was relatively new to the restaurant and had made it clear that he was unaccustomed to working with female wait staff. It was obvious that he considered her his inferior, even though they had barely exchanged more than a few words.

"There you go." The chef nodded over to a shriveled piece of burnt meat in the corner of the square white plate.

"But I can't serve—"

"The customer is *always* right," he had snarled, waving a knife as if to drive home his point. "Give her what she wants."

"Fine." Caroline picked up the plate and, holding her head high, marched back into the dining area and sweetly said, "Here you go."

"What is this?" barked the old woman.

"Your filet mignon." Caroline could hardly bear to look at the blackened steak.

"I wouldn't give this to a dog. It's burnt to a crisp."

Caroline heard snickering from the kitchen.

"You take it back," the woman ordered. "And I want to see the management."

Caroline nodded. "Fine."

Of course, "the management" wasn't around on Sunday, which meant the chef was in charge. "The customer refuses to eat this," Caroline told him as she set the plate at his elbow. "And she would like to speak to you."

"Tell her I'm busy," he said as he tossed some scampi into a hot pan.

"Tell her yourself," she shot back at him.

"I'm busy!" he shouted.

That was when Caroline decided she'd had enough. She untied the strings of her short apron, then removed and neatly folded it, dropping it on the butcher block counter. "I quit," she told him. "Good luck with dinner." And then she left.

She hadn't felt the least bit guilty as she drove home three hours before her shift was scheduled to end. And she didn't regret her hasty decision one bit. In fact she was happy. Almost deliriously happy. Once home she turned on some music, kicked off her shoes, and danced around until she was laughing so hard, she had to sit down.

"Free at last," she had sung, quoting Martin Luther King, Jr., "Free at last. Thank God Almighty, I'm free at last." Then she got on the phone and called an old friend who was also a real-estate agent. "Sandy," she said joyfully. "I want to sell my condo."

"Great!" Sandy sounded eager too. "I'd love to help you."

"So what's the next step? What do I do?"

"How soon do you want it listed?"

"Yesterday." Caroline imagined herself running on the beach outside of Clifden as if she were in a scene from a movie. She could see herself in faded denim jeans rolled up to her knees, a soft white blouse, and running by her side was a gorgeous golden lab with his tongue hanging happily out as the waves splashed nearby.

"Okay then." Sandy's voice had brought her back to reality. "Do you want me to bring over some paperwork today? I can do a walk-through and make some suggestions, you know, things you can do to make sure it's market ready. And we can go over the numbers."

"Perfect." Caroline hung up, then scrutinized her condo. Her housekeeping, while not immaculate, was fairly tidy. She abhorred clutter, which was perhaps one reason she found her mother's hoarding habits so annoying. She fluffed a pale blue pillow, then tossed it back onto the white linen sofa. Noticing a stain on the arm, she ran for her handy spot remover, and within seconds it was gone. She continued going through her place, searching for flaws as if she were playing hide and seek.

A little before seven, the doorbell rang. Before Sandy would come in, though, she made Caroline come out.

"Get rid of that." Sandy pointed to a pathetic, misshapen fake palm covered with dust.

Caroline blinked. "Wow, I didn't even remember that was there."

Sandy laughed. "Homeowners can be so blind." She pointed to the worn-out welcome mat. "And replace that with something pretty."

"Sure."

"And how about some kind of live plant in a nice ceramic pot out here. Something with style. Match it to the new mat. Maybe a bench, too. Something that says, 'Welcome to a wonderful place.'"

"Good ideas." Caroline had nodded as she opened the door wider.

Sandy had even more good ideas. "The place is nice and neat," she told Caroline, "but it lacks color and personality."

"I'm not much of a decorator."

"Yes. I can see that." Sandy frowned. "I have a good friend who's just starting a staging business. We might be able to get a good deal from her."

"Staging?" Caroline imagined a set in a Hollywood studio.

"Don't you watch TV?"

"Of course. I mean sometimes. What do you mean?"

Sandy explained how an expert could come into Caroline's home, decorate it with furniture and other props, and make it look so wonderful that buyers would be lining up with offers.

"Is staging expensive?" Caroline frowned. "Finances are kind of tight for me right now."

"We can make a deal with her to be paid when the condo sells."

Caroline brightened. "Then sure. Why not?"

So they reviewed numbers, and Caroline was slightly disappointed to see that property prices were not as good as they once had been. "I guess I should've sold a few years ago," she said as they looked at the sale prices of similar condos that had closed in her neighborhood.

"The good news is that if you buy something else, you should get an equally good deal," Sandy told her. "Where do you want to move to?"

"My hometown on the Oregon coast." Caroline explained about her mom's need for care. "I actually quit my job today."

"Wow, so are you planning on going up there real soon?"

"As soon as I can get this place ready to sell."

"That means you need to be priced right."

So they kicked around possibilities a little more and finally agreed on a figure. Although Caroline felt a little nervous as she signed the contract, she also felt a huge relief. She was really doing this thing. No turning back. "This just feels right," she told Sandy when they finally shook hands. "It's time for me to do this."

"Your timing is good as far as I'm concerned." Sandy put her paperwork in her briefcase. "We'll get the listing going, and I'll call Lindsey about staging. Then we'll just see how quickly we can get you out of here."

Caroline had been so excited about her decision that she felt certain she'd be awake all night, but to her surprise, she slept peacefully. In fact she had one of the most restful nights she could remember. And then it hit her: She did have a sense of peace about this whole thing, just like she'd prayed—and just like Victor had said she would have if she was doing the right thing. Obviously it was the right thing.

———

Less than one week later, Caroline's condo looked so amazing that she almost didn't want to move. Almost. "Wow," she said as Lindsey artfully arranged some sunflowers in a large clear vase. "This doesn't even look my place anymore."

Lindsey set her creation in the center of the dining-room table. "And that's a good thing, right?"

"Absolutely." Caroline walked around, admiring how Lindsey had brought in color and life by using simple things like artwork, pillows, candles, rugs, and lamps. Also, she'd painted a couple of walls, switched out some furniture, and rearranged everything to make the condo look much more spacious than its eight hundred square feet.

"I think it's ready for the open house tomorrow." Lindsey glanced around one last time, nodding with what seemed to be satisfaction.

"And I'm ready to get out of here." While Lindsey had worked on the condo, Caroline had worked on packing. Other than a few pieces of large furniture that would be sent to her after the condo sold, she had packed all but her personal items and clothing into a PODS container, which would be transported to a storage facility in Clifden sometime next week. After that, Caroline wasn't sure where she'd put her things. Not in her mother's house. Not without bringing in a bulldozer to clear the place out first.

The last time Caroline had spoken to Beverly, the social worker, she found out that her mother had been approved for admittance into Evergreen Nursing Care Center, but Mom was not budging. "We can use force if we need to," Beverly had told her, "but I'd like to see if you can talk her into it first. She mentioned you yesterday."

"Me, she mentioned me?" Caroline was pleasantly surprised.

"She called you the hamburger girl."

"Oh." Caroline had explained that she would be in Clifden by the end of the week and would do what she could to sort things out.

Her phone conversation with Abby hadn't been much more encouraging. First of all, Janie's house wasn't anywhere close to finished yet, although Abby said she was working like a dog on it—those were her words. Besides that disappointment, Abby also explained that Janie might not list the little house after all. On the positive side she told Caroline that Marley had decided to move back to Clifden as well. Apparently she was on the lookout for housing too.

"Is it still okay for me to crash with you for a while?" Caroline asked hopefully. "I plan to get there on Sunday." She didn't want to admit that she was tight for cash and that she'd be even tighter until her condo sold, but she wasn't sure what she'd do if Abby had changed her mind. Her only option might be to clear out one of her mom's jam-packed bedrooms and attempt to "live" there.

"You're welcome to the guest room," Abby had told her. "But I'll warn you: Paul and I are, well, not exactly on friendly terms."

"Oh dear." Caroline felt bad now. "Are you sure you want—"

"Yes. It might be a good thing," Abby said. "In fact I think I'd enjoy your company. Please, do come."

"Okay." Still, when Caroline hung up, she was uncertain. She sure didn't want to get in the middle of a marital spat. She was surprised that Paul and Abby were capable of a squabble. They seemed so compatible. Plus they'd been married for forever. Maybe Abby was exaggerating. Or maybe Caroline would just need to find accommodations elsewhere.

That afternoon, as she drove her fully packed mini-SUV north on the first leg of her trip, she realized that none of this was going quite as she had hoped it would. She had no idea when her condo would sell, or even if it would. Not only that, but her checking account was frighteningly low, and her credit cards, which she had maxed out during her cancer treatments, still carried hefty balances. Yet she felt strangely at peace … and that made up for everything.

==Chapter 23==

ABBY

Abby poured herself a cup of coffee. She knew she should've told Caroline that her arrival was really bad timing. Having a house guest right now, while Abby and Paul were barely speaking, was not wise. Telling people no had never been Abby's strong suit.

Paul had already left the house, presumably for an early golf date. He slipped out of bed while he thought she was still sleeping, but she listened to every step he took. As usual, he did the exact same things he did every Saturday morning when he was getting ready for golf. She heard him using the toilet, brushing his teeth, and taking his Prilosec, but no shower, because he never showered before golf. Then he went into the closet, where he stayed briefly, emerging in his favorite golf pants and a yellow polo shirt, athletic shoes in hand. She watched with one eye as he tiptoed out of the bedroom.

This stealth preparation was not unusual. He had always been thoughtful to let her sleep in on Saturdays when he got up early to play golf. This habit began when the girls were young and Abby got up before six all week long in order to have everything ready for everyone before the day began. Saturday was her one chance to sleep in, because back then they often went to church on Sunday. This morning Abby had listened from her bed as Paul made coffee, probably had some orange juice and toast, then eventually headed for the garage and started up his Corvette.

Now, as Abby sipped her coffee, she replayed the conversation they'd had last weekend after Paul returned Lucy to her parents. Abby had used the two hours of his absence to strategize her inquisition. When Paul got back at seven, exactly when she expected him, she calmly began.

"That was quick," she observed as he hung his Blazers ball cap on the hooks by the back door. "Hopefully you weren't speeding with Lucy in the truck with you."

"Not with Lucy." He grinned obliviously. "But I pushed it a little on the way back."

"Good thing you weren't in the Corvette."

"I wouldn't drive the Corvette in this weather." He leaned over to see what she was cooking. "Not that green spaghetti," he said with disappointment. Abby knew he didn't like pesto pasta, which was exactly why she made it.

"But you drove the Corvette yesterday," she reminded him.

"Yeah, and I didn't think it was going to rain."

"The paper predicted afternoon showers."

"Well, I didn't know that I'd still be in the Corvette in the afternoon."

"So what did you do after golf?" She turned away from him to fuss with the boiling pasta and to keep him from seeing her face.

"Work."

"You went to work in the Corvette?" She turned back around, eager to see his expression.

"I went to meet a client."

"Oh?" She tried to look only mildly interested. "Who?"

"No one you know. A friend of Rob's wanted me to give him an estimate."

"For what? New construction, a remodel?"

Paul frowned at her. "Since when are you so interested in my work, Abby?"

She turned back to the pasta, removing it from the stove and carrying it to the sink to drain. "If you'll remember, I used to be pretty involved in your work, back when you were just starting out."

"Well, that was a long time ago. Why the big interest now?"

She took a deep breath, steadying herself. She was determined to follow this thing through, to voice her concerns and ask her questions. It would be so easy to back down, to smile and pretend that nothing was wrong, to sweep it under the rug the way she handled things like this in the past. She turned to face him again. "Where were you yesterday afternoon, Paul?"

"I told you. With a client." He looked uncomfortable, almost as if he was squirming. He turned from her and opened the fridge, removed a Corona, and popped the lid. "When will dinner be ready?"

"Wait." She set down the colander of pasta. "Where did you go with the client?"

He shrugged then took a swig. "To the building site."

"Where's the building site?"

"Right here in North Shore."

She frowned. "You spent hours at the building site?"

"Why are you obsessing over this?"

"Because. Because I saw you in Newport."

Now he looked like he'd been caught. "In Newport?"

She just nodded.

"What were you doing in Newport? Spying on me?"

That made her mad. "Why would I do that? Or maybe I should ask, do I need to do that? Are you doing something that should be spied on?"

"No, of course not."

"So why are you so reluctant to tell me why you were in Newport?"

He looked confused now. "You really saw me in Newport?"

"Yes." She glared at him. "I had picked up Lucy, and she decided she wanted to go to the aquarium. I saw your car and then I saw someone in the passenger seat, and it was not some guy friend of Rob's, either." She could feel her heart racing, and she felt lightheaded. Her blood pressure must've been high. She grasped the edge of the countertop to steady herself.

"Are you okay?" he asked.

"Of course I'm not okay. I'm mad, Paul. First you lie to me, and then you won't even answer me. Who were you with yesterday?"

"I told you. A client."

"You said it was a guy." The dizziness wasn't going away, and so she sat down at one of the island stools. "The person with you was not a guy."

"Well, the friend of Rob's is a guy. But I was with his sister-in-law."

"Whose sister-in-law?" She had no idea why she asked this. Perhaps to stall until she gathered her wits.

"Rob's friend Glen's sister-in-law."

"So why were you with Rob's friend Glen's sister-in-law?" And why did she feel as if she were questioning a six-year-old?

"Because she's the one who wants to build a house."

"Well, why didn't you just *say so*?" Abby could hear the volume in her voice.

He matched her volume. "Because you didn't just *ask*."

Now she was confused. She thought she had asked. Hadn't she?

"Her name is Bonnie Boxwell." His voice was stiff and his sentences clipped. "She wants to build in North Shore. She's already picked out the lot. She asked me to look at a house in Newport. One that she wants to replicate. She wants me to give her an estimate." He took another swig, then sighed in exasperation. "But maybe you think we don't need money anymore, Abby. Maybe you think I should pass up a job just because there's a woman involved?"

"I didn't say that." She stood and glared at him. "But you were being evasive and dishonest with me."

"I had no idea what you were talking about. You were playing some kind of mind game, asking your paranoid questions, acting like you were catching me in the act of something." He swore. That was something he didn't often do, at least not in front of her. "If you're going to be suspicious and jealous all the time, maybe I should just go out and have an affair." He put his face close to hers. "Is that what you want? Would that make you happy?"

She didn't know what to say.

"Because it seems like nothing I ever do makes you happy. I work my butt off so you can live in this beautiful home, but does that make you happy? No! Do you know how many women would like your life, Abby? And yet you just sit around and feel sorry for yourself, and when you get tired of that, you decide to go after me, accusing me of sneaking off with a woman who just wants me to build her a house, not *sleep* with her." He swore again, then tossed his half-drunken beer into the trash compactor. "And if you think I'm going to eat your green spaghetti for dinner, you better think again!" He stormed out, started his pickup, loudly revved the engine, and left.

Abby had cried as she dumped the unwanted dinner down the garbage disposal. She blamed herself for everything. Paul was right; she was ungrateful. She cried even harder as she cleaned up the kitchen. Cried as she got ready for bed. Cried as she went to the spare room—the room she had shared with Lucy the previous night, having told Paul that Lucy was having nightmare problems and couldn't sleep alone. Finally she had cried herself to sleep.

Now Abby refilled her coffee cup, trying to make sense of what felt more and more senseless each day. She and Paul had seemed to adopt some kind of unspoken agreement by Monday. Both gave each other the silent treatment. By midweek Paul quit stomping around angrily. And by Thursday, Abby returned to sleeping in their bed, mostly because it was far more comfortable than the guest bed. Also, she didn't want Paul to get used to having the master suite to himself.

Friday morning they had an actual conversation. She supposed it might've been Paul's way of saying he was sorry. Her way of saying she was sorry was to cook a dinner that he liked. Caesar salad, T-bones, twice-baked potatoes, corn on the cob, and blackberry cobbler à la mode for dessert. Not exactly heart-smart, but it must've warmed Paul's heart, because he uncorked an expensive bottle of merlot, and when dinner was finished, he asked if he could draw Abby a bath.

Abby could probably count on one hand how many times he'd "drawn her a bath," and she'd have fingers left over. Still, she had accepted. She even accepted another glass of wine as she luxuriated in the bubbles. Part of her was a bit skeptical and suspicious. Did Paul plan to get her intoxicated so that he could quietly drown her, then run off with Bonnie the brunette?

But after Abby finished her bath, undrowned, Paul continued to be sweet and attentive, and the evening culminated in lovemaking. Abby had been surprised at how good it was, which was what worried her this morning. It was like it was *too* good. And that was bad.

She'd heard about this exact thing on a talk show not too long ago. She couldn't recall which show, but she remembered how a guest "expert" had described common patterns of husbands who cheat. He listed things like a sudden interest in hygiene, unexplained absences, and too much time on the computer, or mysterious cell-phone calls and bills. But the one that caught her attention, perhaps because it didn't really make sense, was when the cheating husband became unusually attentive and generous toward the wife he was deceiving. She thought of it as a distraction technique, or maybe even a guilt offering. Now all Paul needed to do was to show up with the routine diamond bracelet, and she'd really be suspicious.

On the other hand, what if he was just being sweet? What if this female client was simply that? And what if Abby was blowing this whole thing totally out of proportion?

One good thing that had come out of all this was that Abby had a reason to throw herself into Janie's renovation project. No one would be able to tell by looking at the place, but Abby had been lining up workers, ordering materials, and she expected the house to

turn a corner by mid-September. And if all went well, it might even
be habitable by early October.

———————

The golf course wasn't on the way to the grocery store, but Abby
drove her SUV as if it were programmed to go there of its own free
will. It was just past noon when she found herself cruising through
the parking lot at Shore Links, scouring the parking lot for a certain
red Corvette. She eventually spotted it parked by the clubhouse, and
she was about to drive away when she was seized with the urge to
find a private spot where she could lurk and spy on her husband.

Her impulse was ridiculous, but it was there just the same. So,
feeling like a stalker, she went over to a shady corner of the parking
lot and backed into a space that was screened by a club cab. She
considered waiting for Paul's car to leave so that she could follow.

Her phone rang, startling her so badly that she jumped. "Hello?"
She glanced over her shoulder as if she might have been spotted
doing surveillance.

"Hey, Abby, it's Marley."

It took Abby a moment. "Oh. Marley. How are you?"

"I'm great, but you sound odd. Did I catch you at a bad time?"

"No. Not really."

"So what are you doing?"

"Stalking my husband." Abby actually giggled. She knew it was
crazy—that she was slightly crazy—but she just didn't care.

"Seriously?"

"Yes. I think I may be losing my mind."

"Hey, welcome to the club. Want to meet for lunch?"

"In Seattle?"

Marley laughed. "No, darling, in Clifden. I hope you're not too disappointed."

"Actually Seattle did sound rather exciting."

"More exciting than stalking Paul?"

"I don't know. Espionage might agree with me."

"Okay, now you really have to meet me for lunch. I'm dying to know what you're up to."

So they agreed to meet at The Wharfside in fifteen minutes. Abby, still feeling like a double agent, looked furtively about before she started her vehicle and then quietly exited the parking lot, taking a back road to make her getaway. Really, what had she been thinking? Thank goodness for Marley. Who knew what Abby might've done if Marley hadn't called?

As Abby drove to town, she told herself that she, once again, had been making a mountain out of a molehill. She was scouting trouble for no good reason. From now on, she vowed, unless she had real evidence, she was going to put her suspicions about Paul behind her.

Chapter 24

JANIE

If Janie had thought the previous weekend was hard, this one was far worse. It was no wonder; her week had been catastrophic. She'd known she wasn't ready for her court case, but she had counted on her normally faithful legal assistant to fill in the missing pieces. Unfortunately Holly had let her down. Whether it was intentional sabotage or simple neglect was unclear, but Janie had been infuriated with the young woman. In what was arguably not her smartest move, Janie had lashed into Holly outside the courtroom, reducing the poor girl to tears. Janie wasn't proud of her actions, but at the time she was too angry to make amends. She'd hoped Holly would forgive her later, and bygones would be bygones.

As it turned out—and this had been news to Janie—Holly was Grant Weisner's niece (on his wife's side). Grant Weisner was the most senior partner of Weisner, Potter and Sorenson. In fact it was Grant's grandfather who had started the firm nearly one hundred years ago. Holly, feeling terrorized, had told her mother the whole horrifying story. Naturally Holly's mother relayed it all (and then some) to Mrs. Weisner.

So it was that after losing the case on Wednesday, Janie was called into her brother-in-law's office Friday morning. Ross's expression was grim. "Is everything okay with you, Jane?"

"Okay?" She frowned at him. "I just lost a big case, but I'm sure you heard about that."

"As a matter of fact, I did." He cleared his throat. "I also heard about Holly."

"Holly?" Janie felt blindsided. "What do you mean?"

So Ross had explained Holly's connection to Grant. Janie sank into a chair. Bending over, she buried her head in her hands and then began to cry. Back in the old days, she would've defended herself. She might've even questioned the ethics of a senior partner hiring a family member, then clandestinely sending that person to work for some unknowing soul without disclosing the relationship. But on Friday she just sat there and cried.

Ross handed her several tissues and waited. Finally she sat up and shook her head. "I can't do this anymore."

He nodded, but his eyes were full of sympathy.

"It's not the same ... without him."

Ross reached for a tissue for himself now. "I know."

"Every day that I come to work, I feel lost and alone. I tell myself I can do it. I tell myself that I'm strong. But then I walk by Phil's office, and it feels like part of my soul is missing, like part of me was buried with him. Like I'll never be the same."

Ross sighed. "I feel some of that too, Jane. Not as much as you do, I'm sure. But I do understand."

"I can't go on."

"At first I thought it would be good for you to continue here," Ross said sadly. "I thought it would be therapeutic, make you stronger. But I've watched you and it's as if … as odd as this sounds, it's as if you're shrinking, kind of fading away."

She nodded. "That's how I feel. Like someday I'll disappear altogether. To be honest, there are times I wish that would happen."

"At first I felt certain that Phil would've wanted you to stay on here."

"He said as much before he died. I'm sure he always assumed that I would continue practicing with the firm."

"But if Phil could see you the way I've seen you, I know what he'd tell you, Jane." Ross paused to wipe his nose. "I know this from the bottom of my heart."

She looked at him through tear-blurred eyes. "What?"

"He would tell you to go. He would tell you to start over, to move on, and to live again. To breathe. To laugh. And love. I know he'd say that, Jane." Ross was crying almost as hard as she was now. He came around the other side of his desk and hugged her. "That's what I want you to do too."

She choked out a sob. "So do I."

When their emotions subsided, they both sat down. Ross blew his nose again. "You know, I don't consider myself an emotional man, Jane. But I think I've kept a lot of grief inside too. I think I needed that."

She made a weak smile. "Glad I could be of help."

"I'm sorry it was at your expense. But I stand by what I said. I honestly think Phil would want you to go somewhere else."

She nodded as she twisted the tissue in her hand. "I agree."

"And despite this week's court session and this little incident with Holly, which shall go unmentioned from this day forward, rest assured you will get excellent references from this firm. You're not being fired. You understand that, right?"

"Yes." She took a deep breath. "So I guess this is it, then?"

He nodded. "For you and the firm, it is. But as far as Edith and I go, you're always family. You know that."

"Thanks."

"And if Matthew ever decides that he wants to pursue law, there'll be a place for him here. You guys know that, too."

"I appreciate that. Although, Matthew hasn't made any decisions yet."

"That's all right."

She stood. "Wow, this is kind of weird."

"You've been here a long time, Jane."

"I know." She looked around his office and sighed. There had been a time when she'd hoped to have an office like this for herself. Now she didn't care.

"There's no hurry to pack your things up. Take your time. Say good-bye and do, well, whatever."

"Thanks." She reached for the door. "And I mean that, Ross. I really appreciate your honesty and your kindness."

He had nodded. Then she left and, without saying good-bye to anyone, because there was no one she felt especially close to, she packed what she wanted from her desk and exited the building.

She had felt surprisingly light as she rode in the cab to her apartment. And yet it was a surreal sort of lightness, almost as if she were walking through a dream, and perhaps just as fleeting. She paid and generously tipped the cab driver, nodded to the doorman, then went to her apartment, kicked off her shoes and, with her work clothes still on, climbed into bed and slept. She didn't wake up until Saturday a bit past noon, and yet she still felt tired. Or maybe she felt sad. Or perhaps empty. Just plain empty.

She paced around her apartment like a caged animal, though she was free to leave—free to do whatever she wanted. But what did she want? Of course, she was thinking of Clifden. She couldn't deny that she wanted to be there. But what would she do there? Fix up her parents' old house and just hide out? What would she be hiding from? And what about practicing law? At one time she had believed that was what she wanted to do for the rest of her life. But if she was painfully honest—and this seemed the time for honesty—she probably chose law because of the accolades that came with it.

There, she had admitted it. She had become an attorney just to get pats on the back, just so people would say, "Look at her, isn't she something!" Certainly she'd had the intelligence to pursue this profession. She'd always been an academic. A geek. She even had the temperament to practice law. But now she wasn't so sure. In fact she wasn't sure she wanted to go back into law at all.

Janie picked up the phone and, without really thinking it through, called Abby. "Sorry," she said after Abby answered in an angry voice. "Did I catch you at a bad moment?"

Abby laughed in a way that sounded slightly diabolic. "Honey, that's all I'm having these days. Bad moments. Lots and lots of bad moments."

For some reason this made Janie feel better. "What's going on?"

"To start with, I was stalking my husband. Then I took a back road and got a flat tire, which was rather aggravating. But after a while a handsome young man came along, and right now he's changing it for me."

"Sounds kind of fun. Well, except for the stalking part, but I'm sure you're joking."

"Oh yeah." Abby's tone bordered on sarcasm.

"So maybe this wasn't such a good time to call."

"No, it's fine. I think I'm over the worst of it. Guess where I'm heading as soon as the tire's fixed?"

"I have no idea."

"To meet Marley at The Wharfside."

"Marley's in Clifden?" Janie suppressed images of Thelma and Louise. But something about Abby stalking Paul, getting a flat, a young man helping out, and now meeting Marley at The Wharfside just smacked of dark comedy.

"She just got here today," Abby explained. "She's quit her job in Seattle and is moving here."

"Really?" Janie felt another glimmer of hope. "Both Caroline and Marley are moving back?"

"Is that weird or what?" There was some background noise now. "Here, you take this for your trouble," Abby was telling someone, probably the young man. "Well, thank you!"

"So your tire is fixed?"

"And I'm ready to roll. Such a nice kid. I told him I had a pretty daughter about his age." She chuckled. "Turned out he knew her! The way he blushed, I could tell he liked her. Probably why he refused my money."

"Well, you're probably ready to meet Marley now." Janie felt envious. "Wish I could join you."

"Me, too."

"Before you go, I wanted to tell you that I quit my job this week. And I think"—she paused to weigh her words—"I think I may be coming back to Clifden too."

Abby squealed so loudly that Janie held the phone away from her ear. "Oh, Janie, do you know what this means?"

"What?" Janie waited.

"The Four Lindas are being reunited for real! Not just a short gig this time. You'd come back here to stay, right?"

"Well, I'm not sure if I'll sell my apartment here yet. I think I need to test the waters per se. But I'll definitely stay long enough to see my house to completion."

"Oh, Janie, this is so exciting. I can't wait to tell Marley."

"Give her my love."

"And Caroline will be here tomorrow."

"Give her my love too."

"Let me know when you're coming, Janie. We'll have a Four Lindas party."

"Sounds great!" They said good-bye, and when Janie caught a glimpse of her image in the oversized mirror above the fireplace, she almost didn't know that person. She was smiling. And it felt good!

Chapter 25

MARLEY

"For someone who sounded borderline psychotic earlier, you're sure looking pleased with yourself now," Marley said as Abby sat down.

"I think it's because I had a complete breakdown."

"A breakdown?"

Abby nodded. "I was so stressed about Paul. And then I get this flat tire and I'm stranded on a road that hardly anyone uses. So I think, *I'll just change it myself.* I mean, I used to do that sort of thing back in the day." She held up a dirty-looking hand in need of a manicure. "Three broken nails later, I was swearing like a sailor." She laughed. "And then I started crying. I was about to phone Paul for help, although that meant I'd have to explain why I was out on that stupid road, and along comes this handsome guy in his old blue pickup."

"And now you're in love?"

Abby laughed. "He's Nicole's age."

"Then why are you so happy?"

"Like I said, I cried and threw a fit. It must've been good therapy." She grinned at Marley. "Plus I knew I was meeting you. And *then* Janie called to tell me she quit her job and is moving back here too. Can you believe it?"

"That's wild."

Abby held up her hands, which looked like they belonged to a mechanic. "Order me an iced tea and I'll go clean up, okay?"

Marley leaned back in the well-worn booth and sighed. Here she was back in Clifden, about to have lunch with an old friend, about to embark on what she was calling Act Three of her adult life. Act One included meeting John, and their bad marriage. It was, unfortunately the longest act. She'd literally given that man the best years of her life. Of course, the payoff was Ashton. She thought of Act Two as the last years of a very bad marriage, moving out onto her own, and the transition era. Now she was ready for Act Three. She had no idea what it would contain or how it would end, but she was ready to meet it head-on.

"All cleaned up," Abby announced as she slid into the other side of the booth.

"So tell me, why were you stalking Paul?"

Abby waved her hand. "Temporary insanity."

"Really?"

"Yes. I'm sure I was having a case of hormones." Then Abby launched into a tale of how Paul had romanced the socks right off her last night.

"You're kidding? He even drew you a bath? And today you're stalking him?"

Abby laughed, then tapped her index finger on the side of her forehead. "I told you it was insane."

"I'll say. Some women would kill for a guy like him."

"Yes, that's kind of what Paul said too."

"Well, I'm glad you two are okay. It's so reassuring to know there's at least one couple who's been happily married for as long as you two. It gives the rest of us hope." Marley decided to change the subject. "So have you ever been in the One-Legged Seagull?"

Abby cocked her head slightly. "Oh, the new gallery."

"How new is it?"

"About ten years I'd say."

"That's new?"

"Well, compared to the others."

"Right." Marley sipped her water. "So do you know the owner?"

She nodded. "Jack Holland."

"Yes. I just met him. He's looking at my portfolio." Marley giggled. "I am so nervous. You'd think I was sixteen and waiting for my first date to show."

Abby's brows lifted. "You're interested in Jack?"

"Oh, no." Marley shook her head. "I didn't mean like that. I was referring to the nervousness of having someone looking at my art. It's kind of like being naked."

Abby laughed lustily. "There you go with another sexual metaphor. Are you sure you don't like Jack?"

Marley felt slightly irritated. "Abby, I told you I only met him. We barely spoke."

"But your eyes lit up when you started to talk about him."

"That's because *he's looking at my art.*" Marley wanted to ask Abby what she'd been smoking. "Good grief, Abby, don't make it into something it's not."

"Sure." Abby picked up the menu.

"Sorry, I didn't mean to sound so hostile. It's just that it was unnerving to stand there and ask a perfect stranger to look at my work."

Abby's expression grew thoughtful. "Yes, I can understand that."

"Besides, I'm sure Jack is married or has a girlfriend or—"

"See!" Abby held up a triumphant finger.

Marley made a face. "Okay, I'll admit he was interesting. But that's just because he seemed genuinely kind. That's what caught my attention."

"Yeah, yeah. Paint it how you like. You're the artist, Marley."

Marley realized it was time to change the subject again. "Here's my big problem, Abby," she said after they placed their order. "I can't find a place to live."

"Is Lois helping you?"

"Yes. But she just doesn't seem to be finding anything. Do you think I should look for a different realtor?"

Abby frowned. "I don't know."

"I'm sure my budget must look like pretty small potatoes to Lois. But there's nothing I can do about that. She probably thinks I'm being stubborn because I want something on or very near the beach, but I refuse to do an old mobile home. I'm sorry, but that's just creepy to me."

"Paul would agree. Those old ones are pretty hard to work on. And they definitely have a shelf life."

"It's not that I'm unwilling to do some fixing up. I'm not afraid to paint or do some minor repairs. I was home alone so much when John was flying that I got fairly handy. I'd settle for something tiny and—"

"I know of a place." Abby's eyes lit up.

"Really? That's for sale and in my price range?"

"Well, I don't know your price range, but trust me, it's cheap. And it's for sale by owner, so Lois might not even know about it."

"Seriously?" Marley grabbed Abby's list. "Is it near the beach?"

"It's on the beach."

"Let's go!" Marley was grabbing her purse.

"But we ordered our—"

"I don't want to lose it, Abby. What if someone else snatches it up before I can get—"

"Hush, hush." Abby had her cell phone out now. She hit a speed-dial button and smiled mysteriously. Marley waited on pins and needles and wished that she were a praying woman.

"Hi, Mom," Abby was saying. "Is the Lowenstein cabin still for sale?"

Marley felt like she was about five years old. She wanted to bounce up and down on the old booth's springy seat.

"Really?" Abby listened with a thoughtful brow. "Oh, that's too bad." More listening. "Oh, I didn't know." And then finally, "Okay, Mom. I'll call you later. Bye." Then she hung up.

"It's sold?"

"No." Abby closed her phone. "But Mrs. Lowenstein passed away a couple of weeks ago. I knew she'd been in a nursing home in Salem but I—"

"Yes, yes, and I'm sorry, that's too bad. But the house, Abby, *what about the house?*"

"So Mrs. Lowenstein's daughter was over here checking on the house, and she was worried that it would be sitting vacant all winter.

You know how vandals can wreak havoc on beach houses. So she was thinking about renting it and—"

"And is it still for sale?" Marley demanded.

"Mom isn't sure. But she's going to walk over."

"Walk over where?"

"To the Lowenstein cabin."

"Which is where?"

"Next door to Mom's cabin. I thought you knew that." Abby frowned.

"It's next to your mom?" Marley's hopes soared.

"Yeah, that little cedar-sided boxy looking place. It's tiny."

"It's perfect."

"When did you last see it?"

"I don't know. When we were kids maybe."

"And you know it's perfect?"

"When's your mom calling back?"

Abby rolled her eyes and waited as the waitress set their orders of fish and chips down. "Don't worry, Marley. Mom's on it now. There's not much else you could ask for."

Marley shook some vinegar onto her fish, then smiled to think of Doris Lund out there acting as her realtor. Abby's mother was one tough but highly likeable woman. "Yeah, I guess you're right." As much as Marley tried to pace herself, she ate quickly, and she was full after just one piece of fish and a handful of fries. She motioned for the check and paid it before Abby could argue.

"Okay, I get the hint," Abby reached for her purse. "Let's get this over with."

"Is it okay to go over there before your mom calls?" Marley

didn't want to do anything to jinx this thing. "I don't want to step on any toes."

"We'll just park at Mom's and see what she's found out. And let's take just one car. We can drop mine at the tire shop and hopefully get it fixed while we're gone."

"This is starting to feel magical," Marley told Abby as she drove them toward the beach.

"Magical?"

"Well, remember when I told you I wanted to be like your mom when I grew up?"

"Oh yeah. Maybe you can start wearing baggy old men's clothes and get yourself a black skull cap too."

Marley just laughed. "Maybe I will."

"To be honest, I'd love to see someone in the Lowenstein house."

"Even me?" teased Marley. "I might ruin the neighborhood."

"Especially you. Mom's getting up there, you know. She sometimes needs help. I'll tell her to just call you."

"Hey, if I get that house, I'll be glad to give her a hand now and then."

"That'd be great. I don't like her sitting out there with nothing but vacant houses all around her. It feels unsafe."

"Why are they all vacant?"

"They're not always vacant, but remember most of them are vacation cabins."

"Oh, that's right."

"So it can be lonely."

"Sounds nice and quiet to me."

"It can be very quiet," Abby warned.

"Yes, but it might be inspiring to an artist. That's what I was thinking."

Soon they arrived, and to Marley's delight, Abby's mom and another gray-haired woman were waiting outside to greet them. Doris introduced them to the Lowensteins' daughter. "Barb's in charge of the property," Doris explained.

"Go ahead and look around," Barb told Marley and Abby. "Not much has been fixed up since Mom went into nursing care, but her personal things are gone. You can have the furniture if you want. I doubt that you will. It's in pretty bad shape."

Marley stood on the road and stared at the house. It was tiny and it was old. The trim and shutters needed painting. But she loved it. She absolutely loved it.

"How's the roof?" Abby was asking.

"I have no idea," Barb called back. "But it wasn't leaking when Mom was there."

"And the plumbing?"

"Try it out if you want."

"Come on," Marley urged Abby. "Let's look first and ask questions later."

"It's definitely musty in here," Abby turned her nose up.

"Of course it's musty," Marley said defensively. "It's old. It's been shut up. What do you expect?"

"I was just saying."

Marley walked around the small space, imagining where she would put her things, what colors she would paint the walls, and then she pulled open the tattered drapes to see the ocean. "Oh-mi-gosh!"

Her hand covered her mouth as she stared out the grimy windows. "I want this house."

"Marley," Abby said in alarm. "You haven't even looked at the bathroom yet. Or tried the—"

"I don't care. I want this house."

"Not until we check it out more closely," Abby told her. "Come on." Marley felt herself being tugged away from the view, and the next thing she knew, she was staring into a toilet that looked like it hadn't been scrubbed in decades. "Let's make sure it works," Abby said. She pushed the handle and, although it was slow, it did flush.

"It really smells in here," Abby observed. "And this sink! Well, it's ancient."

"I like it." Marley tried the tap and it worked.

"How about this ugly tile?" Abby picked up a broken yellow tile that must've fallen off the wall.

"Tile can be replaced."

"But this shower can't be." Abby gave a tug on a piece of the flimsy plastic wall, which was falling apart.

"Sure it can." Marley noticed the bathroom was large relative to the size of the house. "But I could fit a claw-foot tub there if I took out the shower."

Abby nodded, almost as if she was seeing it too. "You could rig it with a European shower, too, and a nice curtain."

"Yes!" Marley said eagerly.

"Let's go look at the kitchen," Abby suggested. "You were so fixated on the view, you didn't even see it. I have to admit the cabinets could be kind of cute with some fresh paint and hardware."

Marley grabbed Abby's hand. "See! You're getting it!"

Soon they were in the kitchen, and Marley was imagining the small space painted in bright tropical colors and decked out with new tile—maybe even something handmade. "It could be so cheerful, Abby," she said as Abby tried the kitchen tap and then the lights.

"Everything seems to work," Abby admitted. "Maybe it just needs a face lift."

Marley patted the old-fashioned white ceramic sink. "This old girl is kind of like me, Abby; she needs some TLC and someone to believe in her."

"I know it's useless to try to talk you out of this, Marley." Abby opened a door that revealed a small pantry. "But can you at least have Paul come over to give it a look? Just in case there's something you've overlooked."

"But I *want* this house!" Marley felt ready to stomp her feet and shout. "I want it, Abby!"

Abby laughed. "Yes, I understand."

"And I don't want Paul to say or do anything to mess this up."

"He won't, Marley. He'll just give you the facts."

"Maybe I don't care about the facts." Marley planted herself in front of the window again and stared hypnotically at the sand and waves.

Abby put an arm around Marley's shoulders. "Listen, Marley, there's probably no reason you won't get this house. But what if you could get it for less money?"

Marley considered this. "Less money?"

"Yes." Abby nodded. "If Paul finds things that aren't working, you might be able to bid low to compensate for repairs you'll need to make. That's how real estate works. Have you ever purchased a house before?"

"Not really. We only bought one house, and that was when Ashton was still in diapers, so John kind of handled it."

"Well, Mom told me the price of this cabin, and we both think it's a little high, which might be why it's still on the market. Plus not being listed with a realtor is sometimes a flag that something could be wrong."

"Like what?"

"Oh, I don't know. It might just be overpriced, or there might be a lien on it, or something could be in serious disrepair."

"How do you know all this?"

"I almost got my real-estate license when the girls were in school. I studied and was ready to take my exam, but we decided it was more important for me to be home." She smiled sadly. "But I still know a thing or two."

"Do you know what Barb is asking?" Marley wasn't sure she wanted to know, especially after hearing that it was priced too high.

"Mom said she wants close to three hundred thousand."

Marley knew that figure would wipe out all of her savings. "Oh."

"Is that outside of your budget?"

"I wouldn't have anything left to live on."

"So you wanted to pay cash? No financing?"

"I don't have a job, Abby. How do I get financing?"

"Do you get alimony?"

"Just enough to cover my living expenses. If I have a house payment as well, and no job." Marley shrugged. "It might be dicey."

"Right." Abby frowned. "On top of that, you'd still have the expense of fixing the house. Who knows what that might cost?"

Marley's hope was plummeting. What had made her think she could do something like this? Perhaps Lois was right. She should just settle for one of the old mobile homes not far from here. She could still walk to the beach. And she wouldn't be starving or forced to take a job she didn't like. "I guess I'm just dreaming," she admitted to Abby. "I thought I could swing this, but in reality, probably not."

"Oh, don't give up." Abby looked worried. "I wasn't trying to rain on your parade. I was just trying to be realistic."

"That's what I'm being. Realistic. It is not realistic to carry a loan and empty all my savings on a house that obviously needs some work, probably more work than I know. It's crazy."

"But what if the house *is* overpriced? And what if Barb is more desperate than we think? And what if you didn't have to empty out your savings?"

Marley considered this. What if?

"What if this really is the best house for you? And what if you let it go?"

Marley made up her mind. "I know what I'm going to do. I'm going to go out there, and I'm going to make Barb an offer. A cash offer that will leave me with enough money to pay for the fix-ups and a little nest egg as well. Really, what do I have to lose?"

"Let's take it a step further," Abby said. "Let's make the offer contingent on an inspection. You can have Paul come out or hire a real inspector, but before you hand over your savings, you must have this place inspected. Okay?"

"Okay. So what do I do, Abby? Just go out there and tell her what I can pay, tell her to take it or leave it?"

"I have an idea. How about if I represent you?"

"Like a real-estate agent?"

"One who won't ask for a commission."

"It's a deal." Marley stuck out her hand and they shook.

"So what do you want to offer?"

Marley thought hard. The truth was she was willing to offer her entire savings, and yet she knew that wasn't terribly smart.

"Don't forget that Barb might counter your offer." Abby was digging something out of her purse.

"Counter, meaning she'll want more. Right?"

"Right." Abby withdrew a small notebook and pen. "Here, you write down whatever figure you think is best. And give yourself some room to raise your offer in case she counters."

"Kind of like an auction?"

Abby nodded. "Kind of."

So Marley wrote down a figure that she was absolutely comfortable with. Of course, she didn't expect Barb to accept it. But at least this would start what felt a bit like a game. "Here." She handed the notebook back.

"Okay. You stay here and dream about what you'll do with this place, and I'll start this ball rolling."

Marley was surprised at how nervous she felt, as if she were about to hyperventilate. First she paced, and then she went to look out the window again. After a minute or two of gazing at the ocean, she began to relax. She could actually feel her heart rate slowing, and her breathing became even. The ocean really was good medicine.

Abby came back in the house with a strange expression on her face. "You're not going to believe this."

"What?" demanded Marley. "Did she laugh in your face?"

"She accepted your offer."

"Seriously?" Marley felt like hopping up and down.

"But before you start doing the Snoopy dance, let me explain."

"Explain?"

"Barb said she'll accept your offer, but if you come back after getting the house inspected and ask to reduce the price any more, the deal is off."

"That's okay." Marley hugged Abby. "Thank you so much!"

"Want me to go tell Barb the good news?"

"Absolutely!"

After Abby left, Marley really did do the happy dance. There wasn't a lot of room to dance, but she did the best she could. This beach house would soon be hers!

====Chapter 26====

CAROLINE

"It's so good to see you," Caroline said as her old friend Claudia handed her a glass of iced tea. "I'm glad you talked me into stopping for the night."

"I can't believe you considered driving right past us." Claudia frowned. "Especially when we're halfway between LA and Clifden. It's been way too long."

"I really appreciate your hospitality," Caroline said. "And your house is gorgeous." During their twenties Claudia and Caroline had shared a tiny apartment. Both had big-screen dreams and restaurant jobs, but then Claudia met Dale and ditched her dreams in exchange for comfort. At the time, Caroline thought she'd settled, but now she wasn't so sure.

"When Dale heard you were coming, well, he did something." Claudia had a mysterious expression.

Caroline felt confused. "He *did* something? What did he do? Throw a fit?" But that seemed ridiculous. She'd always gotten along well with Dale.

"No, nothing like that. He invited Mitch for dinner."

"Mitch?" Caroline tried not to look as shocked as the felt. "Mitch Arenson?"

"Is there another Mitch?"

"Why is Dale in contact with Mitch?" Caroline felt slightly unsteady, as if the earth had shifted ever so slightly.

"Mitch works for Dale."

Caroline was still trying to wrap her mind around this. Mitch was coming to dinner? Mitch worked for Dale?

"Remember? They were both computer geeks. About fifteen years ago they bumped into each other at an electronics show. Dale hired him, and he's been around ever since."

"Oh."

"Okay, I can tell you're shocked. I told Dale this was not a good idea."

"But I thought Mitch got married. Is his wife coming to dinner too?" Caroline took a long sip of tea.

"They divorced several years ago."

"Oh."

"So do you want me to call Dale and tell him it's a no-go?"

Caroline thought about this. "No. Actually it might be interesting to see Mitch. And therapeutic."

"If you're sure." Claudia frowned. "I know how he hurt you."

Caroline nodded.

"But Dale doesn't know the whole story."

"Thanks. I appreciate that." Caroline stood and stretched. "After all that iced tea, I need to visit the ladies' room." She felt unsteady as she walked through Claudia's spacious house, as if she needed to hold on to things to avoid tipping over. She used the bathroom in the suite Claudia had shown her earlier. She stood in front of the mirror, slowly breathing deeply, telling herself to relax and let go. Relax and let go. Mitch was part of her history, but that's all it was. History.

Okay, it was more than that. Mitch had been the love of her life. She had desperately wanted him to propose to her. She wasn't even all that concerned when she became pregnant with his child. Certainly she was young. They both were. But even in her early twenties, she felt ready to be a mom and wife. She was willing to let go of her Hollywood dreams in exchange for Mitch. She imagined them with the little house and the white picket fence and a couple of kids and a dog. The possibilities had seemed idyllic.

But Mitch had burst her bubble by insisting he wasn't ready for any of that. Not marriage, not kids, and absolutely no white picket fence. He had been so adamant about it that she worried she was going to lose him, and she couldn't bear that. They'd been so happy together—everything was so perfect. Or so it had seemed.

To keep Mitch, Caroline had agreed to get an abortion. Then, just a few months after the abortion, Mitch moved on. He told her that he wasn't in love with her anymore, like love was a switch he could turn off and on at will. She heard later that he'd married. And then she'd worked to forget him.

Caroline looked at the clock hanging above the towel rack. Nearly four. If she left now, she could make it to Clifden by—she counted the hours on her fingers—around two in the morning. Where would she stay? Abby wasn't expecting her until tomorrow. No, maybe she should just stay put and go through with this and hope she felt better afterward.

"You're not upset, are you?" Claudia asked when Caroline rejoined her in the kitchen. "We don't have to—"

"No." Caroline said firmly. "I want to do this. It might be good for me."

"If it's any comfort, Mitch has changed. A lot. I like him much more than I used to. A little maturity and a few hard knocks have been good for him."

"What kind of hard knocks?" Caroline didn't like to rejoice over other people's sufferings, but in Mitch's case … well, she was only human.

"He and his wife, Teresa, lost their only child, a daughter, to leukemia several years ago. In fact Dale thinks that's what messed up their marriage."

"That's too bad. How old was the girl?"

"Just eleven."

Caroline felt guilty for her ill wishes toward Mitch.

"Mitch did everything he could to salvage their marriage, but Teresa got involved with another guy."

"Wow, that's hard too. Poor Mitch." Now Caroline felt really guilty.

"Anyway, you'll see. He is different. And Dale said Mitch was actually looking forward to seeing you again."

"So no pressure, right?" Caroline laughed nervously.

"Right. No pressure." Claudia returned to peeling cucumbers.

"Need some help?" Caroline offered.

Claudia paused to look at her. "You look tired to me, Caroline. I know you've been working hard to get your house listed and your stuff packed, and it was a long drive here. Plus you have a full day of travel tomorrow. Why don't you just go take a rest? It's a couple hours until dinner. Just relax."

"Really?"

"Absolutely. Everything's under control."

So Caroline returned to her suite. After a nice long shower, she did relax, and it did feel good. Almost good enough to get Mitch off of her mind. But not quite. She remembered his dark wavy hair and chocolate brown eyes, his straight Roman nose and full lips. He had the kind of face that she could look at forever. Of course, that was almost thirty years ago. There was no telling how he looked now. After so much hard stuff in his life, he could be bald or paunchy or old. Yet if his spirit was still there, and if he had changed in good ways like Claudia had suggested, Caroline might enjoy getting reacquainted even if he was bald, paunchy, *and* old.

She slept for about an hour, then got up, did her hair and makeup, and spent about twenty minutes trying to decide what to wear. As ridiculous as it seemed, she felt as if she were in high school again, getting ready for a big night. Finally she settled on an aqua-blue sundress and her favorite turquoise-blue sandals. Not too casual and not too overdone. Comfortable yet classic.

"Need any help in here?" Caroline found Claudia still in the kitchen, although she must not have been there the whole time, since she too had changed her clothes. She wore orange capri pants and a bright floral top that matched.

"Not really," Claudia told her. "The salad is made, the halibut is ready to go on the grill." She removed a bottle of sauvignon blanc from the fridge. "Let's take this out to the deck and relax a bit until our male guests arrive."

Caroline knew she could use some more time to relax and didn't argue as she followed her host outside. The view from their house was lovely. The home was not next to the ocean like Abby's, but on a hill where the ocean could be seen in the distance.

They spent this time catching up. Claudia spoke of her four kids, all of whom sounded like they were perfect. Or perhaps it was simply Claudia's happy spin.

"Our baby, Jordanne, won't graduate until next spring. Then they'll all be on their own, and with the money we'll save from not paying tuition, we plan to do some traveling."

"That sounds nice."

"Yes. Before we get too old to enjoy it."

They chatted on, and Caroline felt more at ease. By the time Dale and Mitch arrived, she told herself that the four of them were simply old friends getting together. No history. No future. Just a one-time event.

"Caroline," Mitch actually reached out and took both her hands, helping her to her feet before he embraced her in a warm hug. "You have no idea how good it is to see you!"

She nodded and smiled as she stepped back. He was definitely older, but not in a terrible way. His hairline had lifted quite a bit, but for the most part his locks were still dark and wavy, with some silver running through it. His eyes, while still chocolate, looked sadder than she remembered. And time, combined with sun, had etched some wrinkles into his face. But, all in all, for a man his age, he looked quite good.

"You're looking well," she told him.

"And you look as if you've barely aged at all."

"Of course you knew that's what I wanted to hear."

"It's true!"

Dale greeted Caroline, welcoming her to his home. "It's like old times, isn't it?" he said. "Except we're older." Then he excused himself to see if Claudia needed anything.

"So what brings you here?" Mitch asked Caroline.

She explained her relocation to Clifden.

"Finally giving up the fast lane, are you?"

She shrugged. "I guess." Then she explained a bit about her mother. "She would never admit she needs help. My mother, bless her heart, thinks she's just fine on her own."

"I went through something like that with my father recently," Mitch told her. "My mom passed on in '98, and my dad did pretty well on his own for a while. But then he started getting forgetful, of little things at first. He'd put his wallet in the freezer or the ice cream in the pantry. But it got worse. And finally he was so bad off, he would actually walk outside stark naked."

"I guess I should be thankful my mom's not gone there yet."

"Yes, the neighbors can be unappreciative."

"So did you put him in a care facility?"

"I tried, but he refused to go."

"So what did you do?"

"Fortunately the law intervened. The next time he went flashing the neighbors, minus the overcoat, the police picked him up and took him to a nursing home. That made it a lot easier."

"So I should hope that my mom will decide to go streaking?"

Mitch laughed. "Maybe you'll come up with an easier solution."

"I hope so."

Dinner went smoothly, and anyone observing would have assumed Mitch and Caroline were old friends. Indeed they were. Except that Caroline hadn't felt warm or friendly toward Mitch in years. After dessert Claudia seemed to nudge Dale, and the two left Mitch and Caroline alone again. Caroline suspected this was not a coincidence.

"I asked Dale and Claudia to give me a few minutes alone with you, Caroline. I hope you don't mind."

"Not at all."

He reached for her hand now, almost in the way a man does when he's about to propose, although he didn't get down on one knee. That was a relief. Still, Caroline braced herself. What was he doing?

"I just wanted to tell you how sorry I am for the way I treated you back in LA."

"Oh, that." She sort of waved one hand. "That was—"

"Don't brush it away," he told her. "It was a terrible thing to do. And I'm really sorry I was so spoiled and selfish. When I think of how I acted, I feel nothing but shame. And I would appreciate it if you would forgive me."

She didn't say anything.

"I know I don't deserve to be forgiven, but I'm asking."

"Of course I forgive you."

"Thanks. I know it can't undo what was done. But it does take a load off my shoulders."

Caroline considered this. "You know, I feel better too."

He squeezed her hand, and then let go. "Good."

She considered telling him the rest of her story, about how the abortion prevented her from having children, and how that ended her marriage, but that would sound bitter. Really, especially after his apology, she felt no bitterness. Sadness, yes, for what might've been. But she wasn't bitter.

"When Dale told me you were coming here, I thought he meant to live." Mitch looked disappointed.

"This seems like a lovely place to live," she told him. "But my mom needs me in Clifden. It's a lovely seaside town too. Kind of like here, only much, much smaller. And I think I'm going to like that."

"You mean the smaller size?"

"Yes. I'm tired of the noise and the fast pace. I'm ready to go to the grocery store and expect to see people I know. I think it'll be fun."

"It does sound nice." He sighed. "Would you have any objections if I came by to visit sometime?"

"Not at all."

"Do they have an airport?"

"No, they're much too small for that."

"Not even a municipal?"

"What's that?"

"You know, for small private planes."

Caroline thought for a minute. "You know, I believe they might, now that you mention it."

"That way I could fly up and save some travel time."

"You have your own plane?"

"Well, nothing fancy. But if the weather's good, it gets me where I want to go."

"Then by all means, come on up."

They talked some more, and to her relief, they didn't talk about the past too much. At least not about their past relationship. They did fill in other details surrounding their lives, and by the time Mitch announced he should go, Caroline felt like they were good friends. And she liked that.

He kissed her on the cheek and promised to look into flying up to Clifden when he got the chance. Then he left, and Caroline assured Claudia and Dale that the encounter had gone well. "I'm actually grateful that you guys did this. It helped me to bury some old things."

"So what do you think?" Claudia asked hopefully. "Any chance you two could get back together?"

"Oh, I don't think so." Caroline shook her head. "Besides time and location factors, well, I just don't think so."

"But you never know."

"No. I suppose not."

"Well, we won't keep you up. I know you want to make an early start in the morning."

Caroline hugged them both, then went to bed. Of course, she couldn't sleep at first. No, her mind was fixated on Mitch. Although she continued to tell herself a relationship with him was not only impossible but impractical as well, she still couldn't help but wonder. What if?

=Chapter 27=

ABBY

"You did what?" Paul demanded on Sunday morning.

Abby poured coffee beans in the grinder. "You heard what I said," she calmly told him.

"I just can't believe I heard you right, Abby." He looked truly angry. "Did you really tell Caroline McCann that she could stay here until she finds another place to live?"

"Something to that effect." She turned the grinder on to drown out his yelling. She ran it a little longer than usual, and when she quit, the kitchen was quiet and she turned to see that Paul had left. Well, fine, let him be that way. She wasn't about to disappoint Caroline in order to appease Paul. She continued to make coffee, slowly and methodically, as if one false move would ruin the brew.

Finally she clicked the on switch, but before the water started to drip, she pounded her fist on the countertop. Why did Paul have to act like this? Caroline was his friend too. Besides that, Abby reminded herself, this wasn't only Paul's home. She had the right to share it if she wanted. Why did Paul think he should be the only one to call the shots? Abby poured herself some coffee as she continued to have this mock argument with her husband that she was sure to win.

She could hear the TV in the den, so she knew he hadn't left the house altogether. She also knew she needed to tread carefully; she wanted him to keep his promise to check out Marley's beach cabin. Already he'd complained about that.

"I thought you hated for me to work on Sunday," he had said when she asked him last night. He'd come home late again, after supposedly "just playing golf."

"Helping a friend isn't really *work*, is it?" she persisted.

"Helping *your* friend, you mean."

"So now I have *my* friends and you have *your* friends?"

"Fine, Abby. I'll do it, okay? Now will you get off my case?"

"I just don't see why you're making it into such a big deal." She knew she could've held back that last comment. It wasn't smart to push him too hard, not if she really wanted him to help Marley. But it was too late.

"Crawling around beneath a house, poking around electrical wires, checking plumbing and septic tanks? If you don't think that's a big deal, why don't you do it?"

That's when she'd backed down, showing approval, smoothing his ego, and applying all the little "management" techniques she'd mastered over the years. She didn't even ask him about where he'd been all afternoon. But, just the same, she wondered.

The phone rang and, suspecting it was Marley, Abby grabbed it before the second ring. She didn't want to disturb Paul. "Hey, girlfriend," Marley said happily. "I'm on the way to the cabin. You guys want to meet me there?"

"Let me check with Paul," Abby told her. "If I don't call you back, it means we're on our way." Then Abby hung up and filled Paul's favorite mug with coffee, adding cream and sugar the way he liked it. She set this on a sandwich plate, then set two oatmeal-raisin cookies (Paul's favorite) next to the mug. She'd made the cookies yesterday afternoon, planning to use them to sweeten him up to doing this inspection for Marley.

"Sorry to ask so much of you," she said when she handed him the plate.

"Huh?" he looked surprised. "Oatmeal-raisin cookies?"

"Uh-huh. I made them for you yesterday."

"A bribe?"

"Maybe." She smiled. "I'm sorry if I have friends who seem a little needy right now, Paul. But if you only knew how much I need them. You might be more willing to help them because you'd be helping me."

He actually smiled now. "Since you put it like that." He picked up a cookie. "And since you sweetened the deal."

She reached down and ruffled his hair. "I'm going to head out to meet Marley at Mom's," she told him. "You come along whenever you're ready." Hoping that had done the trick, she took off.

Abby wondered what the other Lindas would think if they knew about the games she played with her husband—the ways she humored him, placated him, took the blame for his shortcomings. What would they say? They were all single, independent, and smart. Would they think she was stuck in their mothers' generation?

Sometimes that's how she saw herself. And yet her mom was as liber-
ated as any woman. After a relatively brief period of grieving after
Abby's father died more than twenty years ago, her mom had been
on her own and happy as a clam. Despite her troubles with Paul,
Abby was not so sure she'd be that strong if he died suddenly from
a stroke.

When she pulled in front of her mom's house, Marley's little
car was already there. Abby found the two of them sitting in the
well-worn Adirondack chairs on the back deck. "Nice day," she said
as she joined them.

"So is Paul here?" Marley asked eagerly.

"He's on his way." Abby leaned back against the chair's wood
slats and sighed.

"No hurry," her mom said. "That little cabin's not going anywhere."

"Unless there's a tsunami," Abby pointed out. "Have you ever
noticed how much closer to the water you are here?"

"Isn't it nice?" her mom murmured.

"And you have a key, right?" Marley asked.

"Barb gave me a key to let you in." Mom chuckled. "I didn't
admit that Bernice gave me a key a long time ago. That's what neighbors do."

"And if I become your neighbor," Marley looked hopeful, "I'll
want you to continue keeping that key."

"You mean you won't change the locks?" Abby asked.

"Why should I?"

Abby shrugged. "I don't know."

"My daughter is slightly paranoid," Mom told Marley quietly.

"I am not paranoid." Abby frowned.

"I'm just teasing, sweetie. But you are extra careful, you have to admit that."

"Well, Paul's like that. I have to take his needs into consideration." But even as Abby said this, she knew it sounded odd.

"But here's the thing," her mom continued, aiming her words at Marley. "If you want to be a woman alone, living on the beach, you need to be strong in your self-confidence and slightly unconventional to boot."

Marley laughed. "Hey, that sounds like me."

"Yes, you seem the independent type. I don't see you needing a man, like some women do."

Abby felt left out. Also, she was still a bit out of sorts after her argument with Paul. "But Marley was married for a long time," Abby pointed out.

"Legally married," Marley told them. "But John had been stepping out on me for years. And because of his flight schedule, I was independent most of the time. It was an odd sort of marriage." She laughed. "And I don't miss it a bit."

"See?" Abby's mom said. "She is an independent woman."

Abby felt angry. Were they suggesting that she was not, just because her marriage hadn't failed and because Paul was still alive? That seemed a little unfair. Before she could respond—and who knew what she was going to say—she heard Paul's pickup pull in.

"Sounds like Inspector Gadget is here," she told them. They all got up and went out to meet him. Naturally, with an audience, Paul was his sweet, charming self.

"Here's the key," Abby's mom said as she handed it over.

"Do you need any help?" Abby asked.

"Not unless you want to climb under the house to see the spiders or smell the septic tank."

"I'll pass," Abby said.

Marley looked torn.

"You can go if you want," Abby told her.

"That's the problem. I don't want to." Then Marley broke out into an old tune. "'I don't like spiders and snakes, and that ain't what it takes to love me.'"

"So I'm on my own." Paul looked relieved. "Well, it'll take about an hour or so. You ladies sit back and relax, and I'll be back with my report."

After about thirty minutes Abby had an idea. "You know that Caroline is coming today?" she said to Marley.

"That's right. I almost forgot."

"Well, since everything seems to be under control here, I think I'll run to the store and pick up something for dinner. Everyone can come. You, too, Mom."

"Thanks, honey, but tonight's card night for me and the girls."

"Sounds fun," Marley told her.

"Maybe you'll want to join us sometime."

"Sure." Marley nodded. "I might."

"So come by around six," Abby told Marley.

———————————

While at the store Abby got a call from Caroline saying that she'd make Clifden around five. "Marley's coming for dinner," Abby told her as she shook the water from a head of leaf lettuce.

"Sounds great." Caroline's voice was happy. "Can't wait!"

As Abby waited in the checkout line, she tried to imagine how it would feel to be starting all over. Not that she wanted to leave Paul. She really didn't. But sometimes she just wondered.

By the time Abby got home, Paul's truck was there too. There was another pickup backed in as well, and it was blocking Abby's side of the driveway. She parked on the street and went inside to see if she could get someone to move. But when she called, no one answered. She heard men's voices out on the back deck and went out to see that Paul and two other guys were putting what appeared to be a hot tub in place.

"What is that?" she cried as she went closer.

"You weren't supposed to see this yet." Paul held up his hands like he was trying to hide something, which was ridiculous, since the hot tub was the size of a small elephant.

"You got a hot tub?" she said incredulously.

"You've been wanting one for ages," he told her.

"You got it for me?"

"Who else?" Now he came over and gave her a hug.

She was totally shocked. What had made him do this? "But it's not my birthday or our anniversary or anything."

He kissed her forehead. "Can't I just get something because I want to?"

She smiled up at him. "Of course."

"Don't you like it?"

"You know I love it."

Now he frowned. "See why I was a little disappointed that Caroline was coming to visit?"

"Why?"

"I wanted it to be just the two of us to try it out."

"Oh."

"How's this look?" one of the guys called out.

"It needs to move back a little." Paul went over to help them.

"Well, I've got groceries to get out of the car," she called out. She was still stunned as she unloaded the car. She couldn't understand why Paul was being so nice. Especially since she had given him the cold shoulder for most of the week, thinking the worst of him. As she put the groceries away she mulled all this over, trying to make sense of it.

She almost dropped a bottle of dressing when it hit her. A hot tub probably cost about the same as a nice diamond bracelet. Was this some sort of guilt offering?

She looked out the window to see Paul happily filling his hot tub, as if he hadn't a care in the world. Suddenly she felt irked. If the man was trying to salve his guilt, she wanted diamonds, not a gift he could use himself! She was about to go out and give him a piece of her mind when the doorbell rang. It was too early for Caroline, but she hurried to get it anyway.

"Marley," Abby said when she opened the door. "What's wrong with you?"

"Didn't Paul tell you?" Marley looked like she'd lost her best friend.

"Tell me what?"

"He proclaimed my house a disaster area."

"He did?" Abby reached out and pulled Marley inside. "Why? What happened?"

"He hates my house. That's what happened."

"But why?" Abby led Marley to a stool at the island in the kitchen. "Sit down and tell me about it."

"He said the septic tank had to be replaced, and that there was dry rot, and the windows were no good, and"—Marley sniffed—"and he called it a scraper."

"A scraper?" Abby frowned.

"As in it should be scraped off the beach and thrown away."

"Oh, I don't think he—"

"He said the smartest move would be to tear down the house and start over. He even offered to build it for me. But I can't afford that."

"I know." Abby patted her shoulder. "Maybe it was a mistake having Paul look at it. He never has liked old houses." Abby remembered his final verdict on the Victorian house that she had loved.

"I thought about it, and I suppose he's right. But it seems so sad to just tear the house down. I really wanted to rescue that house. She was starting to feel like a metaphor for my life. How can I just turn my back on her?"

"Did my mom have an opinion?"

Marley kind of smiled. "Yes."

"What?"

"She said Paul was full of beans."

Abby laughed. "Yes, that sounds like what she'd say."

"And she said that house was in as good a shape as her own house, and she wouldn't have the slightest qualm about living there herself."

"So see? Maybe Paul's just throwing out the baby with the bathwater."

Marley looked surprised. "That's exactly what your mother said!"

"So we'll get you a second opinion."

Marley seemed to consider this. "No. I don't think I need a second opinion."

"You don't?"

Marley shook her head. "I've been driving around town thinking about it all afternoon. Barb gave me a pretty good deal. I was ready to pay about twenty thousand more. So if I use that extra money to take care of the things that Paul said need to be fixed, I should end up with a fairly sturdy little beach cottage. Don't you think?"

"That actually sounds rather sensible."

"I won't hire Paul to do any of it."

Abby laughed. "I'm sure he'll consider that a personal favor."

"But it would be nice if he could give me some names."

Abby waved her hand. "Let's leave the poor man out of this. I can give you some names."

"Even better." Marley shook her head. "Paul's a nice guy, but hearing him going on about my house like that, well, if he'd been my husband, I would've let him have it."

"Yes. I know how you feel."

Marley laughed.

Paul must've sensed that he wasn't particularly welcome in the kitchen, and so he seemed to be lying low. Abby was relieved. She was still feeling uneasy about the hot tub, which she'd secretly named Diamond Lil. If this was his way of making up for infidelity, she wanted to get to the bottom of it. Just not while they had company around to witness the mess.

At a little past five Caroline arrived. The three women exchanged a group hug, and to make the Four Lindas complete, Abby called Janie, putting her on speaker phone so they could all hear. "We wish you were here," Abby said.

"That's right," Caroline chimed in. "It feels like a new beginning."

"I wish I were there too," Janie told them. "But just knowing I'm coming makes such a difference."

"When will you come out?" asked Marley.

"As soon as I get things figured out here. I'm trying to decide whether to sublet my apartment or just sell it. Either option should happen quickly since I'm in a pretty desirable neighborhood. It's just hard to let go completely. It's a big step."

"Do you think you'll ever want to go back there?" asked Caroline.

There was a long pause. "No." Janie said slowly. "I really don't think so. I honestly think I'm done here."

"Then just sell the place," Marley told her. "Get free of it and get yourself over here so we can start having some fun!"

Janie laughed. "You make it sound so easy."

"We're all in the same boat," Caroline said. "Well, except for Abby. She's in a luxurious yacht."

"And Abby just got a hot tub today," Marley announced.

"Ooo, that sounds nice," Janie said. "Maybe you'll let me try it out when I get there."

"You bet. Just do what you need to do, and do it in your timing," Abby advised Janie. "Don't let us influence you the wrong way."

"Don't worry. You're mostly confirming what I feel in my heart."

They chatted a while longer, then all said good-bye. Caroline wanted to see the new hot tub, and Abby suggested Marley show her while Abby got chicken ready to be grilled. After the two were gone, Abby considered Caroline's "luxurious yacht" remark. She knew Caroline meant that as a compliment, but for some reason it stung. Her life probably looked like a luxurious yacht to an outsider, but it felt more like a leaky yacht to her. If she had to choose between a leaky yacht and a rowboat, she'd grab the rowboat in a heartbeat.

=Chapter 28=

JANIE

Janie knew that the way to torture a workaholic was to give her unexpected time off. Usually, *tortured* was how Janie felt when she had excess free time on her hands. But now it was different. Instead of feeling frantic and displaced, Janie felt *almost* relaxed. Although that feeling was going to take some getting used to, she liked it. For that reason she forced herself to do practically nothing on Sunday. Of course, while she by all appearances was doing "nothing," her brain was cheating.

While Janie drank an espresso at her favorite coffee shop, she attempted to read a novel that she'd started long ago. Her mind bypassed the storyline, though, instead strategizing where she would begin tomorrow. She set aside the book and decided to go for a walk. As she strolled through the park, her brain jotted down mental lists of what she would pack and store, and when she would book her flight. By late afternoon, as she was dipping into boysenberry gelato, all she could think about was what she had begun calling The Great Escape.

Eventually she gave in to it. She returned to her apartment and began making a real list. She went online and purchased an airline ticket with a departure on Friday, which meant she'd be in Clifden for Labor Day weekend. Then she began to pack. She packed some things in a bag to check onto her flight. She sorted other things into piles to be shipped before she left town. She couldn't believe how much she accomplished by Sunday evening. And yet, for a workaholic, it was simply run-of-the-mill.

The payoff for her efforts, besides being organized for The Great Escape, was that by the time she fell into bed, she was utterly exhausted and as a result she slept well.

The next day, she continued getting ready for The Great Escape by arranging to have her mail forwarded, gathering packing materials and several boxes, filling them with things she felt she might need on an extended visit, then labeling them to be shipped to her parents'—make that her—address in Clifden. By the end of the day, there wasn't much else to be done.

Tuesday, she decided to pack more things up. She knew it might be premature, since she wasn't certain that she was moving to Clifden for good. And yet she liked the idea of having her own dishes and pots and pans and furnishings and whatnot in her Clifden house. Besides, she would need these sorts of things if she ended up living there. So she called several moving companies until she found one that was willing to give her an estimate and pick up her things before her flight on Friday. It was time to really get busy.

By Thursday morning Janie had packed up most of her apartment. Naturally she had left Lisa's and Matthew's rooms intact, and she planned to leave some of the larger pieces of furniture that she didn't think would fit in the Clifden house. She carefully tagged and labeled everything, so there would be no confusion when the movers arrived in the afternoon.

It was nearly two when she heard someone at the door. Thinking it was the movers, she called out, "Just a minute," but then heard someone enter the apartment. Scrambling to find the phone to call for help, she realized it was her son.

"Matthew!" she cried in relief as she attempted to make her way to him through the maze of boxes.

"What's going on in here?"

Ignoring his question, she hugged him. "Oh, it's so good to see you!"

"Yeah, but …" He backed away and frowned. "What are you doing?"

So she attempted to explain her plan, but he seemed seriously troubled by it. "But this is our home, Mom. It's where I come when I'm not in school."

She wanted to point out that his visits were a rare occasion but didn't. "I'm not getting rid of the apartment," she assured him.

"It looks like you are." He frowned at the boxes.

"Go look in your room, and you'll see everything's there. Lisa's room, too. And I'm leaving some of the larger furniture as well."

He still didn't look convinced. "It feels like you're tearing up our home."

She placed a hand on his shoulders. "I'm the only one here most of the time, Matthew, and when I'm alone, all I can think about is your dad and how much I miss him. Every room is a reminder. Sometimes it feels like I'm suffocating in here. I couldn't admit it before, but I realize now that I've been depressed. Even Uncle Ross could see it."

"But what about your position at the firm?"

She told Matthew what had happened last week. "It's like I've been slowly breaking down. That was the last straw. And really, it's for the best," she said.

"So you won't be practicing law anymore?"

"I don't know." She sighed. "All I know is that I'm useless as an attorney right now. At least in New York. Maybe with a fresh start, I'll reconsider."

"Wow." He shook his head. "I had no idea."

"I know. And that's my fault. I've hidden my feelings for so long, it's no wonder I'm such a basket case."

His serious expression warmed a bit. "My mom, telling me she's a basket case. That's a new one."

"It's the truth. It felt like I hit the wall, like I couldn't function anymore. The answer seems to be for me to leave."

Matthew ran his fingers through his sandy hair, the same way his dad used to do when perplexed. "I don't know, Mom, it just feels strange to me. I can't imagine you anywhere else. Are you sure you're doing the right thing?"

"I realize I should've told you first, Matthew. And I did try to call, but you weren't answering and I didn't want to leave a message, because I figured it might be a little upsetting."

He nodded. "Yeah, it's not easy seeing your home dismantled like this."

Janie felt guilty, as if she'd just taken away her children's last shred of security. Why hadn't she considered that? Why was she so self-centered? Her children had suffered a loss just as much as she had. And here she was, tearing down their happy home. Tears began to form in her eyes. "I'm sorry, Matthew, maybe I was just being selfish. I just wanted a fresh start, to get away from the pain. But maybe it's all a mistake."

Now they were both silent for a long moment.

"It's not too late for me to cancel the movers." She went for the phone. "I'm going to call them right now."

"No, Mom." Matthew put his hand on her shoulder as if to stop her. "If you really think this is the right thing, you should do it. I'm just being a spoiled kid who wants it all."

She considered this. The truth was Matthew's visits had become more and more infrequent, so much so that she suspected he, like her, felt a sense of sadness in this place. "You can come visit me in Oregon," she assured him. "I'm getting Grandma and Grandpa's house all fixed up. Remember how much you and Lisa used to like going there when you were kids?"

He brightened. "Yeah, it's a pretty cool place."

"Like I said, I'm not selling the apartment. Not yet anyway. We'll see. But I didn't want to buy new furnishings and things for the house in Clifden. This just seemed easier and more economical."

"Does Lisa know?"

Janie grimaced. "I haven't heard from her in several months, Matthew."

"She called me a few weeks ago."

"Really?" Janie felt hopeful. "How did she sound?"

"Like Lisa."

"Oh."

"She was still in Arizona. It sounds like she's got a boyfriend."

"And?"

"And what?"

"Did she ask you for money? Do you think she's still using?"

He shrugged. "It's not like you can do a drug test over the phone, Mom."

"I know."

"She didn't ask for money either. She actually sounded okay."

"Really?"

"You shouldn't worry so much." He patted her shoulder.

"So you're really okay with this move?"

He grinned. "Yeah, as long as I can still come here and crash if I need to."

"Sure, why not?"

He glanced around at the bare walls and the jumble of furniture and boxes. "Do you care if I put some things in here?"

She considered this and laughed. "Let me guess: This is going to become Matthew Sorenson's bachelor pad?"

"I might invite some friends to do a weekend here, now and then."

"Just remember this is a co-op, Matthew. Keep the noise down, and abide by the rules. And take responsibility for your friends if they come."

The doorbell rang again, and this time it was the moving guys. By five o'clock the place was mostly cleared out. Janie took Matthew to dinner and told him more about the changes in Clifden and why she wanted to live there. She even told him about her old friends, the Four Lindas, but she didn't tell him about Victor. Really, what was there to tell?

"Maybe this is a good thing," Matthew said as they walked back to the apartment. "I mean, you seem a lot happier than you've been since Dad got sick and everything. That's pretty cool."

She nodded. "It's like I can see the light at the end of the tunnel now." She linked her arm in his. "I just hope it's not a train coming my way."

He laughed. "No, Mom, I think it's just the end of the tunnel."

Chapter 29

MARLEY

"My house closes on the day after Labor Day," Marley told Caroline and Abby as they met for coffee on Friday morning. "I'm so excited I can hardly stand it. Finally I'm going to own a home of my own." That wasn't the only thing making Marley happy this week. Jack had agreed to hang a painting or two of hers in his gallery. Upon hearing this news Tuesday, she shot up to Seattle on Wednesday, gathered her paintings, loaded them into her car, then drove back yesterday.

"I'm trying not to be envious," Caroline told Marley.

"Envious?" Marley was confused. "About what?"

"About the fact that you've already found a house." Caroline laughed. "Although Abby took me by to see it the other day, and I have to admit it's a little too rustic for my taste."

Marley just smiled. "Well, it suits me to a T."

"And you'll probably turn it into something wonderful," Caroline told her. "I could never do that. Besides, I can't really buy anything until my condo sells, and who knows when that will be?"

She turned to Abby. "In the meantime I'm staying at a pretty swanky bed-and-breakfast."

Abby made a half smile. "I was thinking about offering Janie a room too, but I'm afraid Paul will think I really am turning our home into a B and B."

"When does Janie get here?" Marley asked.

"She arrives in Portland this evening, and she'll drive down here tomorrow." Abby's tone sounded flat and unenthusiastic and completely un-Abby-like.

"Are you okay, Abby?" Marley asked.

"Yeah," Caroline chimed in, "you seem kind of down."

"I'm fine."

The way she said *fine* made Marley think all was not well. Still, if Abby didn't want to talk about it, why should they push her?

"How's your mom?" Marley asked Caroline.

"She's actually a little better. I've been giving her these mineral supplements that were recommended for dementia patients, and I honestly thing they're helping her memory just a little. Either that or I've been around so much that she's actually remembering who I am. Or maybe I'm just getting a bit senile myself."

Marley and Caroline laughed, but Abby just sat there staring out toward the docks with a glazed expression.

"Hey, you," Marley nudged Abby with an elbow.

"What?"

"You just don't seem like yourself today," Marley told her. "Are you sure you're okay?"

"I don't know." Abby sighed. "Things with, well, with Paul … It's been a little strained lately."

Caroline's blue eyes got bigger. "It's not me, is it? Does Paul resent me staying with you guys?"

Abby shrugged. "It's hard to say. Paul's just been acting differently. It's probably nothing, but it just makes me sad."

"I'll bet it is me," Caroline said with conviction. "Like yesterday, when you and I were in the hot tub. It seemed like his nose was out of joint."

"But that's silly," Abby told her. "Why should he care?"

"Maybe because he wanted to be in the hot tub with you?" suggested Marley.

Abby laughed, but her eyes were sad. "I doubt that."

"But it's possible," Caroline said.

"I doubt it." Abby's eyes narrowed slightly. "Do you know that I've named that hot tub?"

"Named it?" Caroline frowned. "What?"

"I call her Diamond Lil."

"Diamond Lil?" Marley was confused too. "Why?"

"Because I think the hot tub is my diamond bracelet."

"Are you saying what I think you're saying?" Caroline asked. Abby nodded.

"What *are* you saying?" demanded Marley.

"I think she's saying that the diamond bracelet is some kind of payoff." Caroline glanced at Abby. "Am I right?"

Abby nodded again.

"A payoff for what?" Marley asked.

"Do you think Paul's seeing another woman?" Caroline asked gently.

"Is that why you were stalking him?"

"You were stalking your own husband?" Caroline looked shocked.

Abby had tears in her eyes. She picked up a paper napkin and blotted them. "Her name is Bonnie Boxwell. She's probably ten years younger than me and very pretty."

"And you know for a fact that Paul is seeing her?" Caroline handed her a real tissue.

"I know that he's *seeing* her. I've seen them together."

"You've seen them together?" Marley flinched to imagine Abby finding her husband in the arms of another woman.

"Paul says she's simply a client. That she wants to build a house in North Shore. But I think she wants more than just a house."

"Meaning she wants your husband, too?"

Abby shrugged. "Maybe so."

"Oh, Abby." Marley reached over and grabbed her hand. "I'm so sorry."

"Me, too." Caroline looked like she was about to cry too.

"I confronted him once, and he accused me of being paranoid. I have to admit the stalking incident was a bit crazy."

"But it does make you nutty when you find out your husband's been cheating," Marley told her. "Trust me, I've been there, done that."

"I just can't believe after thirty-five years of marriage, and all the ups and downs we've been through, that he'd do something like this."

"But what if he hasn't done it?" Caroline suggested. "What if he's telling the truth and you really are being paranoid?"

Both Abby and Marley turned and scowled at Caroline.

"I'm not trying to defend him," she said. "But I've seen him with you, Abby. I've seen him acting like he really cares about you. And it's sweet."

"But what if it's just an act?" Abby shot back.

"What if it's not?" Caroline said.

"Caroline's right," Marley told Abby. "You could be wrong about him."

"What you really need to do is to sit down and talk to him," Caroline declared. "Have a real heart-to-heart."

"That's easier said than done," Abby told her. "Paul can be hard to pin down."

"And even harder when you have a house guest," Caroline said sadly. "I'm going to find another place to stay."

"No, no, you don't need to do that," Abby protested.

Caroline nodded. "Yes, I do. I remember my grandma used to say, 'Three days for company and fish.'"

"What's that supposed to mean?" Marley asked.

"In three days they both start to stink."

"But you don't need to leave," Abby persisted. "Really, Caroline, it has nothing to do with you."

"Except that I'm in the way. I give you someone to talk to besides your husband, and now that I think about it, I haven't seen you and Paul in a real conversation since I arrived."

"We probably won't have a real conversation after you leave either."

"But you need to try," Caroline ordered. "You need to do your part, Abby. You can't just assume the worst and then play the victim."

"Do you think that's what I'm doing?" Abby looked slightly defensive.

Caroline reached for her hand. "I'm sorry. That came out wrong. But I do believe you have to fight for your marriage, Abby. You can't just roll over. I mean, you guys have been happily married for thirty-five years, right?"

"More or less."

"And you don't want your marriage to end, do you?"

Abby shook her head.

"Well, do you know the main reason men cheat?"

Both Abby and Marley were staring at Caroline with interest, although Marley couldn't get over the irony that Caroline, who'd been married more briefly than any of them, was dispensing marital counsel.

"Okay, I'll admit I saw this on a talk show, but it made sense: The main reason men cheat is because they're lonely."

Marley laughed. "Yeah right."

"I said the main reason, not the only reason."

"I can tell you the reason my husband cheated," Marley said. "It's because he couldn't keep it in his pants."

"People assume that's true of all men. But according to this guy, a lot of men are lonely, and they don't get the kind of attention they need from their wives, so they go looking elsewhere for it."

"So you're saying this is the wife's fault?" Marley felt angry.

"That's what it sounds like," Abby said. "Are you suggesting that if I were more attentive and affectionate, and if I said and did everything Paul wanted, my marriage would be affair-free?"

"I know," Marley teased, "you can start meeting Paul at the door wearing nothing but an apron!"

"With a martini in my hand," Abby said wryly.

"Then you ease him into his recliner," Marley joked. "And fetch his slippers and pipe."

"And I should probably have a chocolate cake in the oven." Abby laughed.

"Fine, fine." Caroline held up her hands. "I'm just telling you what I heard. You don't have to shoot the messenger."

"I'm sorry," Marley said to Caroline. "But you hit a sore spot with me. I used to try to do all that, and John cheated anyway. In fact John had been cheating on me right from the beginning. I only found out a lot later."

Caroline nodded. "I realize there are men like that. They cheat because they want to. It has nothing to do with the wife. Believe me, I've run into a few of those."

"Married men, hitting on you?" Abby asked.

"Oh yeah." Caroline sighed. "Sometimes I think I'm just one of those women who attract the worst kind of jerks. Although time and age have taught me to look for certain signs."

"Like a wedding ring?" Abby suggested grimly.

"Or the thin white line where a wedding ring should be," Caroline told her. "But it's more than just that. There are lots of signs if a person is willing to look."

"Yes, but you're a decent human being." Abby frowned. "I'm not so sure about Bonnie Boxwell."

Marley looked at her watch. "Oh, I need to get moving. Jack offered to meet me at the gallery at ten thirty."

"So no hard feelings?" Caroline asked Marley. "You don't think I was blaming you for your husband's infidelity?"

"No hard feelings." Marley blew kisses to her friends, then left.

Once she got in her car, where her paintings were being "stored," she took time to check her appearance in the visor mirror. She fluffed her hair slightly and even applied a bit of lipstick. Of course, she then questioned why she was making this effort. *To appear professional*, she told herself. Although she wondered if it might be something more, too, something to do with the owner of the One-Legged Seagull. But she wasn't going to think about that now.

As she drove the few blocks to the gallery, her nervousness grew. It was one thing for Jack to show interest in a portfolio based on snapshots of her work. But seeing the full-sized art was another story. He might change his mind. Still, she told herself, she would take any rejection like a professional. She would even invite him to offer critique. Of course, she might have to bite her tongue to keep from defending herself, but she thought she was grown up enough to do this.

She parked by the back entrance, as Jack had instructed, and was getting a painting out of the car when he came out to help. Before long they had all eight paintings unloaded and spread out around the back room. And like Marley had said, she might as well have been standing there in her underwear. Totally exposed. She had never even shown her work to Kevin. She'd heard his critiques before and had the self-awareness to know she couldn't have listened to him tear into her art and then continued working for him.

Jack rubbed his chin as he scrutinized an acrylic she'd done on the heels of being separated from John. She called it *Seattle Night on the Waterfront*, but looking at it now, she could see how some people might describe it as moody, depressing, overly emotional, or just plain bad. "Interesting style," he murmured as he moved to the next painting.

Marley flinched. *Interesting* was one of those words that could go either way. In her experience, while working at the gallery, it usually meant someone didn't care for a piece but didn't want to admit it. She tried to think of a response, but everything that came to mind sounded either defensive or rude. So she just nodded.

Now he was looking at one she called *Seattle Cityscape*. She remembered the foggy night she'd taken the photos that inspired the image. That was shortly after the divorce became final. "You're definitely into impressionism."

"Yes." She wished she could think of something more intelligent to say. She considered excusing herself and making a run for it. She could sneak back to pick up her art sometime when Jack wasn't around.

He moved on to study a still life she'd painted the previous summer. She simply called it *Poppies*. Unlike the other two, this one was cheerful, and possibly amateurish. It was so hard to judge one's own art.

She felt a hot flash coming on. She didn't get too many of those, but when she did, it was as if her inner thermostat had been turned to high and before long her face would be flushed. To make matters worse, she'd forgotten to apply her deodorant that morning.

"Excuse me," she said as she pulled out her cell phone. "I forgot that I need to make a call about my house."

He nodded and she hurried out the back door and down the alley a ways, where she held the phone to her ear and pretended to be deep in conversation as she waited for her heart rate to slow and her temperature to drop. She decided to call her son. She pushed speed dial, and to her relief, Ashton answered.

"It's your mom," she said, "frantically calling you for some reassurance."

"Reassurance?"

"Yes. You know I'm relocating to Clifden, but I've just done something incredibly dumb."

"What?"

"I'm letting a man who owns a gallery look at my art. And I'm so nervous I'm having hot flashes."

Ashton laughed. "Good for you, Mom. It's about time you took a serious risk."

"So you don't think it's ridiculous for me to have someone looking at my art?"

"Your art is *good*, Mom. I've told you so lots of times."

"But you're my son. What else can you say? It's kind of like when I used to tell you that you were good at sports."

He laughed. "No, it's nothing like that. We both know I sucked at sports. But you really are good at art. Leo thinks so too."

Marley took a deep breath. "Okay. Thank you."

"So hold your head high, and even if the gallery rejects your work, remember how subjective art can be. And remember that you have talent."

"Thanks, darling. Give my love to Leo."

"Are you still coming for the drumming concert on Sunday?"

"I wouldn't miss it."

Then they hung up, and Marley took her son's suggestion seriously. Taking in several deep breaths, she held her head high and returned to the back room of the gallery, where she would handle her rejection like a grown-up. After all, Ashton was right. Art was entirely subjective.

When she came into the back room, she heard laughter. And there, in front of her paintings, stood Jack and a dark-haired woman who looked to be in her thirties. They were laughing, it seemed, at her work.

"Oh, there you are," Jack called to her.

Marley was incensed but determined not to lose her temper. "I can see my art isn't right for your gallery." She picked up a smaller painting and was reaching for another.

"No, I like your work," Jack said.

"So do I," the woman said.

Marley turned and looked at them skeptically. "Then why were you laughing?"

"You didn't think we were laughing at your paintings, did you?" Jack looked surprised.

"Well, I ..." Marley wasn't sure what to think.

"I'm sorry, Marley, I should've introduced you to Jasmine," Jack said. "She works for me, and I asked her to come in and see your art."

"And you were laughing," Marley reminded him.

"Not at your work," Jasmine told her. "I think your art is lovely."

"We were laughing at a funny thing that just happened in the shop."

Jasmine started chuckling again. "I kid you not—a woman just came in here and asked if we had any velvet paintings. I wasn't sure what she meant at first, so I asked her to explain, and she said, 'You know, those pictures that are painted right onto velvet fabric.' And then she told me she'd seen one with a bullfighter once, and she wanted to hang it in her bedroom."

Marley couldn't help but laugh. "Seriously?"

Jasmine nodded. "And seriously, I was just telling Jack that I like your art."

"That's the truth." Jack nodded. "I'll take all eight on consignment, if you like."

"All eight?" Marley felt slightly lightheaded.

"Of course, that means work for me," Jasmine told her. "I'm the one who gets to rearrange things to make room for them."

"Would you prefer to have just a few?"

"No," Jack said. "I told Jasmine that I want her to find a space for all of them. You'll be our featured artist for a while." The bell on the door sounded, and Jasmine excused herself.

"I'm so embarrassed to have assumed you were laughing at me," Marley said after Jasmine left. "Now you know how insecure I am."

He chuckled. "Trust me, I know how that goes. Imagine how I feel—I work in a gallery where my own art is hanging, and I can overhear people saying that a piece looks flat or unrealistic or whatever."

Marley nodded. "And art is so subjective."

"So I've developed some rather thick skin." He removed the painting from her hands and set it on the counter. "You said you were calling someone about a house. Does that mean you've already found a place to live in Clifden?"

"I have." She smiled sheepishly now. "But the truth is I was using the phone as an excuse to get away before I suffered a total meltdown. It's so hard having someone look at your work."

"It's sort of like they're looking at your soul, isn't it?"

She nodded. "I know that's not really true. Most people just look at the surface of art, thinking about whether or not they like it."

"Well, I do like your work." He grinned. "I suppose that means I like your soul, too."

Marley felt another hot flash coming on. But she didn't run this time. Pretending that all was well and that it was natural to be flushed and hot, she took her time to fill out the consignment forms and agreed to let Jack frame her work at her expense, whether they sold or not. Then she shook Jack's hand and, feeling the third hot flash coming on, she thanked him again and went on her way.

Once she was in her car and a few blocks away, she let out a loud hoot of happiness. At last it seemed that things were starting to happen for her!

==Chapter 30==

CAROLINE

Caroline wouldn't let Abby talk her into staying in their home, not for one more day. This was not because Caroline blamed herself for their marital troubles; she simply knew they'd need some privacy to resolve anything.

"I don't want to hear about you inviting Janie to stay here either," Caroline warned Abby as she carried her last load out to her car. "You and Paul need your space."

Abby just sighed. "I really don't see what difference it would make."

Caroline locked eyes with her. "Look, Abby, if I had a marriage with as much going for it as I think yours does, I would be willing to fight for it."

Abby looked slightly surprised. "You would? Really?"

"You bet I would. Paul is a good guy. Oh, he's got his faults. But I really think he loves you, Abby. And you guys have built a great life together. Would you really want to lose that?"

Abby started crying again. So Caroline dumped her load of

clothes and whatnot into the back of her car, then wrapped her arms around her friend. "Abby, listen to me. I wouldn't tell you this if I didn't love you. But, seriously, if you don't do your part to make this marriage work, I know you'll be sorry later."

"But what if I do my part and it still doesn't work?"

Caroline released Abby. "At least you'll know that you tried your best. You won't have anything to feel guilty about later."

Abby sniffed and nodded. "You're probably right."

"I'll be in touch." Caroline closed the hatchback.

"I almost forgot to ask, Caroline." Abby squinted in the sunlight. "But where are you staying?"

"At Mom's."

Abby blinked. "You're kidding."

"Nope."

"Oh, Caroline, now I feel really bad."

"Don't. I think it's going to be a good thing."

"But her house, you said it's horrible—a dump site."

"Oh yeah. It is. But I promise you, before I go to bed tonight, there will be one room in that place that's not a health hazard."

Abby just shook her head, but Caroline gave her a bright smile. "I think it'll be good for Mom to have me there. It might help to bring her back to reality, you know?"

"I suppose that could happen."

As Caroline drove across town to her mom's house, she suspected this plan might bring her back to reality too. She just hoped that she and her mom didn't end up in some kind of knock-down, drag-out fight when Caroline started clearing out her old bedroom and throwing junk into the trash. Worst-case scenario: her mom would throw such an out-of-control fit that Caroline would simply call 9-1-1 and get some professional assistance. Really, she hoped it wouldn't come to that.

Caroline stopped by a one-stop-shopping store on her way to her mom's. She gathered things like garbage bags, cleaning materials, and an electric fan that was fifty percent off.

After that she swung by McDonald's again. Only this time she got food for both of them. Her plan was to sit in the kitchen and peacefully eat together. Hopefully her mom would relax and be content to snooze in front of the TV like she usually did in the afternoons.

To Caroline's relief, that's exactly what happened. Knowing her time was limited, Caroline went directly to her old bedroom as soon as her mother nodded off. Opening the window wide, which was no easy feat, she pushed out the old screen and began shoving boxes of magazines and paper, old clothes, and mostly plain-old garbage directly out the window. She could only imagine how the yard would look when she was done, but she would eventually bag up all the junk and get it out of sight.

Midway through this nasty clean-out, Caroline almost screamed when she discovered a dead mouse. Using two old magazines, she scooped the critter into a box of ratty-looking old clothes, muttering, "Rest in peace," as she laid an old sock over him. She wished she'd had the foresight to purchase rubber gloves and a surgical mask, because it was obvious that other critters, including spiders, had inhabited this space over the past several decades. It took an immense amount of self-control, or maybe it was just plain desperation, to continue.

"I can do this," she kept telling herself as she hefted box after box out the window. At least she was in fairly good shape, thanks to Pilates and yoga. Even so, she knew she'd be sore afterward, and she tried not to think about how good it would have felt to have a date with Abby's Diamond Lil tonight.

After the room was cleared of everything except the bed (which looked questionable), a bedside table, her old dresser, and a wooden chair, Caroline tiptoed down the hallway to discover that her mom was still snoozing. Caroline went out to retrieve the cleaning supplies from her car. She cringed to see the heap of garbage outside of her window.

"What are you doing there?" A boy who looked to be about twelve looked curiously at her from the sidewalk. "Having a garage sale or something?"

Caroline laughed. "No. I doubt anyone would want to buy any of that trash." Then she got an idea. "Hey, would you like to make some money?"

He looked at her suspiciously, as if he was remembering some parental instruction about stranger danger.

She pulled out the package of black trash bags and held it up. "I'll give you twenty bucks to bag that stuff up and carry it over to the side of the garage for me."

His eyes lit up. "Twenty bucks?"

She nodded and held out the bags.

"Let me go ask my mom first," he told her.

"Sure." She tossed the box of bags over by the frightening pile. "I'll just leave those there in case you want to do it. But if you do it, be quiet, okay? My mom's sleeping in the house and she can be kind of grumpy."

He nodded. "I know. My mom's afraid of her."

"I am too sometimes," Caroline admitted.

Then he dashed down the sidewalk and disappeared into a blue house. Meanwhile, Caroline gathered up what she thought she'd need for round two of this cleaning match, then quietly slipped inside. Once again, she was relieved to see her mom was still sound asleep. She filled a bucket with warm water, then returned to the stark-looking bedroom, where she plugged in the fan and set it on the chair by the open window. She began scrubbing the lower half of the spotty walls with a product that was supposed to eradicate mildew. When the pale yellow walls were spot-free, she started to clean the old linoleum floor. She began by sweeping up old mouse droppings and other debris into a dustpan. As she dumped this out the window, she observed the boy dragging a big black bag across the lawn.

Using the same cleaner she'd used on the wall, she attacked the floor. As she scrubbed, she remembered how she used to hate this floor, complaining to her parents that she needed pink wall-to-wall carpeting. Not that they listened. But now she was thankful for the old yellow linoleum. At least she knew that when she finished, it would be clean.

By the time the room was sanitized, Caroline was not only exhausted but filthy. As much as she disliked using her mother's bathroom, she did her best to clean herself up. Maybe the bathroom would be her next project—if her mother didn't catch on and throw her out first.

"What are you doing in there?" Mom demanded when Caroline emerged from the bathroom.

"Using the bathroom," she told her. "Is that not allowed?"

"What's that I smell?" her mom persisted.

Caroline held up her hands, which still smelled of bleach. "My hands?"

Her mother sniffed, then nodded.

"I just washed them," Caroline said, as if that explained everything.

"I need to use the bathroom." She pushed past Caroline.

"And I need to go get us something for dinner," Caroline said lightly. "I'll be back in about an hour."

Her mom didn't respond, just shuffled into the bathroom, still sniffing as if she thought she were a bloodhound. Caroline hoped she wouldn't go sniffing in the bedroom and throw a hissy fit.

"How's it going here?" Caroline asked the boy outside.

He kind of shrugged. "Okay."

"I need to go to the store," she told him. "But I'm going to pay you for half your work now, just so you'll know I'm not stiffing you." She dug into her purse, then handed him two fives. "I'll be back in an hour or so."

"Thanks!" He grinned happily.

"By the way, I'm Caroline," she told him.

"I'm Jacob."

"See you later, Jacob." Caroline felt a strange mixture of exhaustion and happiness as she drove back to the store. She was actually somewhat impressed that she'd accomplished so much. She was even looking forward to finishing up. She just hoped—and even prayed— that her mother would not open that bedroom door. Caroline considered getting some kind of lock.

As Caroline filled her cart with a deluxe mattress pad, high-thread-count sheets in pale yellow, two pillows, a white-and-yellow comforter, a couple of matching pale-yellow throw pillows, white curtains, a white shag throw rug, a small bedside lamp, and several other "comforts," she tried not to worry about the expense. After all, if she wasn't staying at her mom's, she'd be paying for a hotel, and what she was purchasing today wouldn't even be the cost of two nights in a hotel. Plus it would allow her to be on hand for her mother. And maybe that would help. She hoped so.

Next she went through the grocery section, where she got herself some yogurts and fresh produce and a few other things. Finding something her mother would eat was a challenge. Plus, due to the unsanitary conditions, Caroline wasn't eager to cook in her mom's kitchen. And so, after gathering some basics like canned soups, saltine crackers, and more of the protein drink that she'd been encouraging her mom to consume, she decided to keep things simple by hitting McDonald's again.

Jacob was finishing up when she got back. She paid him the other ten and then a couple more bucks as a tip. "Thank you so much!"

"Let me know if you need anything else done," he said eagerly.

Caroline looked at the overgrown grass and shrubbery. "Do you do yard work?"

"I do at my house."

"Why don't you check with your mom about doing yard work here?"

He nodded eagerly. "All right!"

Leaving her bedroom purchases in her car, Caroline carried her groceries and takeout food into the house. She found her mom in the kitchen, staring blankly into her rather sparse refrigerator.

"I got dinner," Caroline said cheerfully.

Her mom jumped. "You scared me."

"I'm sorry. But I brought you something." Caroline dangled the McDonald's bag like bait, and her mother closed the refrigerator and came over, sat down, and waited for Caroline to set things out. Then Caroline sat down and pretended to eat with her mom. But the truth was, she just couldn't stomach any more fast food. Her plan was to eat something after her mom went to bed. As usual, her mom ate very slowly, almost as if each bite was painful to chew. Maybe it was. But Caroline decided to put this time to use by straightening the kitchen.

"What are you doing?" her mom demanded.

"Just cleaning up a little," Caroline said cheerfully. "Do you remember when I was a girl and I hated to clean the kitchen?"

Her mom frowned.

"You should be glad that I grew up and don't mind doing it now."

"Don't break anything," her mom warned.

How Caroline would break anything in here was a mystery. Almost everything she could see was either plastic or melamine. But she told her mom that she'd be careful. Finally her mom was done eating and rose from her chair.

"Do you want to go for a walk?" Caroline asked.

"A walk?" Her mom looked at her like Caroline had taken leave of her senses.

"Sure. It's nice outside and—"

"No!" Mom firmly shook her head. "No walk." She shuffled back into the living room, made a *harrumph* sound as she sank into her old recliner, then clicked the remote and found her favorite game show.

Caroline continued cleaning the kitchen. She was surprised and yet thankful that Mom wasn't lurking, watching over Caroline's shoulder and questioning every move she made. Caroline wondered if this meant her mom had started to trust her more. Or maybe it was just a fluke. Whatever the case, Caroline was determined to make the most of the time she had.

Using some of the old grocery sacks that her mother must've been saving for years, she bagged up piles of old Styrofoam containers, empty glass jars, and all sorts of junk that normally cluttered the countertop and hogged cabinet space. She took the full bags out to the garage, adding them to the dump site that was already there. She hoped to hire someone to clear out that whole space before it went up in smoke. Hadn't her mom ever heard of internal combustion?

Then, knowing she was already asking for trouble, she loaded the seldom-used dishwasher with all the gritty dishes and cups from the cabinets and, after a long search through all the junk stuffed beneath the kitchen sink, she finally located an ancient box of dishwasher soap. Of course it was solid as a rock. But she knocked it around until it finally released a couple of large clumps, which she tossed into the full dishwasher. Next she gave the countertops, sink, and appliances a much-needed scrubbing. And when she was done, she thought the kitchen was almost clean enough to fix food in.

She had no idea how her mom would react to these changes. Caroline decided to play dumb if questioned about it. She also decided that this would be the way to test whether her mom needed to be moved out of the house or not. If she could accept help without blowing her top, there was hope.

Caroline went into the living room. She was hoping that her mom had fallen asleep again, but she appeared to be wide awake. "Why are you still here?" she demanded when she noticed Caroline.

"Because I live here, Mom."

Her mom frowned as if trying to process this.

"You're my mom. I'm your daughter. Don't you remember?"

Her mom nodded but looked uncertain. "Of course I remember. You're Caroline."

Caroline went over to her mom and stroked her hair. "That's right," she told her. "Do you remember how you used to put my hair in pigtails when I was little?"

"What are pigtails?" she asked.

"Braids. One on each side." Caroline tried to show her.

"I don't remember." Now she looked sad.

"That's okay." Caroline stroked her mom's hair again. "Maybe you'll let me fix your hair someday."

Mom seemed to consider this, then she turned back to the TV. "My show is on."

"I'm going outside for a while," Caroline told her.

"To play?"

"Yes." Caroline smiled.

"Don't be out after dark," her mom warned.

"I won't."

So Caroline went out to her car and fetched some of her bedroom purchases. Checking to be sure no one was watching, she went to her open bedroom window and dropped them through. She made a soft landing pad of the quilt and pillows before dropping the lamp. Then she locked her car and actually did take a nice long walk. Although it seemed strange to be in her childhood neighborhood, it felt good to breathe the fresh air. And she made it home before dark.

When she entered the house, her mother was no longer in the living room. Worried that she might've been discovered, Caroline went directly to her bedroom, but everything seemed to be as it should. So she listened at her mother's door and could hear Mom rustling about in there, probably getting ready for bed.

Caroline went into her room and quietly began putting her bed together. Although the bed seemed small, it actually looked rather inviting when she was done. And after she'd hung the white linen curtains, laid down the rug, and turned on the little bedside lamp, the place was almost cozy. She decided to wait for Mom to fall asleep before she brought in her clothes and things from the car.

Sitting there in her old bedroom, Caroline remembered how often she had retreated to this place as a girl when her dad was in one of his rages, beating her mom with his words and occasionally a fist. Sometimes Caroline would try to intervene on her mother's behalf, using her smile and charm to defuse a situation. Other times she would simply put on her earphones and music and tune the whole thing out. She still felt guilty about that. But she had been a child. She had needed her parents to care for her, not the other way around. Maybe some things never changed.

=Chapter 31=

ABBY

"Where's Caroline?" Paul asked as he sat down to what was obviously a dinner for two.

"At her mom's." Abby handed him the salad bowl.

"You mean she's staying at her mom's?"

"She thought it might help." Abby almost added, *our marriage*, but couldn't bring herself to say the words.

"So have you lined up any other unexpected house guests?" he asked as he sliced into his steak.

"No." Abby studied him as he focused his attention on his food. "Are you saying that it's not okay for me to invite friends to stay with us?"

He looked up. "No. I'm just saying I'd like to be in the loop."

"Meaning I should get permission first?"

He frowned, then took a bite.

"Because that's how it feels sometimes, Paul. It feels like you're the only one who calls the shots in this marriage. Like you think I'm the little woman and that I should cater to your every whim and need."

"That's how you feel?"

"Sometimes." She forked into her salad with a vengeance.

"Well, do you know how it feels to me?"

She set down her fork and stared at him. "Probably not. Tell me, how does it feel?"

"It feels like you don't appreciate a single thing I do for you. It feels like I work hard to provide everything you could possibly want and all I get in return is complaints and nagging."

"Complaints and nagging?" Abby was indignant. "You honestly think I nag you?"

He nodded, then took another bite of steak. How he could make such mean accusations and continue eating was a mystery to her.

"What on earth do I nag you about, Paul?"

"You're always wanting to know where I've been, who I've been with, when I'm coming home, where I'm going. All the time you're on my case, treating me like you're the mom and I'm the errant little school boy. I call that nagging."

"What if I took off whenever I liked? And what if I never communicated with you regarding my whereabouts? Would you like that?"

He shrugged, then returned to slicing his steak.

"No, of course *you* wouldn't even care," she answered for him. "You assume that your frumpy little housewife couldn't manage to get into any sort of real trouble."

"I never said that."

"You don't *need* to say it, Paul. It's written all over your face."

He set down his knife and fork. "Are you suggesting that I shouldn't trust you, Abby? Is there something you're trying to tell me?"

"Even if there were, I doubt that you'd care."

"I don't understand why you'd say something like that, Abby."

"Because it's the truth. You take me for granted, Paul."

"Same back at you, Abby."

"I'm not the one with the mysterious secret life, the one who goes off for hours at a time without any explanation."

"No, you just go for days, acting like everything is perfectly fine, then out of the blue you start attacking me like you're doing right now." He frowned. "Let me guess. It's hormonal."

Abby stood up, threw down her napkin, stomped to her room, then slammed and locked the door. Not terribly mature, but at least she hadn't said what she wanted to say. Abby had never cared for foul language. She sat down on one of the club chairs and, too angry for tears, simply fumed. She'd handled that all wrong. Nothing had come out how she'd meant it to. She had actually planned for them to have a civilized conversation tonight. She had even planned to tell him that she appreciated him. That's why she'd fixed a dinner that she knew he'd like. Now he was out there eating alone, and probably enjoying it. That made her even madder. It was obvious he didn't care about her. He'd probably be happy if she just up and disappeared. Then he could openly date Bonnie the brunette, maybe even marry her, and they'd both live happily ever after.

She quietly opened the French door to the bedroom deck and walked out. Maybe it was hormones or anger or just plain insanity, but Abby walked out onto the beach, where she removed her shoes at the water's edge, then actually went into the ocean. She stopped when it was knee deep, high enough to get the bottom of her capri pants wet. She stood there in the cold water, looking out toward the horizon. If she had more nerve, she would just keep going straight out into the sea, just like her mother had jokingly said she'd do if Alzheimer's ever kicked in. Abby wondered if she might have the onset of Alzheimer's herself. Perhaps she'd simply imagined that Paul was seeing another woman. Except she *had* seen them together. She remembered that vividly. She also remembered how he had tried to keep her from knowing about it. Obviously he wanted to cover it up.

Instead of walking straight out to sea, Abby began to walk north, staying in the shallows. She just kept going and going until she was surprised to observe that the sun was setting and her feet were numb.

She had walked so far that she'd actually gone a ways past her mother's house. And she sure didn't want to go crying to Mommy. But that's when Abby got an idea. Barb had told Marley and Abby where a spare key to the Lowenstein cabin was hidden, in case they needed to check anything out before the sale closed on Tuesday. So Abby went up the beach and circled back around to Marley's beach cabin, where she found a sandy key beneath the flowerpot, unlocked the door, and went inside. It still smelled musty, but she didn't really care as she locked the door behind her.

She didn't turn on any lights, but simply went into the little bedroom and lay down on the squeaky bed, pulling a wooly blanket up over her, and hoping that a sense of feeling might return to her feet more quickly than she expected it to return to her heart.

Chapter 32

JANIE

On Saturday morning Janie sat on the edge of her hotel bed and turned on her BlackBerry. She hoped it wasn't too early to call Caroline, but she was eager to connect with someone—she wanted her friends to know she'd finally made it into town. "Hey, Caroline, it's Janie," she said pleasantly.

"Janie, where are you?"

"I got to town really late last night. I decided I'd rather be here than Portland. I'm at the hotel and I tried to call Abby, but they must be out—"

"Abby is missing."

Janie sat down on her bed. "Missing? What do you mean?"

"It's just terrible, Janie. Paul called last night to see if she was with me, and of course she wasn't. Then he told me that they'd gotten into a little fight. Abby went into her bedroom, but when Paul went to check on her, she was gone."

"Did she take her car?"

"No. This is the hard part, Janie."

"What?"

"Paul said the bedroom door, the one that looks out to the beach, was open, and although it was getting dark, he saw her tracks and they led straight to the ocean. And he found her tennis shoes and they were all wet."

"Oh no!"

"She was gone all night. Paul called the Coast Guard, and we've all been out looking for her."

"Do you think she … she did something crazy?"

"I don't know. She's been really depressed over their marriage."

"Oh, poor Abby!" Janie felt sickened. "Is there anything I can do?"

"If you want, you can join Marley and me. We're just walking the beach."

"Where are you?"

"About a mile south of Abby's house. You remember where Bear Cove is, that picnic spot by—"

"Yes. I'm coming now."

"We'll meet you in the parking lot."

Janie felt shaky as she drove to Bear Cove. What if Abby really had done something crazy? If she was so depressed, why hadn't her friends noticed? Of course, Marley, Caroline, and Janie had all been consumed with their own troubles and challenges. Trying to relocate and reinvent their lives wasn't exactly easy. They probably all assumed that Abby was lucky because she already lived in Clifden. And yet she'd given them clues. She'd always said her marriage wasn't as good as it looked on the outside. But whose marriage was?

Janie parked the car, got out, and immediately spotted Marley and Caroline. They all ran to meet each other for a group hug. "Any news?" Janie asked as the hug broke up.

"Nothing." Marley frowned. "I just can't believe Abby would do something like this."

"I can't either." Janie just shook her head.

"She was depressed," Caroline reminded them.

"That's true," Marley agreed. "She was fairly sure that Paul is having an affair, and it was tearing her up."

"Poor Abby." The three of them walked out toward the beach.

"I have to admit that Paul has done some suspicious things lately," Caroline told them.

Marley told Janie about Diamond Lil. And Caroline filled her in on Bonnie the brunette.

"Even so," Janie said, "I can't imagine Abby taking her own life."

"Paul said she was hormonal," Caroline told them.

"And that's what every woman wants to hear from her husband," Marley said bitterly.

They walked in silence for a while, looking up each time the Coast Guard helicopter made a pass overhead. Meanwhile a cutter was out in the ocean, also searching. It didn't help that the sky was gray with a band of fog hanging out on the horizon.

"I assume Abby's mom hasn't heard from her," Janie said.

"No. She's on her way to Abby's house, where she plans to look for clues."

"Clues?" queried Janie.

"Like a note or something," Caroline explained.

"Oh, right."

"And I'm sure you've tried her cell phone," Janie asked.

"It's in her purse."

Janie took a deep breath. "Do you think this is the end of the Four Lindas?"

"Before we even really began." Marley sniffed loudly.

Caroline handed her a tissue and then gave one to Janie. "We need to think positively," she told them. "I mean, really, Abby is not the type to commit suicide."

"But she was hurting," Marley reminded them. "She and Paul have been together since high school. It would be hard to see that all fall apart."

"She has her daughters," Janie pointed out. "And her grand-daughter."

"And she has us," offered Caroline.

Suddenly Marley stopped walking. "I have an idea!"

"What?" Caroline and Janie asked simultaneously.

"My beach house. What if she's there?"

"Wouldn't her mom have noticed?"

"I don't know, but I'm going to find out." Marley had turned around, and Janie and Caroline followed. Soon they were in their cars, and Janie followed Marley up the beach road, going north, until they finally reached Abby's mom's house.

They all got out and ran to the door, where Marley picked up a flowerpot. "The key isn't here," she said as she began pounding on the door. "Abby!" she cried. "If you're in there, open up!"

Caroline knocked on the window, yelling for Abby to come out. Janie just stood there watching, wondering if she'd made the mistake of her life to relocate to a place where a good friend would run off and drown herself in the ocean.

The door opened, and sleepy-looking Abby blinked at them. "What are you doing—"

All three of them nearly tackled her with hugs.

"We thought you were dead!" Caroline cried.

"That you'd drowned yourself in the ocean," Janie added.

"The Coast Guard is out there looking for you," Marley told her.

"Oh dear." Abby's hand flew to her mouth. "I never considered any of that. I just wanted to teach Paul a lesson."

"By faking your suicide?" demanded Caroline.

"That's not what I was *trying* to do." Abby's forehead creased. "But I can see how it might've looked like that. The truth is, I wasn't in my right mind last night." She actually smiled. "But I feel much better now."

Marley was already on the phone. "I'm going to let everyone know you're okay, Abby."

"Thanks," Abby told her. "And I'm so sorry. I didn't mean to scare everyone."

"We love you, Abby," Caroline said. "We couldn't bear to lose you."

"We wouldn't be the Four Lindas anymore," Janie added.

Abby sighed. "I'm truly sorry that I upset everyone. But at the same time, I'm glad I ran away from home."

"Why?" demanded Caroline.

"Because in a weird way, it showed me that I have some control over my life. I don't have to settle for being a little house frau, cooking and cleaning and catering to my husband while he's off doing only God knows what." Abby led them around to the beach side of the house, where they sat down on the rustic wooden benches that flanked the deck.

"Is that how you really feel?" Janie asked her.

"A lot of the time."

"Paul's on his way here," Marley informed them. "He's letting the Coast Guard know that you're okay."

Abby scowled. "I'm not sure I want to see Paul."

"But you need to talk to him," Caroline urged.

"Yes," agreed Janie. "You need to tell him how you feel."

"I tried to do that last night." Abby sighed. "But it just turned into a big fight."

"I'm sure he's sorry about that now," Marley told her.

"Don't be so sure." Abby leaned forward with her elbows on her knees. "He's probably mad that the Coast Guard got involved. This is so embarrassing! I'll bet the Coast Guard is mad too."

"They'll be relieved that you're okay," Marley told her.

Abby's head was hanging down. "I don't want to talk to Paul."

"Come on, Abby." Janie put her arm around Abby's shoulders. "You need to tell Paul how you feel. And you need him to be honest with you. Don't keep running from this."

Abby turned and looked at Janie hopefully. "You're a lawyer. Would you sit with me and sort of act like a mediator?"

"If you want me to."

"That's a great idea," Caroline told them.

"I think I hear Paul's truck now," Marley said. "Maybe we should split, Caroline."

While Marley and Caroline made their getaway, Janie explained a few things to Abby. "As a mediator I can't take sides. My purpose will be to facilitate discussion and negotiate some kind of settlement."

"Wow." Abby looked impressed. "You really do know how to do this."

They could hear Marley and Caroline talking to Paul. He sounded agitated.

Janie thought for a moment. "I think I should speak to Paul first."

"Go right ahead," Abby told her. "I'll be right here."

So Janie went around the house, meeting Paul halfway. "I need to talk to you," she said.

"Why?"

"Abby has asked me to act as a mediator."

"Are you going to be her lawyer?" He looked concerned.

"I just want to help facilitate an open discussion between the two of you. From what I've heard, you guys can use some help in that area."

"No kidding."

"So are you willing to do this?" she asked.

"If you think it will help."

"I don't think it could hurt."

So they returned to Abby. Paul sat on the bench opposite her, and Janie took the one beside them. "Okay," Janie began, "here are my ground rules. Questions must be answered honestly. Accusations will only be addressed if they are made reasonably. No name calling or mudslinging. Only one person is allowed to speak at a time. And I'm in charge. Do you agree to that?"

"I do," Abby said.

"Of course you would." Paul looked angry. "She's *your* friend."

"I thought I was your friend too," Janie said.

He shrugged, then let out a long sigh.

"Like I told Abby, as a mediator I won't take sides. I'm impartial."

He didn't look convinced. "So when do we start our little kangaroo court?"

"See?" Abby said. "He's not going to cooperate."

"Sorry." He pulled off his ball cap and ran his fingers through his hair. "It's just that I still feel angry."

"Why do you feel angry?" Janie asked.

"Because of what Abby put me and everyone else through. I called out the Coast Guard and everything. We thought you'd drowned."

Janie turned to Abby. "Do you have a response?"

Abby told Paul the exact same story she'd already told her friends. "It's not like I planned it all out," she said finally. "I was so emotionally spent that I fell asleep and didn't wake up until they knocked on the door."

"Why didn't you go to your mom's house?" Paul asked.

"I didn't want to disturb her."

"Yeah right."

"I think you'd be happier right now if they were pulling my cold, lifeless body out of the ocean!" she said loudly.

"Abby," Janie warned, "remember the rules."

"I'm just being honest. That's how I feel."

"Do you have a response to that, Paul?"

His expression was a mix of anger and sadness. "That's ridiculous."

"What is ridiculous?" Janie prodded.

"That I'd be happy if she were dead." He looked at his wife. "I was worried sick, Abby."

"I find that hard to believe."

"Why?" he demanded. "I'm your husband. I love you. Why would I want you to be dead?"

"Because of Bonnie Boxwell."

He smacked his forehead. "Oh, so that's where we're going again." He turned to Janie. "Abby has this crazy obsession that I'm cheating on her with a client."

"Are you?" Janie asked.

"No, of course not."

"Then why do you think Abby feels the way she feels?" Janie persisted.

"Because she's insecure and has too much time on her hands."

"Are you saying that you've done nothing to make Abby feel the way she does? You bear no responsibility?"

"Okay, she saw me with Bonnie. But I explained that to her already."

"Not really," Abby jumped back in. "You mostly swept it under the rug."

"How so?" he demanded.

"For starters you tried to deny it at first. Like you didn't want me to know."

"I *didn't* want you to know. I knew you'd be jealous."

"How did you know that, Paul?" Janie asked.

"Because that's how she is."

"I am not," Abby burst out. "He's always—"

"Stop!" Janie held up her hands. "Let's start over. Paul, I want you to honestly describe your relationship with Bonnie Boxwell."

"Like I said, she's a client. She wants me to build a house for her."

"And how many times have you met with her?"

"I don't know."

"More than once or twice?"

"Yeah."

"Did you tell Abby you were meeting with Bonnie?"

"No. She'd just get mad."

"So you kept that information from her?"

"I suppose so." He looked helplessly at Abby now. "But only because I knew you wouldn't like it."

"Why do you think it bothers her so much?" Janie asked.

"Because she's insecure and jealous."

"Has this happened before?" Janie persisted. "Has Abby been jealous of other female clients?"

He seemed to consider this. "Not that I can remember."

"That's true," Abby agreed. "This is a first."

"So, Abby, why are you jealous of Bonnie?"

Abby bit her lip as if she was thinking hard. "Well, to start with, it was shocking to see him with a strange woman in another town, especially considering that he'd told me he was doing something else. Plus he was driving his Corvette in the rain. He never drives his Corvette in the rain."

Janie turned to Paul. "Your response."

"I drove my Corvette to play golf. It was sunny and—"

"But the forecast was for rain," Abby interrupted. "You knew that."

He shrugged. "Anyway, Rob introduced me to Bonnie."

"She was at the golf course?"

He nodded.

"Why was she at the golf course?" Abby asked.

"Because she's a golfer."

"Does she golf with you?" asked Janie. "Honest answer, please."

Paul looked uncomfortable. "Sometimes. We'll invite her to play if she's there alone. There's no law against that."

Abby stood up now. "Paul, why don't you just come out with it?"

"What?" He held his hands up.

"Tell us what's going on between you and Bonnie," Abby said calmly. "Just get it out in the open, once and for all. Please!"

"Abby's right, Paul. Let's quit playing twenty questions. What exactly is going on between you and Bonnie?"

"I don't know." He looked like he felt cornered, but Janie didn't really care. All she wanted was for the truth to surface.

"How can you possibly not know?" Abby demanded. "Do you honestly expect me to believe that?"

"Paul, you *do* know," Janie pressed. "Abby is begging you to tell her the truth. Last night was a desperate move on her part, because she's almost certain you are cheating on her. She has the right to know the truth."

"Okay. This is the truth: Bonnie is a nice woman. She's fun to be with. She likes to play golf. She's very appreciative of anything I do for her."

"What do you do for her?" Abby's face looked pale.

"You know, I help with planning her house. Sometimes she calls with a question. Sometimes she calls because she's lonely. We're just friends, Abby. I swear that's all there is to it."

"So you've never considered taking it to the next stage?" Janie locked eyes with Paul.

He just shrugged.

"Of course he's considered it." Abby sat back down, dejected.

"I suppose it's crossed my mind. Sometimes Bonnie says little things ... you know ... that make it sound like she's thinking about it."

"And yet you continue to be in relationship with her?" Janie asked.

"She wants me to build her house."

"Would you build her house at the risk of losing your marriage?" Janie asked.

Paul didn't respond.

"I can't take this." Abby stood up.

"Wait, Abby." Janie reached for her hand. "Don't you want to know the truth?"

Abby sat back down and nodded.

"Do I need to repeat the question, Paul?"

"No. And the answer is no." He looked at Janie. "I don't want my marriage to end. I love Abby. But sometimes it's not much fun being married. Abby takes me for granted. She's never happy. And sometimes it's tempting to look beyond my marriage."

Abby was crying now, quietly, with her head hanging low.

"I don't love Bonnie," he said to Abby. "But I'm not happy about how our marriage is. I mean sometimes it's great. And other times it feels like you don't even know I'm alive."

Abby looked at him with tears in her eyes. "I'm not happy about how our marriage is either. And that's how I feel too, like you don't even know I'm alive."

"But you both want your marriage to work?" Janie asked.

"I do." Paul went over and sat by Abby now, wrapping an arm around her. "I do love you, Abby. I always have. I always will. But sometimes it feels like you're pushing me away."

Abby sniffed. "I love you too, Paul."

Janie sighed in relief. "Okay. Here's what I recommend."

They both looked at her.

"You continue to talk this out, keep these rules in mind, and go to some marriage counseling sessions. Can you do that?"

"I'm willing," Paul said.

"Me, too."

"Great. Because I want to come to your fiftieth wedding anniversary." Janie smiled at them. "And now I'm going to leave you guys to make up. Paul, I expect you to tell Abby how you felt when you thought she had drowned. And Abby, you need to tell Paul how it felt to run away from home."

Janie felt a real sense of accomplishment as she drove back to her hotel. Negotiation wasn't something she'd done much of in the past, but she thought it might be something she'd enjoy doing in the future.

For the first time since Phil had died, she thought perhaps she really did have a future!

=Chapter 33=

MARLEY

"Thanks for coming to the concert, Mom." Ashton told Marley on Monday morning. They'd just finished a late brunch, and she was getting ready to head back to Clifden.

"I thoroughly enjoyed it," she told him. "Let me know if you have another one, and maybe I'll bring my friends." She wasn't sure that the other Lindas would appreciate a drumming concert, but it might be fun to see their reaction to the colorful drummers, dreadlocks, tie-dye, and all.

"I'm really glad you decided to relocate to Clifden. I can't tell you how cool it is to have my mom only ninety minutes away."

"You wouldn't have said *that* ten years ago," she teased.

"Yeah, well, I've grown up some."

She smiled and ran her fingers though his curly hair, just like she used to do when he was small. "Yes, you have."

"And now you don't have any excuses for not coming to visit." Ashton opened the car door for her.

"That works both ways. You'll have to come see me too. I want you to come over as soon as I get my little beach house ready." She reached out to give him a hug, asking him to tell Leo good-bye for her.

Soon she was on the highway, and she couldn't believe how good it felt to be going home—home to Clifden. Oh, sure, the beach bungalow wasn't ready for her to move in. In fact it wouldn't officially be hers until she signed papers tomorrow morning. But in her heart it already belonged to her. It was home, and she couldn't wait to start fixing it up. She knew it wasn't going to be as easy as she'd originally hoped. Paul had made that crystal clear. Even so, she could imagine it all finished. Her plan was to go shabby chic with pizzazz. She just hoped she had enough elbow grease and finances to bring her dream into the realm of reality. Really, what other choice would she have once she signed the papers and handed over her money?

What if she was in over her head? What if everything went wrong? What if she was about to waste her nest egg on something totally hopeless? As she drove along the winding coastal highway, her emotions felt like a ping-pong ball being smacked back and forth. First, she'd feel elated and excited to think about how well this new adventure might go for her. She could imagine herself living out her dreams in her charming beach bungalow, creating wonderful art that surpassed everything she'd done before. Maybe she'd get better acquainted with Jack. Yes, she couldn't quit thinking about Jack. In fact she'd even mentioned to Janie that she wanted to invite Jack to today's Labor Day picnic at Victor's house. Janie had said, "Why not?" but Marley had chickened out. No need to push things.

About halfway home more doubts began to set in. In her mind she'd just painted the old kitchen cabinets a bright coral shade, only to see them falling off the wall. And suddenly she was imagining her bungalow being in such disrepair that it would be condemned and bulldozed, and all she'd have left was a small patch of sand. To make matters worse, her artwork would be criticized as amateurish and not fit to sell, and Jack would be so disappointed that he'd never want to speak to her again.

Marley turned on the radio to distract herself from this emotional roller-coaster ride. Really, her imagination sometimes got the best of her! Fortunately the oldies station was rocking out for Labor Day, and she soon became lost in the lyrics of The Beatles, The Rolling Stones, and Fleetwood Mac. Before she knew it, she was pulling up to Victor's house, where a number of cars were already parked. Some she recognized. Some she didn't.

As Marley was retrieving her canvas bag of nonperishable goodies, her contribution to today's gathering, she heard a car pulling up behind her. She turned to see Abby and Paul in the red Corvette. That they had come together in the same vehicle seemed a good sign.

"How's it going?" Marley quietly asked Abby while Paul was busy getting something out of the trunk.

"Okay, I think."

"Is this it?" Paul held up a picnic basket and blanket.

"Yes," Abby nodded. "And those enchiladas should go in the oven."

"I'm all over it." He grinned at Marley. "She tells me to jump and I ask how high."

"Now that's an exaggeration." Abby made a face as Paul went into the house.

"It seems like you guys are doing better." Marley studied Abby's eyes.

"I suppose things are better. But I still think Janie's probably right. We do need counseling." She sighed. "But already Paul is dragging his feet. His theory is as long as we're acting somewhat civilized to each other, everything is just fine."

"Oh."

"I think we're still on thin ice. I just wish Paul would tell Bonnie Boxwell to go take a hike." Abby chuckled. "Well, not like that exactly. But I wish he'd ask her to find another contractor."

"Have you told him that?"

"Not in so many words. I've hinted. And he hints back that business is business and he can't afford to let go of any clients."

Marley nodded. "Yeah, you guys probably do need marriage counseling."

Abby stood up straighter. "But let's not think about that today. We're here to have fun—and I want to celebrate the Four Lindas being together again. Paul and I will work this thing out. I'm sure of it."

As they went inside, Marley hoped Abby was as sure of it as she made it sound. But, like Abby, Marley didn't want to dwell on it. Today was supposed to be a celebration.

"Two more Lindas," Janie said as they entered the house. "We're almost all present and accounted for."

"Where's Caroline?" Marley asked as she set her bag on the counter.

"MIA," Janie told them. "I tried calling her last night but it went straight to voice mail. Same thing this morning. I actually drove by her mom's house to make sure she was okay."

"Like maybe her mom knocked her off in the middle of the night?" Marley was only partially joking.

As Young As We Feel

"To be honest, something like that went through my mind. I know that Mrs. McCann is pretty unpredictable. If she found out that Caroline had gotten rid of her things while clearing out a bedroom, well, it could mean trouble."

"So was Caroline there?" Abby looked worried as she finished unloading her picnic basket.

"Her car was gone. And I just couldn't muster the nerve to go up to the door and ask. I'm sure it would've only upset the poor old woman."

Janie glanced outside to where the guys were gathered around the grill. "I'm actually a little worried this could be my fault," she said quietly.

"Your fault?" Marley felt confused. "How could it possibly be—"

"Because I know Caroline was interested in Victor."

"So?" Abby frowned.

"Well, Victor invited me to meet him for coffee yesterday. It was the first time I'd seen him since getting back."

"And?" Abby sounded impatient.

"And Caroline walked into the Coffee Company and saw us."

"But why should that—"

"Well, I'm sure it looked like we were there as a couple." Janie's cheeks looked pinker than usual.

"What were you doing?" Marley teased. "Making out?"

"No." Janie got a stern look. "We were simply talking. But Caroline took one look at us, then pulled her phone out of her purse—very coincidentally it seemed—then she turned around and walked away."

"Maybe she was just being polite," suggested Abby. "I hate it when people use cell phones in restaurants."

"Yes, that occurred to me. But she never came back. Doesn't that strike you as odd?"

"Maybe she forgot something." Even as Marley said this, she knew it sounded weak.

"Do you think I hurt her?" Janie looked seriously worried.

"Caroline is a big girl," Abby said confidently. "She can handle it."

Marley looked curiously at Janie. "So, pray tell, is there something going on between you and Victor? Something we should know about?"

Janie waved her hand dismissively, but there was a twinkle in her eyes that suggested something more.

"Well, let's not obsess over Caroline. I'm sure she'll be here soon." Marley glanced outside. "Besides, it's a gorgeous day, and we should go out and—what the—"

"What's wrong?" Abby turned to see.

"Is that Jack Holland?" Marley lowered her voice, although she knew the men couldn't possibly hear through the closed glass door.

"Yes." Janie nodded with a sly expression. "I just happened to visit the One-Legged Seagull yesterday and I met Jack, and we were just talking, and the next thing I knew, I'd invited him to come today. You're not mad, are you?"

Marley wasn't sure how to respond. On the one hand she wanted to hug Janie. On the other hand a little heads-up would've been nice. She might've taken more time with her appearance, washed her hair, or even shaved her legs. "I'm just a bit surprised."

"Is there a problem with that?" Abby asked.

"No. I mean Jack's a friend and he should—"

"Hey, there's Caroline," Janie announced.

The three of them turned to see Caroline coming into the house with a bag in her arms and a good-looking man trailing behind her. "Who's she with?" Marley asked quietly. Abby and Janie seemed to be as much in the dark as she.

"Hey, Lindas!" Caroline sang out. "I want you to meet a friend." She proudly brought the attractive stranger, who seemed to be about their age, into the kitchen. "This is Mitch Arenson, an old friend from my past." Her expression was slightly mysterious. "I ran into him on my way to Clifden, and he totally surprised me by flying up here yesterday." She turned to Mitch and said, "These are the women I've been telling you about—the other Lindas: Marley, Janie, and Abby."

He grinned and shook all their hands. "The Four Lindas, together again. I almost didn't believe Caroline when she told me about your little club."

"We're definitely a unique sort of group," Abby admitted.

"And the way you've been reunited in your hometown after all those years," he continued. "Well, I told Caroline it seemed nothing short of a miracle."

"A miracle?" mused Marley. "I guess that's one way to describe it."

"I'd describe it as a blessing," Janie said quietly. "Without the encouragement of these women, I'd still be stuck in New York, feeling lonely and sorry for myself."

"Well, I agree with Mitch," Caroline proclaimed. "It is *a miracle*. And I believe that God has a reason for reuniting us. I can just feel it in my bones. There are some good things ahead for us girls."

Mitch looked slightly uncomfortable. He glanced outside.

"Do you want me to take you out to meet the boys?" Caroline offered.

"That's okay. You stay here with your Lindas," he told her. "I can introduce myself."

As Mitch was going out, Abby grabbed a pitcher of lemonade and began filling four plastic cups. "Okay, Lindas," she said, "time for a toast."

"Here's to being reunited," Janie began.

"And here's to new beginnings," added Abby.

"And here's to the future," said Caroline.

"And here's to the Four Lindas," declared Marley. "We're going to rock this little old town!"

The End

Or is it just the beginning?

... a little more ...

When a delightful concert comes to an end,

the orchestra might offer an encore.

When a fine meal comes to an end,

it's always nice to savor a bit of dessert.

When a great story comes to an end,

we think you may want to linger.

And so, we offer ...

AfterWords—just a little something more after you

have finished a David C. Cook novel.

We invite you to stay awhile in the story.

Thanks for reading!

Turn the page for ...

- **Discussion Questions**
- **An excerpt from *Hometown Ties***

DISCUSSION QUESTIONS

1. What qualities of childhood friendships can't be duplicated in adult friendships? In what ways are the bonds of childhood stronger? Weaker?

2. If you were reunited with a close childhood friend, would you be friends today? How might your experience be similar to or different from the Four Lindas?

3. Abby, Marley, Caroline, and Janie all face a critical period of discouragement and disappointment, but for different reasons. What do they have in common that allows them to have empathy for their differences?

4. How did Cathy's death affect the way each of the Four Lindas thought about this season of life?

5. Abby and Janie both grapple with depression of varying degrees. Using their stories, discuss whether you think depression can be avoided or whether it is at times inevitable—perhaps even helpful. What, if anything, could Abby and Janie have done to get through to the other side of their depression with less collateral damage to themselves and the people they love?

6. Caroline has an adventurous spirit, a forgiving and gracious heart, and a can-do attitude in spite of the suffering she has experienced. Do you attribute these qualities to personality, to conscious effort, or to something else? Can anyone develop such a perspective on life, or only certain people?

7. What kept Marley from working on her art while she lived in Seattle? In what ways were these obstacles legitimate? In what ways were they excuses that protected Marley from pain or fear?

8. How could Janie feel jealousy toward Caroline and Victor while still grappling with grief over her husband's death?

9. "You can't go home again," the saying goes. What kinds of risks are Marley, Janie, and Caroline taking by moving back to Clifden after so many years away? What are the potential rewards?

10. Which of the Four Lindas do you most closely identify with? What about her choices do you find surprising? Disappointing? What would you have done similarly or different if you were in her shoes?

Chapter 1

CAROLINE

Caroline knew better than to trust her mother. Even before Alzheimer's, Ruby McCann was undependable at best. Now she was unpredictable, unreliable, and sometimes she was downright sneaky. Today she was just plain missing. Caroline had been less than an hour at the grocery store, getting some milk, eggs, bread, and fresh produce in the hopes she could entice her mother to eat something. She'd left her mother contentedly watching a dog show on Animal Planet. And now she was gone.

But Caroline wasn't that surprised. Her mother had wandered off twice last week, and both times Caroline found her on the front porch of what used to be the Wilson house. Marge Wilson had been her mom's best friend, and Caroline supposed that some old wrinkle in her mom's brain sent her there for coffee or a cup of sugar or something. Each time, the current homeowners had appeared to be at work and, despite her mom's incessant ringing of the doorbell, no one responded. However, Caroline's mother was not on that porch this morning.

"Don't come undone," Caroline told herself as she continued through her mom's neighborhood—the same neighborhood Caroline had walked through hundreds, maybe thousands, of times while growing up in the sixties. It should have been as familiar as the back of her hand, and yet it was different … changed by time. She looked at the back of her hand. Well, that had changed some too. And what appeared to be the beginning of a liver spot had her seriously concerned. Hopefully her hands weren't going to go all blotchy and speckled like her poor old mother's. Good grief, Caroline was only fifty-three. That was ten years younger than Goldie Hawn, and Goldie still looked fantastic. Of course, Goldie had lots of money to keep her good looks looking good. But what Caroline lacked in finances, she hoped she could make up for in savvy. Which reminded her: Wasn't lemon juice supposed to bleach age spots?

"Caroline!"

She turned to see a figure on a bike zipping toward her and waving frantically. Jacob, her mother's neighbor, the preteen boy who'd rolled up his sleeves and assisted her with the clandestine emptying of her mother's pack-rat-stuffed spare room, was quickly coming her way.

"Hey, Jacob," she called out. "What's up?"

"I think I just saw your mom," he said slightly breathlessly.

"Oh, good. Where is she?"

"Down by the docks in Old Towne."

She frowned. "Really, that far? Wow, she was feeling energetic. Thanks for tipping me off."

"Yeah … but … I … uh …" Now Jacob appeared to be at a loss for words, and his cheeks had blotches of red, which might've been from a hard bike ride … or was it something else?

"What's going on?" Caroline studied him. "Did my mom do something weird?"

He nodded with wide eyes.

She braced herself, hoping that her mom hadn't gotten into some kind of verbal dispute with some hapless bystander. Her mother, who'd always been a reserved and somewhat prudish sort of woman, was now capable of swearing like a sailor. Just one more unexpected Alzheimer's perk. "Okay, tell me, Jacob, what's she done this time?"

"She, uh, she doesn't have her clothes on." His eyebrows arched and he made an uneasy smile.

"Oh." Caroline felt like the sidewalk was tipping just slightly now, like she needed something to grab onto to keep her balance. "You mean she doesn't have *any* clothes on?"

He just shook his head. "Nope."

"Nothing?" Caroline tried to imagine this, then shook her head to dispel the image. "Not a stitch?"

"Nothing. Not even shoes."

"Oh." She turned around and started walking back toward her mom's house, still trying to grasp this. "Well, now that's a new one."

Jacob nodded as he slowly half walked, half pedaled his bike alongside her by the curb. "People are trying to help her," he explained, "but she keeps yelling at them to stay away or she's gonna jump."

"Jump?"

"Yeah, into the bay."

She started jogging now. "I better hurry."

"She was heading out on the dock, the one by the big tuna boat, when I last saw her."

Caroline ran faster now, glad that she was still in relatively good shape despite missing her yoga classes down in LA for the past few weeks. "Thanks for letting me know."

He smiled apologetically. "Yeah. Sorry that it was kinda bad news."

"Hey, don't ever be sorry to bring me news about my mom, Jacob. Believe me, I don't even expect it to be good." And now she broke out into a full run.

She ran into the house, which she'd left unlocked just in case her mom wandered back while Caroline was gone. She hurried down the dim hallway, quickly unlocked the deadbolt she'd installed her bedroom (to keep her mother from going through her things) grabbed up her purse and, remembering her mother was naked, she pulled the yellow and white bedspread from her bed. On her way to the front door, she noticed her mom's favorite purple paisley shirt neatly folded on top a pile of old magazines and books cluttering the worn coffee table. That should've been Caroline's first clue. Where her mom's other clothes had disappeared to was still a mystery. But Caroline's plan was to wrap her mother in the comforter, escort her to the car, and quickly get her home.

It only took a couple minutes for Caroline to drive her SUV down to the docks, where she parked in a no-parking zone near a patrol car then jumped out and, with purse in hand and the bed-spread flapping behind her, she ran down the boardwalk toward the tuna boat. A small crowd of spectators had already gathered on the wharf to witness this interesting event, and a couple of uniformed policeman with perplexed expressions stood at the edge of the dock.

"Hello," Caroline called breathlessly as she hurried toward them, peering past them to see if she could spot her mother. She cringed at the idea of spotting a naked old woman wandering around with that bewildered expression in her faded blue eyes.

"Stay back," the female officer yelled at Caroline, as if she were about to perpetrate a crime.

"I'm here for my mom," she told them, pointing down the dock. "I heard she's down there."

"That's *your* mom?" The woman looked at Caroline suspiciously, like Caroline was somehow responsible for the bizarre behavior of a senile parent.

"Yes. She has Alzheimer's and—"

"Hey, are you Caroline McCann?" the other cop asked.

She nodded, peering curiously at him. He appeared to be about her age, although he wasn't familiar. "Do I know you?"

He grinned. "Probably not. Steve Pratt. I was a couple years behind you in school. But I remember you, all right. Coolest senior cheerleader at CHS and—"

"And don't forget we're on duty here," his partner reminded him.

"So"—Caroline squinted to see down the dock, which was looking alarmingly deserted—"about my mom? Where is she?"

"She's holed up in a fishing boat down on the end," Steve told her.

"Said she was going to jump if we didn't back off," the woman filled in.

"So we left"—Steve glanced over to the parking lot—"and called for backup."

"Backup?" Caroline frowned. Did they plan to take her mother by force?

"A professional," he said quietly, "someone from the hospital is bringing … uh … a counselor-type person to talk her into coming peacefully."

"Well, that won't be necessary," Caroline said as she folded the bedspread over her arm and moved past them. "I'm sure I can entice her to come with me." Okay, she wasn't as sure as she sounded, but she would at least try. Sometimes her mother knew and responded to her. Most times she didn't.

"We'll still need to file a report," the female cop called out as Caroline pushed past them and onto the dock. "We need your information."

A report? Caroline tried to imagine filling out their forms with her frightened, naked mother in tow. Didn't they realize this would be tricky at best?

"All I ask is that you try to stay out of the way." Caroline directed this to Steve, since he actually seemed a bit infatuated with her, which might've been flattering under different circumstances. "Police uniforms frighten her," she explained. "And if she sees you two again, she might really jump, and I'm sure it wouldn't take long for someone her age to get hypothermia. You wouldn't want to be responsible for that, would you?"

"We'll keep a low profile," he told her. "You just take your time and see if you can calm her down and get her safely out of there. Just yell if you need help."

Of course she needed help, she thought as she walked down the dock. As calm as she had tried to appear for the sake of the police, she knew her rescue attempt could go a number of directions. And so she whispered a desperate plea for real help. "Please, God, let my mother come peacefully." She was near the end of the dock now. "Peacefully and painlessly. Please!"

"Mom?" she called out in a sweet voice. Not that her mother normally responded to either *Mom* or a sweet voice, but it couldn't hurt to try. "It's Caroline," she called again. Still no answer. At least she wouldn't be catching the poor woman unawares. Her mother hated to be surprised.

Fortunately there was only one boat on the end of the dock, and since it was tied off close, it was easy to climb board. Caroline hopped onto the deck and called out in a pleasant tone, "Ahoy, Mom, are you aboard?" She heard a shuffling sound on the other side of the cabin area and suspected her mom had heard her calling, was fully aware that Caroline was there, and yet didn't want to reveal her whereabouts, which meant this was going to be a game of hide-and-seek. It had been one of Caroline's favorite games as a child. Not that her mother ever had time for such games back then ... back when Caroline could've appreciated it. Now her mother liked to play it a lot. Unfortunately it was never much fun now.

"It's okay, Mom. It's just me—your daughter—*Caroline.*" She noticed a dirty bait bucket and wished she had something to tempt her mother with, something to entice her out of hiding. If only she'd had the foresight to bring a Milky Way candy bar, which she tried to use only on the rare occasion when her mom was being completely unreasonable. The best way to her mom's heart was via a McDonald's cheeseburger and fries and, in really desperate situations, a milk-shake. A vanilla shake would come in quite handy right now.

"Are you hungry, Mom?" she called out, hoping it wouldn't backfire on her when her mom discovered that Caroline had come empty-handed. "How about a cheeseburger and fries, Mom? And a vanilla shake too?"

No answer. Just the sound of a westerly breeze snapping the pirate flag on one of the masts. "Are you cold, Mom? I brought something for you to wrap up in." Now Caroline opened the bedspread as if it were a net, deciding to go ahead and make her approach. Worst-case scenario, she could wrap up her mom and forcibly remove her from the boat and herd her back down the dock, calling out for reinforcement from the police. Surely the three of them could wrangle her into the back of the SUV. Caroline tiptoed around to the side of the cabin, careful not to startle her mother by stumbling over the heavy ropes loosely coiled at her feet.

As she quietly rounded the corner and spotted the hunched figure of her mother, Caroline felt a shockwave of recognition run through her. Turned away from Caroline, the old woman was crouched in a fetal-like position with her arms pulled tightly together in front of her, fists clenched in a protective and defensive way. But her parchment skin was so pale and her body so skinny, with shocks of white fuzzy hair sticking off the top of her head, she almost didn't seem human. From a distance, and in a lesser light, she might've been mistaken for an alien.

Caroline felt a lump in her throat and a sickening in the pit of her stomach. Was this what it finally came down to? Was this how Caroline would end up one day? Naked, frightened, alone, and confused? Where was the purpose, the meaning in this? Why did some old people have to suffer so?

"Oh, Mom." The words came out in a quiet sob as she wrapped the bedspread around her mother's scrawny frame and held her tight.

At first her mother struggled against her, but with little strength, she eventually gave in. She was obviously spent, too tired, too cold to resist. Caroline continued to hold her mother in her arms, pulling her close, hoping some of her own body warmth would soak through the bedspread and into her mother. Caroline rocked her gently as if soothing a frightened child. To the tune of an old seventies song she gently crooned, "It'll be all right, it'll be all right." Slowly, her mother relaxed.

The question now was how to get her mom off the boat, down the dock, past the police and curious crowd, and into her SUV. It seemed impossible. And her mother seemed very weak. How far could she realistically walk?

"Do you want to lie down and rest?" Caroline asked quietly.

Her mother nodded with damp, tired eyes.

"Yes." Caroline nodded too. "That's a good idea." She helped her mother to a vinyl-upholstered bench, which ran along the sunny side of the cabin. Grabbing an orange life vest to use as a makeshift pillow, she eased her mother down with the bedspread still wrapped around her like a shroud.

"Just close your eyes and rest, Mom." Caroline sat near her mother's head, tucking the bedspread around her bare shoulders and stroking the fine white hair, wishing for a miracle. Caroline took in slow deep breath in an attempt to calm herself so that she could think more clearly. She leaned her head back, feeling the warm sun on her face and listening to the sound of the water lapping up against the sides of the boat, the flapping flag in the breeze above her, and the haunting cries of seagulls nearby. Yes, it would be all right. Somehow it would be all right.

It wasn't long until her mother's even breathing assured Caroline she was soundly asleep. Quietly and almost reflexively, Caroline reached into her bag to retrieve her cell phone. But who to call? She wished she knew a big strong guy—someone who could simply pick up her mother and carry her to Caroline's car … then perhaps he'd carry Caroline away as well, off to his palace perhaps. But this was real life. She needed real friends, and there listed first in her cell phone directory was Abby's name. Since Abby seemed to know almost everyone in town, she would be a good choice, except Caroline was pretty sure that Abby and Paul had a marriage counseling session today. There was no way she wanted to disturb that.

Marley was a possibility, except that her house was a ways out of town, and Caroline knew that Marley was working feverishly to finish a painting in time for a special exhibit at the One-Legged Seagull. Finally, Caroline decided on Janie. Although their relationship was sometimes strained, she trusted Janie. And having been a smart New York attorney, Janie should have some brilliant ideas for how to handle this.

"It's Caroline," she said quietly after Janie answered. "I need help."

"What's wrong?" Janie sounded alarmed.

"It's my mom." Caroline gave her a quick lowdown of her morning thus far and explained how she was now stuck with a naked and frightened mother on a smelly fishing boat with the police waiting nearby. "I asked them to hold off," she said finally, "but I don't know how long they'll do that. You know how police can be." Just then Caroline noticed her mother's bare feet and gasped to see they were bleeding.

"What is it?" Janie asked with concern.

"Her feet—she might need medical attention too."

"Okay," Janie said crisply. "I'm on it."

"Or just some flip-flops so we can walk her to my car."

"I'm getting in my car right now."

"Hey, could you stop by McDonald's on the way?"

"What?" Janie sounded incredulous. "Are you serious?"

Caroline quickly explained that fast food somehow soothed her mother. "You know, just in case she's difficult when she wakes."

"Okay, I'll call Abby and ask her to pick up the food and to meet us at the dock, okay?"

"What about their appointment?"

"Oh, they should be done with that by now."

"We're on the wharf, out on the dock past the tuna boat. It's the fishing boat on the end with the pirate flag," Caroline said weakly. "You'll probably see a small crowd of spectators and police standing nearby."

"See you in about five minutes."

Caroline closed her phone and looked down to see that her mother was still soundly sleeping. She was probably exhausted from trekking nearly two miles with no clothes or shoes. Or had she slowly disrobed along the way, dropping clothing like Hansel and Gretel's crumbs, perhaps? Was she hoping to use them to find her way back home? And why couldn't she have left her shoes on? More than these questions, Caroline wondered *why*. Why, on a day when the temperature was barely sixty degrees, would an eighty-four-year-old woman want to walk naked through town? Why would she come clear down to the docks?

Alzheimer's was a mysterious disease plagued with a long list of unanswerable whys. Caroline hated to admit it, but perhaps it was time for her to seek some serious help in caring for her mother.

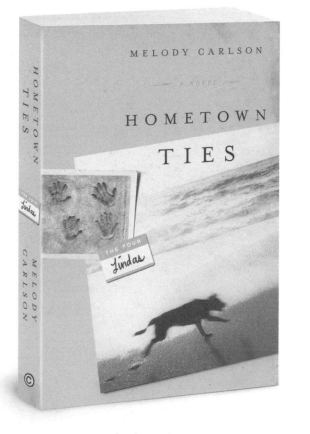